"You're pack now, Jamie. Mine. I always protect my own."

Damian ran a thumb across her cheek. "Next time we'll take it at your pace. I won't push you." She ran her hands up his arms, feeling the tense muscles, the power. Suddenly having this big, bad wolf watch over her made her feel erotic and wanting. Jamie tugged out his shirt and slid her hands up his flat abdomen, feeling him quiver beneath her touch.

"Push all you want," she told him.

His eyes darkened. Damian took her mouth in another drugging kiss. His hips pushed against hers.

"Mine," he said roughly. "No other male will dare touch you and you will not want them. You're mine."

Dear Reader,

What do you do when the woman who tried to kill you turns out to be your destined mate?

If you're Damian Marcel, alpha-werewolf pack leader and ruthless hunter, you pursue her to New Orleans to make her your own.

Jamie Walsh is on the run from Damian, for she thinks he's the Draicon werewolf who murdered her brother. Damian is determined to get her to trust him and surrender to the bond they share. When they discover Jamie is infected with a spell that's turning her to stone, they work together to find a missing book of magick. Only the book has a cure for the stone spell, and if the evil Morphs find it first, they will use it to destroy all Draicon.

As they race against time to find the book while warding off attacks from the Morphs, Damian and Jamie progress from enemies to lovers. When Jamie discovers a profound power lies within her, she must turn to Damian for help in harnessing the magick she's longed for all her life.

I'd like to think Damian and Jamie's story reflects the determination and grit of New Orleans. Like the city's residents, they are survivors who struggle to heal from past tragedies and begin anew. And, like New Orleans, their magick endures even through the darkest times.

I hope you enjoy Damian and Jamie's story of courage, strength and how two strong-willed individuals learn to set aside the past to forge new beginnings formed from love and understanding.

Happy reading!

Bonnie Vanak

ENEMY LOVER

BONNIE VANAK

All the characters in this book have no existence outside the imagination of
the author, and have no relation whatsoever to anyone bearing the same name
or names. They are not even distantly inspired by any individual known or
unknown to the author, and all the incidents are pure invention.

First published in Great Britain 2012
by Mills & Boon, an imprint of Harlequin (UK) Limited,
Eton House, 18-24 Paradise Road, Richmond, Surrey TW9 1SR

© Bonnie Vanak 2008

ISBN: 978 0 263 89593 3

089-0212

Harlequin (UK) policy is to use papers that are natural, renewable and
recyclable products and made from wood grown in sustainable forests. The
logging and manufacturing processes conform to the legal environmental
regulations of the country of origin.

Printed and bound in Spain
by Blackprint CPI, Barcelona

Bonnie Vanak fell in love with romance novels during childhood. While cleaning a hall closet, she discovered her mother's cache of paperbacks and began reading. Thus began a passion for romance and a lifelong dislike of housework. After years of newspaper reporting, Bonnie became a writer for a major international charity, which has taken her to countries such as Haiti and Guatemala to write about famine, disease and other issues affecting the poor. When the emotional strain of her job demanded a diversion, she turned to writing romance novels. Bonnie lives in Florida with her husband and two dogs, and happily writes books amid an ever-growing population of dust bunnies. She loves to hear from readers. Visit her website at www.bonnievanak.com, or e-mail her at bonnievanak@aol.com.

For the uber guild "NOOBS GONE WILD."
Thanks, guys, for all your help with computer
games and for being so riotously funny.
Adam "Billdacat" Persac,
Michael "Pachomius" Bailey,
Drew "Furiousmage" Richardson,
Carlos "Malandro" Plata and
Jerry "Demonslayr" Stetler.

Chapter 1

Once the prey, now he was the predator, Damian Marcel thought as he hunted through New Orleans for the woman who'd tried to kill him. His destined mate, the only female he could impregnate. Jamie Walsh. His draicara.

The scent of fresh river water hit like a hard slap. Damian lifted his nose to the wind, and drank in the smell of the Mississippi. His Draicon senses tasted the water, licked it with a slow, lingering caress. At last, home again.

Twin feelings of joy and deep sorrow pierced him. Home no longer. This place wasn't home. Not anymore. It was a damn tomb, sucking him under, making him scream as he tried to claw his way out.

Damian tried to concentrate on the physical terrain, opening himself up to everything, resisting the instinct to shape-shift into his more powerful wolf form. New Orleans was known for the supernatural, but a werewolf prowling through the bustling French Quarter might scare a few tourists. He gave a mirthless smile.

Another, sharper scent pricked. Honeysuckle and warm woman. His nostrils flared, trying to catch the elusive fragrance. His fingers reached up, traced the air as if stroking a female's soft skin.

"Jamie," he murmured. "Jamie, *chère*. You can run, but you can't hide. I will find you."

He cursed in French as her scent faded. Somewhere in this thicket of narrow alleys, colorful shops and hard-grained nightclubs, she hid from him.

Thrusting his hands into the pockets of his trousers, he ignored the chattering tourists snapping pictures. Across from Jackson Square beneath a shady tree, a thin-shouldered painter dabbled color on a canvas, shifting his weight on a lopsided folding chair. On a park bench, a man in a white shirt and faded khaki shorts played mournful notes on a banjo, accompanied by a saxophone player. The music reflected Damian's pensive mood.

New Orleans still struggled to recover after

Hurricane Katrina, but the Quarter crawled on, pumping music, booze and flavor into the city. And magick, which had been bred into his blood and bones. Good magick, Draicon magick.

Black magick. Morph magick.

Damian grimaced. Morphs, former Draicon who turned evil by murdering a relative, could shape-shift into any animal. They killed ruthlessly and absorbed the terrified victim's dying energy. Jamie had joined with the Morphs to gain magick, but Damian stripped her of power by casting a binding spell. He'd let her escape him in New Mexico, knowing she needed time alone and he could easily track her down. Little danger existed after he'd killed Kane, the Morph leader, a week ago. Anguish had filled Jamie's voice.

"I'll break your spell, Damian. You'll never have me," she'd vowed.

His chest felt hollow with sharp regret even as his desire for her made him restless. Petite Jamie with her pixieish, heart-shaped face, delicate, translucent skin and huge, expressive gray eyes. Her soft, warm lips pliant beneath the hard press of his own.

The air's mild chill braced him. He strode along the sidewalk, his sharp gaze roving over the crowd. Sunshine beat down on the red-necked tourists, glinted off the faded brass of the player's sax. As he passed the painter, the artist regarded him with a mournful gaze. His words stopped Damian short.

"Have you heard the call of the wolf?"

Startled, Damian whirled. He studied the touch of gray at the man's temples and the faded, almost ragged clothes splattered with splashes of gray and black paint. The hollowed cheeks and the thin blade of a nose looked pale and wan in the brilliant sunlight. Not a very successful artist, for the man looked thin as a ghost.

"A wolf, sir?" Damian asked.

The man turned, his large dark sunglasses hiding his eyes. "The *loup garou* will never *fais do-do* in the bayou, *mon frère.* Have a look. Interesting, *non?*"

The werewolf will never sleep in the bayou, my brother. Instantly on guard, Damian glanced at the painting. Near a wood cabin, a wolf howled at a full moon. A distant memory nagged at him. He glanced at the man's gaunt face, but couldn't place him. For a moment he felt dim hope. A former member of his old pack? Could one have survived?

"*Mon frère?* The one who works hard never sleeps. Please, take a look," the man begged.

Hope died. Everyone in his former pack was long dead. He couldn't afford to indulge in memories or he'd lose his focus. The living Jamie was his priority. The man had heard his accent and tried to strike up a camaraderie just to sell a painting. No Draicon from his pack would ever resort to begging. This man was just another starving artist hawking his wares.

A familiar, haunting smell suddenly drew away Damian's attention. The scent was fresh, straight from his boyhood.

"You must have quite an imagination," Damian murmured. "Excuse me."

He scanned the area. His gaze landed upon a wizened elderly man hauling a large red bucket over to a small wood table. The man set the bucket down. For a minute, something dark flashed in the vendor's rheumy eyes. Then it vanished.

"Crayfish," the hawker yelled. "Fresh crayfish!"

Drawn to the sight, Damian strode toward him.

The slate-gray crayfish wriggled in the bucket, claws snapping in a bid for freedom. Damian's mouth watered. Memories flooded him; memories of wading through the clear creek, picking up the crustaceans for a tasty afternoon snack. Suddenly his stomach grumbled. He needed energy from raw food. Fishing out money from his wallet, he paid the man, who dropped the crayfish into a plastic bag.

"Fresh is best," the vendor advised. "All the flavor's in the shell."

Damian nodded. "I know."

Clutching the bag, he climbed the steps and headed for the Moon Walk, a stretch of pavement bordering the Mississippi. Damian watched a barge slowly labor upriver as he leaned against a tree growing in a square planter. No one was around. He opened the bag, and one after another he devoured the batch. Finally he reached for the last crayfish. A little bigger, it did not writhe and struggle, but remained oddly still. Perhaps it wasn't as fresh.

Damian raised it to his lips, and recoiled. The crayfish opened its mouth and hissed. "Draicon," it whispered.

Alarmed, he dropped the shellfish. A Morph. It began shape-shifting and multiplying even before it fell to the pavement. Damian fisted his hands, waiting to see what form it would take.

An explosion of crayfish followed. Some scrambled away. Lightning-quick reflexes kicked in as Damian pounced, killing them. Damn, where was the host?

Hearing a snicker, he whirled, but not before burning pain lanced his side. Better than his back, where the dagger nearly landed. The Morph rushed by. Human, the form requiring the least energy to maintain.

Damian waved his hands. Daggers appeared in his palms. The creature lunged. Releasing an angry hiss, the Morph lashed at his chest with the knife. He sidestepped, twisted. He calculated, swift on his feet as he judged the creature's abilities. Quick, but he was faster, and more alert.

Then the Morph grinned a sickly, yellow-toothed smile. "Too late, Draicon. Your draicara is dying. Your spell failed to work."

Startled, he drew back. The Morph seized the advantage and swiped at him. Damian recovered as the Morph started to change. Talons grew from its fingers and fangs replaced the yellowed teeth. Exerted from the fight, it began to shift much more slowly than normal.

Not so fast. In another animal form, the Morph would be harder to kill.

He kicked out, knocking the Morph to its knees. Damian dropped his knives as he jumped atop the Morph, then slammed its hand against the pavement, knocking aside its dagger.

As humans, they were easier to hurt. Damian pressed hard against the third vertebra of the back of Morph's neck, exerting enough pressure to cause excruciating pain. Pain used up their precious energy and prevented them from shifting.

"Tell me, you gutless coward. Why didn't my spell work?"

The Morph squealed but said nothing.

More pressure. The creature moaned. "Stop,

stop," it pleaded. Spittle ran down the side of its mouth. Damian smiled grimly.

"Talk."

"It slowed the dark magick, not stopped. Her blood... thickening." The Morph twisted, trying to break free.

With a low growl, Damian clamped down on the creature and dug his thumb deeper. Moans came from his enemy. "Okay, please, just stop, stop the pain," it begged. "Dark magick inside her, turning her...to stone. Living stone, alive but dead."

Shock seized Damian, loosening his hold. The Morph tried to escape the punishing grip. Damian seized its arm and twisted it backward. "Details. Now. Or I'll break every bone in your body and you'll wish you remained my meal," Damian threatened.

The Morph sucked in a breath. "The porphyry spell...rarely used. We c-can't absorb the victim's dying energy. Gave her dark magick, and the more magick she used, the f-faster it worked. In weeks, sh-she'll be encased in stone. Dead but a-live—damn, that hurts!"

His mind raced. "You can undo it," he said, twisting harder.

"N-no," the Morph wailed. "Can't...no counter spell. Only the ancient Book of Magick."

He sprang up to release his victim, grabbed his daggers. Time to end this.

The Morph recovered and staggered to its feet. Snarling, it sprang forward, features twisted with hatred. No pity. Damian twirled the daggers and threw. They hit home, straight in the creature's heart.

Acid blood spurted. Damian didn't flinch, only watched the Morph collapse. Grimacing, he rolled the body into the Mississippi, watching it disintegrate into gray ash before it slid into the water.

Dragging in a deep breath, Damian muted pain from his injuries. His magick was powerful and the wounds slowly scabbed over. He waved a hand, replacing his ruined Versace shirt, silk trousers and leather loafers with faded jeans, a black T-shirt and scuffed biker boots. Anonymous New Orleans garb.

The Morph's words rang of truth. Damian felt a sickening jolt to his stomach. He'd heard ancient tales of the porphyry spell. Victims exhibited lethargic tendencies at first. They ate anything to give them energy, especially sugar. Just as quickly as they ingested the food, it passed out of their systems. They cried sweet tears, their blood...

Their blood turned sluggish, their skin gray,

their internal organs eventually to granite. It was an agonizing end.

"Merde," he said softly.

Damian raced back to where he'd bought the crayfish, searching for the vendor. The man had vanished. Hot anger spilled through him. He'd been tricked. The seller must have been a Morph.

Jamie…dying. And Morphs openly roaming the city? What the hell was going on?

Were they everywhere, cloaked as humans? Bad news. Even his powerful Draicon senses couldn't detect them like that.

He lifted his nose and inhaled, trying to track the vendor's scent, when a teasing smell drifted toward him, floating on the wind. Honeysuckle and warm female skin. Jamie.

Instinct kicked into high gear. He had to find her. In weeks, she'd be dead. No, worse. Frozen into stone, a living hell.

Whirling, he dragged air into his lungs. Stronger now, there, coming from the south? He shouldered aside a tour group enjoying the banjo player's music.

The lost Book of Magick had a cure. Containing white and dark magick, the ten-thousand-year-old text held ancient secrets. Damian's father had hidden it from the Morphs. Every seventy years one spell must be used to keep the magick active.

If Damian didn't find the book in the next three weeks, the spells would vanish forever.

If he didn't find the book soon, Jamie would suffer an excruciating end.

I promise I will save you, my beloved draicara, even to my last dying breath.

Wolf senses on alert, he followed Jamie's scent.

How much could someone lose? Jamie Walsh wondered.

Plenty.

So many had died before. Her parents. Her brother. Now, her magick.

She felt numb. Dead inside. Gray, her flame extinguished. Her world. Gone.

Jamie leaned against a broken lamppost to catch her breath. A bone-numbing wind penetrated through her thin *Textually Active* T-shirt. The walk to the grocery store had never tired her. She set down the plastic bag, rubbed her hands against her faded jeans. Lead weights dragged at her feet. No one to lean on. No one to help. She was alone.

A knot squeezed her stomach. Alone was good. She could survive the odds better on her own. She didn't need anyone.

A familiar scent teased her senses. Fresh lake water and warm, sensual spices. The enemy. Damian.

Adrenaline pumped energy into her tired body. Jamie's gaze whipped around. But only tourists wended their way down the street in the bright, sharp afternoon. Wary of exposure, she turned toward home.

Her brother Mark's original French Quarter house near Jackson Square looked innocuous from the outside with its forest-green walls. Jamie unlocked the gate, slipped inside and bolted it. She hurried through the dark corridor, reaching the inner courtyard with a relieved sigh. Dumping the groceries on a wrought-iron table, she sank onto a chair.

Centuries-old walls surrounded her, a safe exposed-brick cocoon. Little could penetrate her refuge, except perhaps Damian. A cold chill snaked down her spine. Draicon were ruthless. What would Damian do if he caught her? Would he exact punishment?

You did try to kill him.

What did he want?

The answer came back in a rush of remembering. Sex. It came back to sex, and mating.

Arousal rasped against fear as she thought of Damian, his large body heavy with muscle. He'd taken her virginity, now he wanted her as his mate. He would hunt her down and never stop until he caught her. Brought her to his bed, pushed his hard, heavy body against her, nudged his hips between her bare thighs and claimed her once more in the most primitive way.

The space between her legs felt tender, wet and ready.

Her brain pushed aside desire and concentrated on self-preservation.

Right now she was a fortress with broken defenses, open to storming by Damian. Damian, who wanted her body, would claim her spirit, as well, drag her back to his dangerous pack of vicious werewolves as his mate. She had no weapon but her wits. A plastic sword against an invading army of sharp, lethal steel.

After trudging upstairs and putting away the groceries, she went to a battered desk cluttered with cables, software, parts and cell phones. Jamie retrieved a new laptop and an aircard and stuffed it into her backpack. She headed for the Petite Maison Voodoo Shop. Mama Renee knew about the secret underworld of magick beings like the Draicon, just like Mark had.

A small brass bell tinkled over the door as Jamie entered. An altar devoted to Marie Laveau sat off to the side, candles burning steadily to honor the long-dead voodoo priestess. Jamie advanced to the back and rapped on the closed door.

Mama Renee opened the door. *"Chère,"* she cried, throwing her arms about Jamie. Jamie hugged her back.

"I brought you a gift. I bought a wireless PC card and put you on my cellular service so you can e-mail your granddaughter. It's time you joined the information age. You're two decades behind."

The old joke brought a smile even as Renee shuddered at the laptop and the slim card Jamie thrust at her. The woman set them down as gingerly as handling a spider and ushered her into the kitchen where she plied Jamie with homemade herbal tea. A large black cat wound around her legs. Giving the silky fur a reassuring stroke, Jamie smiled as Archimedes purred.

"He's looking fat and healthy now," she observed, a little sad as she remembered how she and Mark had found him, skin and bones, living on the porch of a house wrecked by Hurricane Katrina.

The woman's gaze sharpened. "You and your brother worked hard to rescue stranded animals and find them good homes. If not for you, they'd have died. He was a remarkable person, loving and with a good heart, as you are. The world suffered a great loss when he died."

Desperate, aching loneliness filled her. Mark rescued her from a hellish childhood. He was all she had. *And you killed him, Damian. You murdered my brother.*

A lump clogged her throat. Her own heart

wasn't good, but pitch-black. What kind of woman tried to kill her lover?

Renee searched her face. "Something's happened. I see the darkness in your beautiful eyes. But there is still light there, struggling to free itself."

Stricken, Jamie explained everything. She clutched Renee's hand. "Do you have anything, a potion, a *gris-gris,* that can remove Damian's binding spell?"

Renee gently turned Jamie's palm over and studied it. A frown dented her brow as her gaze widened. She shook her head. "Honey, there is no magick to counteract it. You need the source. It's more powerful magick than I can summon."

"I have to get my magick back. I must."

She didn't mean to sound hysterical. Jamie reached for the cracked sugar bowl. She dumped several teaspoons into the china cup and drank.

"Jamie, how many times have I warned you to avoid magick? It's dangerous, and not for you, *chère.* Look at what dark magick did to you."

"But it was the only magick I had. Now it's gone." Jamie set down her cup, hugging herself. "I feel so…lost and alone. Like I've been trying to find myself, and when I had that power, I finally felt comfortable in my own skin, even though I detested how I'd gained it. Every time I felt guilty, I'd use my powers and remind myself of the benefit. I didn't have to rely on anyone. I had magick."

Misery seeped through her. "I don't know who I am anymore. I just want to find my way again. I don't fit in with anyone."

"And the Morphs made you feel like one of them, is that what you wanted?"

Jamie shuddered, remembering the stench of evil seeping into her spirit. "I know they used me, and I hated what they were doing. But the power, oh, Renee, you have no idea! For the very first time, I felt normal. Even if revenge, and evil, was the only way. And now I'm lost again."

The woman sighed. "Revenge brings only darkness. Why would you want revenge on Damian? Why did you try to kill him?"

Jamie bit her lip. Mama Renee was the only woman she'd ever trusted. Perhaps it was time to confide in someone.

"I want you to swear on your life you will not repeat what I say. No one knows."

The older woman looked startled, but nodded.

"I saw him kill my brother."

Shock widened Renee's eyes. "*Non, chère,* the papers said muggers attacked Mark. The police only identified him because…"

"They found his wallet nearby with his ID in it. His b-body…was burned to ashes." Jamie dragged in a deep breath. "Six months ago, I was in a bar on Bourbon waiting for Mark when I met Damian. He was…compelling. It was odd, the chemistry. He told me he was a Draicon, a werewolf. Mark arrived. He got angry when he saw Damian. I could tell they didn't like each other. Mark told me to go home, but Damian had slipped a note into my purse with his room number."

A wry smile touched Renee's mouth. "Let me guess. You're young, enthralled and you went to him."

Jamie nodded. A hot flush filled her face. Her first time, her shyness, his commanding sensuality. His powerful body mounting hers. The wild, uninhibited feeling…their naked bodies straining against each other. The odd feeling that it had been more than sex.

"Damian said he'd teach me magick. I went to the hotel the next day to make him deliver on his promise, but he'd checked out. I felt so used. I went home and Mark was furious. He guessed what happened and ordered me not to leave the house. Draicon were evil werewolves and he would make Damian pay."

Never had she seen her brother so angry, so concerned about her. For the first time he truly cared. And Damian killed him.

"And how did Mark know about the Draicon?" Renee asked.

Shrugging, Jamie stared at the shelves of herbs lining the wall. "Mark knew secrets about the magick world. He was my only family and I trusted him.

"That night, Mark needed help coaxing out a stray dog from this building he'd just bought. Said he would meet me there. He told me to wear new clothing he'd sprayed with this chemical compound to hide my scent so Damian couldn't find me. I was inside the building searching for the dog when I heard motorcycles in the alley. I peered outside and I saw…I saw…Mark. He was facing Damian and these five bikers, all tall and dressed in leather…"

Emotion squeezed her throat. "I heard Damian say, 'That's him, Mark Walsh. Kill him.' Th-the bikers undressed and turned into wolves. I saw Damian shape-shift into this huge wolf and… Mark screamed… Damian, he was…he was…" She squeezed her eyes shut, remembering the snarls, muscled wolves, the awful sounds her brother made as he died.

"I fainted. When I woke, I went into the alley. There was nothing but gray ash." Jamie gulped down a breath. "I reported Mark missing and the police told me a witness saw Mark killed by muggers. Then I just ran, because I didn't know what else to do."

"Oh, Jamie," the woman said softly. Opening her arms in invitation, she beckoned to her.

Oh, she wanted to! Wanted to let the older woman give her comfort she'd needed since Mark's death. But Jamie didn't dare remove the layer of steel she'd erected to shelter her from the uncaring world.

She shook her head. "I stayed in hotels, afraid to go home, afraid Damian would find me. A few days later, I met his friend. Nicolas was supposed to keep me safe until Damian arrived. I told Nicolas I'd go with him if he taught me magick."

A grim smile replaced grief. "He did. And I used it to find the Morphs, gain magick and try to kill Damian. They used my blood to make a lethal disease and I infected him with a kiss."

Anguish touched Renee's expression. "You've suffered a horrible loss. But why would Damian order your brother killed? Perhaps you don't know the full story."

Jamie bristled. "He probably knew Mark was going to go after him for seducing me. I saw my own brother ripped to pieces. Draicon are merciless killers."

The cries still echoed in her mind. The terrible screams of pain and tearing sounds...

Renee gently reached for her palm. "Jamie, you've had a rough life for one so young. You're special, different and you suffered for it. It's time you let go, and learned not everyone is the enemy. Sometimes the ones you think you can trust least are the ones you should trust most. They are your real family."

Shifting in her chair, Jamie felt the rub of old scars against her lower back. Heard the mocking sneers from her cousins, felt the burning sting on her flesh...

Shame flared inside her. Relatives were highly overrated. "You're more family than anyone else." *All I have left.* "So there's nothing you have to give me a smidgen of my old powers back?"

"Nothing." Wisdom shone in Renee's dark gaze. "What is holding you bound is ancient Draicon magick. If Damian did this, he did it to protect you."

"I need an ancient Draicon spell to remove it. The Book of Magick."

Renee looked troubled. "Such texts are meant to lie undisturbed, for they are too dangerous even in the hands of the wisest, most skilled sorceress."

She wasn't wise or skilled. But desperate.

"Promise me if you find the book, you will turn it over to the Draicon," Renee begged. "You've already become a victim to terrible forces. The book could destroy you for good."

"I wasn't a victim, but a willing participant."

The woman gently touched her wrist. "A victim, honey. The Morphs knew you were vulnerable. No matter how you argue the point, they took advantage of your weakness."

Jamie bristled. "Not weak. Never. Thanks, Mama Renee. I can manage on my own."

A cryptic expression touched the woman's face. "Jamie, remember. Even good can come of darkness. The Draicon leader seeks you, and his kind need your healing power."

The words made no sense. She didn't heal, but destroy. Nothing made sense anymore.

The woman offered a sad smile. "And all Draicon are not evil."

Jamie's chest felt tight with emotion as she went with Renee into the main storefront. The little brass bell tinkled merrily behind her as she left.

Feeling lost, she headed for the Pedestrian Mall. Just another average day in the Quarter...

Jamie shrank back, her heart beating double time at the figure stalking toward her. Not Damian, the lean, chiseled face she remembered so well, but another, with cruel, twisted features, wispy hair and black, soulless eyes.

The Morph ambled along, its sallow, shrunken and hunched figure looking like a living nightmare. Couldn't anyone see it? *Run, you fools!*

Jamie blinked hard. Instead of a Morph, she

saw a middle-aged man in khaki shorts, his slight paunch covered by a flowered shirt.

I'm losing my damn mind.

Dragging in a lungful of air, she forced herself to relax. No Morphs stalked the streets. Only people, out for a good time. And one lone were-wolf named...Damian.

Jamie froze in shocked fear.

Wind ruffled his short, dark hair. His elegant good looks made him stand out in the crowd like a sleek sports car among sedate sedans. He prowled with lithe grace toward her, his muscled body moving like a well-honed machine. Oblivious to the crowd, the artists, everything.

Everything but her. His hard green gaze riveted to her like a laser beam. Jamie's heart raced.

Instinct urged flight. She turned, pushed past the crowd. Fast, faster, as she raced beneath the balconies of the Pontalba Apartments, feeling his breath on her like a warm caress of air.

A hand latched onto her upper arm, jerked her to a stop. Jamie gulped, panic racing through her veins, his muscled chest pressing against her as he herded her out of the crowd's way against the brick building. Damian swung her into a faded doorway. Intensity radiated in his gaze.

"Jamie, ah, finally, I found you," he said softly, her name rolling off his tongue in his whiskey-smooth accent.

"Let me go, Draicon. Let me go, now."

She struggled against his steely grip. A hysterical sob rose in her throat. He was going to punish her for trying to assassinate him. Damian crowded her against the doorway, his legs pinning her against the wood. Trapped.

As she opened her mouth to scream for help, he pulled her against his hard body.

His lips descended on hers, cutting off her cry with a kiss.

Chapter 2

His kiss shocked Jamie into immobility. It was gentle, barely a brushing of lips. Damian raised his head, his expression softened. Hysteria fled as he cupped her face with his warm hands.

"Don't scream, *chère*. I promise, I won't hurt you, *ma petite*."

With a mere touch, he extinguished her panic. Damn it, what was this? Draicon magick?

"I'm not going to hurt you, Jamie. That's the last thing I want. I want to help you." His expression grew fierce and intent. "But first…damn…"

He kissed her again.

Jamie sagged in his arms. Feeling the current sparking between them as it had on that night when they'd first met. Her head fell back as he cradled her neck in his palm. Her hands slid up around his neck, feeling rock-hard muscle beneath warm skin. Jamie hung on for dear life like a drowning woman. Tasting him as his tongue boldly invaded her mouth, flicked against hers. Challenging him in return, her tongue tangling in a duet of hot desire and lost passion. It felt as magical and crazy and uncontrollable as when he'd first taken her.

This wasn't real. Or right. Or anything, but the moment, the succulent taste of him in her mouth, claiming it with each firm thrust of his tongue.

Jamie clutched fistfuls of his shirt, drawing him closer. Only then did Damian break the kiss. A low groan rumbled from him as he stepped back, never losing his grip on her. Intent burned in his gaze.

Alarmed and dismayed, Jamie licked her lips. *I just kissed my brother's murderer. The Draicon I tried to kill.*

Damian laid a palm against her cheek. "Hush," he murmured. "I won't hurt you."

"Then lift that damn spell of yours." Jamie stopped moving, stricken by the calming feel of his touch. She stared at him, taking in his strong, square chin, straight nose and high cheekbones. Classical good looks. And a werewolf lurking inside.

She had tried to kill him in New Mexico, but

Nicolas, his beta, had healed Damian. And then Damian had cast a binding spell, prohibiting her from doing magick. The dark powers Kane, the Morph leader, had bestowed on her had vanished. Damian had said it was because the Morphs wouldn't want her without her powers.

But he lied. She knew it.

She then had escaped, but he'd found her. No matter. She would escape him once more.

"I can't. The magick in you is dark. Until I can erase it, the spell remains."

"I'll find a way around it. I can defeat you, Draicon."

A shadow crossed his face. "There are things you must know, Jamie. You're in danger. You need my help."

"Your help? I'd rather kiss a Morph. At least they gave me power."

He gave her a pensive look. "What did Kane do to give you magick?"

"I had sex with him," she taunted.

Now that full mouth flattened into a thin slash. He looked dangerous and edgy. Leaning closer, he seemed to nuzzle her neck. No, he was sniffing her, like a wolf scenting a rabbit. Damian drew back. Male satisfaction gleamed in his eyes.

"You didn't. I can't smell him on you. You haven't been with another male since me."

Her chin rose. "I could. Probably someone

would trade me sex for a way to release your binding spell."

A dark look draped his features. Damian offered a thin smile, but his green eyes spoke volumes. Rage and male possessiveness.

"Don't sell yourself short, Jamie. Your body is worth much more. And if you try it, I'll find the male and make him regret he ever laid eyes on you." He paused, his strokes against her neck gentle compared to the murderous fury flashing in his eyes. "I'll rip him apart. Slowly."

White canines flashed in his dark smile...the teeth elongating as if he were shape-shifting. Jamie tilted her chin up, refusing to show fear.

"And me? What would you do with me?"

Damian's expression shifted. The intensity of his look was strong enough to melt steel.

"What I'd do with you? I'd rip off your clothing and I'd put my mouth all over your body and make you come until you screamed for mercy. There'd never be another male for you, ever, because every time you'd try to get close to another I'd be there, my scent in your nostrils, my taste in your mouth and the feel of my cock inside you."

He released her neck and gave her nose a light, almost affectionate tap. "Understand?"

Jamie moistened her kiss-swollen mouth. A deep, primitive urge rose at the way he stared at her lips. His muscles locked as his pupils got larger, nearly overriding the jade-green irises. Damian might have some odd sexual hold over her, but damn, she had the same over him. She had the odd feeling if she had the courage, she could wield a much greater power. But her lack of experience and inner terror of Damian's power held her back.

"I get it. You stripped my powers to punish me. Fine. Let's deal. I'll make up for it if you get rid of this damn spell. If you don't, I'll find another way. Like a hidden book of magick, Draicon."

Damian lightly trailed long fingertips over her cheek. "My name is Damian, not Draicon." His voice suddenly softened. Was there a note of regret there? She couldn't tell. "There's no need to make up for anything, Jamie. The binding spell is there for your own protection. Trust me, it's best."

"I know what's best for me. I don't need you or anyone else."

Torment flashed in his eyes, then he closed them. Bemused, she stared at the long sweep of dark lashes against his tanned cheeks. Damian opened his eyes, the emotion gone. "Walk with me. We need to talk. It's urgent."

She didn't want to, but the warm palm he cupped on her elbow suggested otherwise. Damian began steering her toward the river.

"Let me go. I don't trust you."

He stopped, giving her a solemn look. "I haven't given you good reason to trust me, either. But we must talk. We'll go to Café du Monde. Very public, so if you feel threatened, there's people around and you can scream for help. Okay?"

The devil offered her an irresistibly sweet deal. Hunger pulled with the image of a crisp beignet coated with layers of glistening powdered sugar.

People crowded the green-and-white-striped canopied café. Damian guided her to a quiet table outside. He pulled a chair out for her.

Torn between wanting to flee and hunger, Jamie sat. Damian took the seat beside her, so close his leg touched hers. She shuffled over; he followed. He seemed determined to stay close. Damian frowned as he examined her dejected expression. Reaching over, he cupped her chin, lifted it to his scrutinizing gaze.

"Hey," he said softly. "Relax. It will get better. The world hasn't collapsed."

My world has, she wanted to say, feeling her throat constrict. Instead she offered a brave shrug that hid her emotions.

Damian gave her a long, thoughtful look. He didn't question her further, but released his grip and gave their order to a tired-looking waitress.

Barely had she left when Jamie ripped a paper napkin out of the holder and spread it over on the tabletop. She shook the glass sugar container over the napkin, then unscrewed it, dumping out the contents onto the napkin.

His green eyes widened as she dug into the snowy mountain with her spoon and gulped down mouthfuls. "Easy," he murmured.

Ignoring him, she continued eating. The rush kicked in, giving her a flood of energy. The spoon clattered to the table. The scarred table-top resembled a white powder explosion. Damian looked deeply troubled.

"Wow, I knew sugar was supposed to give you a rush. I've been so tired lately." She wiped her fingers with a fresh napkin.

His dark, heavy brows drew together. "Jamie, why did you ask the Morphs to grant you the power of flight when there were other powers you could have received?"

"I didn't. Kane infected me with dark magick and told me it would shift to whatever natural form I desired."

Damian's gaze riveted to a fly landing near the sugar on the table. With amazing speed, his palm smacked down, killed the insect. She gave him a bemused look.

"Just a fly," he mused, flicking it away. "But you can't be certain. Not here."

The waitress brought over plates of beignets and steaming cups of coffee. Behind horn-rimmed glasses, her eyes widened at the empty sugar container. "Are you guys nuts? I just filled that," the woman snapped.

His eyes narrowed. "Then get another."

Jamie sank back, watching as he sipped his black coffee. "You wanted to talk, so talk. Then I'm gone."

Jade-green eyes met hers. "How long have you been eating like this, Jamie?"

"Since I dropped Weight Watchers. Any more questions? Are we done?"

"Jamie, how long have you eaten sugar like this?"

Obstinate Draicon. Jamie frowned, bemused at her bizarre behavior. "Today…I guess."

"You're certain this is the first craving you've had?" His voice sounded thick.

Jamie nodded and glanced at her coffee. She stared into the blackness. Black, like her soul had been. Once she would have done anything to hurt Damian. Now the desire for revenge fled, leaving only emptiness. Something inside remained as dark as the beings she'd lived among.

"Why are you here, Draicon?" she whispered. "To make me pay for what I did to you?"

His expression was blank, but he stroked her hand with his fingers as if he couldn't bear not to touch her. "I told you, Jamie, my name is Damian. I'm here to keep you safe."

Doubtful. He wanted something more. She could feel it.

"But, since you've broached the topic, why did you try to kill me? Most women don't kill their lovers when they walk out."

His voice was absolutely gentle, yet his laser green gaze demanded answers. Jamie plucked out a napkin and began twisting it into the shape of a small bird.

"I'm not most women."

"There's something more, isn't there? What?"

Trust no one. Jamie dodged the truth.

"You lied to me, Draicon. At least with the Morphs, I knew what they were. Dark, powerful…"

"Evil."

"But not two-faced. I played along. I thought you, what you did…after we…that night…" She struggled with the words. "I went back the next day to find you and you were gone. You broke your promise to teach me magick."

The napkin twisted in her hands. Words hung unspoken between them.

He clasped her hands in his. The simple touch felt soothing. She stared down at his long, elegant fingers. Hands that crushed, killed.

"I left you a note, telling you where to meet me later."

"There was no note." Jamie wrenched free.

Damian's mouth tightened. "Your…brother probably got to it first. I had to leave. I needed to get rid of a very large problem threatening you. I sent Nicolas, my best warrior, to find and guard you. I was going to teach you magick, but this other matter was more urgent. Now, answer my question. Why did you try to kill me, Jamie?"

"Why did you ground me?" she challenged. "This nonsense about me being your mate is a lie."

"It's not. You are my draicara, my destined mate, which makes no sense because you're human and I'm an Alpha Draicon. We don't bond with human women." Damian looked grim.

"I'm human, so I can't be your mate? Fine. We're done here. Sorry I tried to kill you. Have a nice life."

She pushed back from the table. He hooked an ankle around the chair leg. Jamie stared at his thigh muscles bunching beneath faded denim as he dragged her chair forward. Such power… She quivered, remembering his legs nestled inside hers, the soft hair rubbing against her skin as he thrust inside her.

Her startled gaze lifted to meet his. Damian gave a knowing smile. Little wrinkles fanned out from the corners of his eyes. He touched her hand, frowned.

"I can't read you, even when we touch. Tell me, how did Kane infect you? Did he say anything?"

She glanced away, her stomach knotting. "Kane bit me. Like the bite of the *loup garou*. And he mumbled some words in a strange language."

It had hurt, a lot. And more than the pain and the ecstasy of knowing she had power at last was an underlying shroud of evil. Jamie shivered.

"He was reciting a spell. The magick of a purebred Alpha may help." He gave her a steady look. "My magick, Jamie."

"So if you bite me, it will counter everything inside me? No thanks. One bite is bad enough."

"There are other ways," he said softly. "Much more enjoyable. I can make it very enjoyable."

The meaning became clear in his heated gaze. Jamie drew back.

"Never again. I'm not having sex with you and what we had was just sex. Biology." Afraid to look at him, lest she see a reflection of her own hidden desire.

"It wasn't and will never be just sex between us, *chère*. You know it and I do, as well. It's something neither of us can ignore. But I promise, I will never leave you again."

Damian stroked the back of her hand with his thumb. "What was it like, Jamie? When the darkness came over you?"

Against her better judgment, she slid her fingers up to lace with his. He looked startled. His smile chased the dark shadows beneath his eyes. Just as quickly, it vanished. She raised her gaze, saw his curiosity and worry.

He'd probably never known the gut-wrenching grief, fear and desperation caused by losing everything he cared about. Thinking nothing, not even pure evil, could be as bad. Then finding out what happened before was a spin on a slow carousel compared to the rocketing slide into an oily blackness so deep her soul was a tiny light winking in the vast, empty space.

Her voice rasped like a nail file when she finally spoke.

"It was like being sucked into a black depth, feeling evil invade every single pore. Trapped beneath this vile quicksand. No light, no hope, no way out, nothing but the sounds of your own screams echoing back at you," she whispered.

Damian squeezed her fingers, his jaw tensing. For a moment, turmoil flashed in his eyes as if he'd had a taste of that particular darkness. Then it vanished.

"Care for anything else?"

Their grumpy waitress was back. She looked edgy, fidgety. Probably the end of her shift.

"Hello? Like I said, need anything else?"

Damian barely cast her a cursory glance. "Give me the check and leave us alone."

The woman dropped a slip of paper. As she glanced at their linked hands, her mouth drew back in a disapproving sneer. Lips pulled back, revealing...

Yellowed, razor-sharp teeth, like a crocodile's.

Startled, Jamie blinked. No, just teeth stained from nicotine. The waitress cast another censuring look as she walked off.

What was this?

Trembling, she withdrew her hand, trying to conceal her reaction. She fished into her pocket and threw a fistful of bills on the table.

"My treat. It's getting late. I need to get home." But her legs felt wobbly. "Why am I feeling like this?" she said, rubbing her legs.

"I know why." He glanced around and then reached for her hand. His touch was absolutely gentle. "Jamie, it's very bad. When Kane infected you, he poisoned you."

Disbelief filled her. His green eyes looked serious, his mouth tightened to a slash. "He infected you with his bite, and the porphyry spell. The more dark magick you used, the faster it worked. The reason you feel so lethargic is..."

He dragged in a deep breath. "Your body is turning to stone. The craving for sugar is the first symptom. You're eating for quick energy, but it won't last."

Sharp, intense silence dripped between them. The crowd chattering, clinking china, the clopping of horses' hooves on the street and the roar of traffic were the only sounds. Then she laughed.

"Mark told me you were a liar, but he never said Draicon were great spinners of fantasy."

Anger darkened Damian's eyes. "Your brother was the liar, little one. A dangerous liar. I know it must have been agonizing and terrifying when you lost him…and that's why you ran away."

You killed him, she wanted to scream. Jamie bit her lip. She traced a small pattern in the sugar on the table. "Did you hear how he died?"

"I know how he died. He wasn't who you think he was, Jamie. When you're ready, I'll tell you what I know. I know it hurts to lose a family member."

"You have no idea," she whispered.

A shadow crossed his face. "I do, more than you realize." Damian's green gaze roved around the room. His jaw tightened. "We need to leave. Now. I feel it. You're not safe here. You need to go home and rest."

Rest. The thought sounded lovely. Jamie

got to her feet. Dismay filled her as Damian joined her.

"I'm coming with you. Consider me your guest." He offered her a roguish smile, filled with dark promise. Smooth, cool sheets, warm bodies curling next to each other as they tangled together in passion...

Stop it! Jamie sprinted away, but he easily kept pace.

"Haven't you ever heard of a hotel? Or if you can't afford one, there's an animal shelter around. They take in strays," she grated out.

Six feet of muscled werewolf stared her down, until she was forced to blink and look away. "You're my mate, Jamie. Pack. Pack bands together. It's how we survive. I won't abandon you so get used to the idea of having me around for good."

Damian held her elbow, a courtly, old-fashioned gesture with a greater intent behind it. Trapped, his prisoner. Too weary to fight, she walked. As they crossed over to Jackson Square and neared the cathedral, he ground to an abrupt halt. A cruel, ruthless smile curved his lips.

"Ah, I see an old friend. Stay here," he ordered, guiding her over to a park bench.

Grateful for the reprieve, Jamie sat. Interest sparked as she watched the Draicon stalk over to the doorway near where he'd kissed her. The doorway was open. Odd, because that building was empty and…

The hell with it. She didn't take orders.

Inside, dust and debris littered the empty room. Damian was standing in the far corner, crowding a short, elderly man in faded khaki trousers and a plaid short-sleeved shirt. She recognized him. The vendor who sometimes set up shop on the street near Café du Monde, sold fresh crayfish and then vanished before the police could order him away or question him about a permit.

Nice man, struggling to make a living after his shrimp boat had been washed away during Katrina's awful storm surge. Originally from Slidell, he…

Jamie gasped.

Damian was picking the man up by his throat, shaking him like a rag doll. The vendor uttered a dry squeal. A dagger appeared in Damian's hand. Horrified shock slammed into her as the Draicon thrust it into the man's chest. Then Damian flung him, dear God, flung him, across the room. The little crayfish vendor's head hit the wall with a sickening crack.

He was dead.

A scream died in her throat. Only a strangled moan arose as Damian turned, saw her and sped to her side. He cupped her cheeks in his hands, searching her face.

"Ah, Jamie, I wish you hadn't seen that."

"Y-you killed him," she whispered.

"Watch," Damian said quietly.

Before her eyes, the crayfish vendor's body turned to ash. Gray ash.

"He wasn't human. He was a Morph, disguised as a human."

"But I knew him! I've known him for a year now, I used to buy crayfish from him, he lives in…" Her voice trailed off. Jamie rubbed her arms, suddenly chilled.

"The Morphs killed him, and one assumed the man's identity. This is the second one I've killed today. I think the city is crawling with them, Jamie. Even people you know are really Morphs in disguise." Damian released her.

"How do I know you aren't one, as well?"

He waved his hand and a dagger appeared in his palm. Damian handed it to her, hilt side first. "Cut me. I bleed red, same as you. Not acid. The Morphs disguise themselves as humans, but they can't disguise their blood. That's how I knew the vendor wasn't human. He bled acid."

Hedging, she studied the knife. Calmly, Damian held out his hand. Then she slashed his palm. He didn't even wince. Crimson droplets welled up, bright and viscous. Grimacing, she touched the fluid. Just blood. Fascinated, Jamie watched the wound slowly close.

Damian waved his hand and the dagger vanished. "I suppose that's a good sign that you didn't take the knife and thrust it into my heart," he said with a wry smile.

"The thought occurred to me, but I think it would take a steel drill bit to pierce your hide." Jamie leaned back against the doorjamb, suddenly weary beyond words.

His expression changed to concern. Taking her arm, he guided her out of the building. They went to her house, each step feeling as if she slogged through heavy mud. Finally she reached home. She unlocked the gate and he escorted her inside, taking the key and locking the gate. Damian pocketed the key and released her. Exhausted, Jamie headed for the courtyard and sat in one of the faded wicker chairs.

Approval flared on his face as Damian followed. He looked around, his hand resting on the redbrick wall. "This is a good house. A safe house."

Jamie shoved out of the chair. "Find yourself somewhere else to sleep tonight. You're a Draicon, the ground should suit you fine. Don't howl at the moon. You'll wake the neighbors."

"Howling at the moon is an old wives' tale. I

only howl when I want sex. So don't be alarmed if you hear me in the night."

Startled, she turned to find him offering a charming smile.

"Howl at me all you want, Draicon, but you'll have to force me to get me into bed with you again," she snapped.

"I won't ever force you. You'll come to me. Soon, you won't be able to resist any more than I will," he said gently.

When wolves fly.

Damian followed her upstairs, but she ignored him. The bedroom door locked behind her. Jamie collapsed on the antique four-poster, clutching her pillow and staring at the yellowed ceiling. A cool night breeze drifted through the French doors open to the garden. She always hated this room with its dreary heaviness, but Mark had liked it so she left it alone.

Her body felt leaden. Was she turning to stone? Impossible. *It's a trick to get you to trust him, so he can sleep with you again.*

She hugged the pillow to her chest. Tears didn't come. They weren't allowed. She hadn't cried since, wow, when?

One single tear, shed from guilt and shame when she'd gone to Damian's deathbed and saw him lying there. But real, honest, grieving tears?

Since the day her parents died. Since then

she hadn't wept. Not even for all she'd lost. And doubted she ever would again.

Small sounds barely audible to the human ear alerted Damian. He paused outside Jamie's door. Hovering, he waited, instinct screaming to rush inside and hold her in his arms. She'd bite his head off. Tough Jamie didn't want him seeing her break down.

Her breath was hitching in little gasps.

He broke the lock and went inside. Damian switched on a small Tiffany lamp. The soft yellow glow illuminated a crimson room smothered in ponderous furniture. Much too serious for Jamie.

She needed a light, airy room, with sky-blue walls and whimsical furniture.

Approaching the four-poster bed more suitable for a royal monarch, Damian silently assessed his future mate. Asleep, she lay curled on her side toward him, her shoulder-length black hair mussed. Little snuffling noises came from her, but she shed no tears.

Such delicate features, the pointed chin, the impossibly thick lashes, nearly translucent skin and carved cheekbones and full, mobile mouth and pert nose. She looked so damn young.

Sadness had shone in those expressive gray eyes. Jamie might try hiding her emotions, but her eyes were mirrored pools. He saw himself in the reflection, the arrogant, supremely powerful Draicon who had so much to offer, but instead took so much away. More than her innocence. He'd stolen away her dreams of magick and power.

And in doing so, made her turn to dark forces.

Regret arrowed through him. He would make amends, but had to earn her trust first. Her spunk relieved him. Jamie hadn't lost her spirit or courage, two attributes she'd need in the coming days.

The house was safest for Jamie. He'd felt the ancient, sturdy power. Someone long ago had put a strong shield on it to guard against anyone performing dark magick. Anyone wishing to hurt Jamie would have to drag her outside the structure.

The bed sank beneath his weight. Just to hold her, touch her, if only for a moment. Instinct lashed him to mate. A purebred Alpha, Damian could only procreate with Jamie. He needed her for his pack in New Mexico, ruling at his side.

But he pushed aside lust, brushing back a lock of hair from her pale face. So cold, damn, her skin was icy.

He stroked her forehead. He would save her, at any cost. She was his, and he always took care of his own.

A grim smile touched his mouth. Even if they didn't want saving.

Damian lay down, curled his big body next to her slender one and draped an arm about her waist. She moved back, snuggling against him as if relishing his heat.

He relished the feel of Jamie's slender body. Heaviness flooded his loins. The erection reminded him of the relentless desire chasing him. Damian ruthlessly reined in his control and eased back. She was so slight, yet tough. Tainted from dark magick, yet innocence still clung to her.

Jamie whimpered in her sleep. A single tear leaked out of the corner of one eye. Deeply troubled, Damian chased it away with a kiss. Expecting a salty tang, he recoiled.

Pure, sweet confectioner's sugar.

Growing dread gathered in his chest as Damian abruptly sat up. "It's happening already. What the hell am I going to do?"

I will not let you die. You can't die like my family did. I'll do anything I can to stop this.

Rising out of bed, he left and quietly shut the bedroom door. Damian realized for the first time that he might be too late.

If he couldn't find the book, he'd lose her.

Forever.

Chapter 3

Damian needed answers. His boyhood friend and adopted brother, Raphael Robichaux, could help. He whipped his cell phone out of his pocket, went to punch in Rafe's number. His finger hovered above the keypad. Dialing for help.

Help that never came for his family.

Oh merde, *let's not go there.* But it came back, all in a roaring flood. The phone dropped from his numb fingers to the couch.

Twelve years old, delirious with the power of his first change. Determined to hunt in the bayou. His father had ordered him to remain home. It wasn't safe. Morphs were on the hunt.

Damian wasn't afraid. Hell, he could defeat

Godzilla himself. Annie begged him to stay. "I'm scared, Damian. Please don't leave me!"

He'd told his little sister she'd be fine, tucked her into bed with her favorite stuffed animal. Then escaped to the bayou and run with the night. Powerful. Draicon. Hunter. *No Morph can harm me. Superwolf,* mon ami.

Shortly after, the screams echoed in his mind.

Morphs had stormed into the mansion. Shifting back, his fear and grief scrambling his powers so he couldn't summon clothing by magick, he'd run naked back to his house. He'd hammered his fists on neighbors' doors, but they'd ignored his shouts for help. Cutting his feet on stones, praying he'd make it, his bloodied feet slipping on the pavement, his breath a hot, stabbing agony. The scent of death had poured into his nostrils when he'd bolted through the opened door. His father, on the floor, his body wrapped protectively about Damian's pregnant mother. His brothers, dead. Annie, where was Annie?

He found her hiding beneath her bed. Blood splattered the stuffed dog still clutched in her thin arms. Horror and pain glazed her opened eyes. She was four years old. He'd held her broken body in his arms, rocking her and singing her favorite lullaby until he finally gathered strength to bury his family in the dark of night.

Dragging himself back to the present, Damian

fisted his hands. Never again would he break the rules or abandon those under his protection. When he did, someone paid dearly.

The past was past. He had an adopted family now here in Louisiana, and back in New Mexico his own pack to rule. Soon, he would have his mate, as well. The cell went into his palm again. A loud buzz sounded. He pocketed the phone and headed downstairs, opening the grate that enabled a view of the street.

A petite, dark-skinned woman stood outside. "I'm Mama Renee, Jamie's friend who runs the voodoo shop down the street," she said in a soft slur. "You're Damian."

Startled, he narrowed his eyes. "Are you psychic?"

"But of course. May I come in? I have something for Jamie."

The woman looked nonthreatening. Still…remembering his encounter with the crayfish, he studied her calm features.

"Blink," he ordered.

She did without question. Dark brown eyes, soft and compassionate.

"You don't remember me, do you? But of course, you were only five or so. I remember you. Your father, Andre, he was so proud of you. He called you *loup petit*."

Shock reverberated through Damian. His

nostrils flared as he inhaled the woman's scent. Nothing but a faint fragrance of cologne or perfume.

"My family didn't associate with many... people." He stared at her.

"They only trusted a few. Will you please let me in? I need to see Jamie."

Damian let her inside. Suspicion arose as he closed and locked the gate, then leaned against it. "What do you want?"

"I brought her something to make her feel better." The woman fished a small cloth bag from a pocket in her dress. Damian inhaled the scent of herbs and spices. A *gris-gris*.

Morphs detested the good luck talismans. Still...

"You see everyone as the enemy. What must I do to prove I am a friend?" she asked softly.

Waving his hand, a dagger appeared in his palm. Renee did not look startled, only respectful.

"Cut yourself. I want to see if you bleed red."

His voice was rough with hostility. The woman took the dagger, cut her hand and winced. She gave him back the blade.

A coppery scent of blood filled his nostrils. He jerked his head toward the stairs.

"Follow me."

Senses on full alert, Damian took the stairs

two at a time. He fetched a first-aid kit from the bathroom and returned. Renee put gauze over her wound.

"You don't trust me, which is good. You're very protective of her. She is in big trouble, *mais oui?*" Renee said.

Damian said nothing. He withdrew to the kitchen, out of earshot. He dialed Raphael's number. His adopted brother answered on the first ring. Speaking rapidly in French, Damian told him what happened since his arrival.

"Do you know a psychic named Mama Renee?" he asked.

"Runs a voodoo shop in town. Good people. Why?"

"She's here. I can't leave Jamie alone, but we need to talk. In private so she can't hear us," he said quietly. He wandered back into the living room, leaned against the wall.

"If you need to leave, I will watch her for you," Renee offered.

With Renee's apple-round cheeks, kind smile and ordinary flowered dress, she looked innocuous. Human, but still, humans were dangerous.

"Want me to come over?" Raphael asked.

"Hold on a minute," Damian told him.

She held his gaze. "I was there at your birth."

"T'me dis pas," he said dryly, not believing a damn word.

"I do say," she countered. Then she glanced around. Before his shocked eyes, she shifted into a wolf.

"Mon Dieu," he muttered, watching her return to her human form. "You are family, *non?*"

"There are more of us than you know," she said softly. Renee's eyes grew sad. "My husband and son...they embraced the darkness. Your parents, they kept me safe. I am forever grateful and regret what happened to you as a *bébé*. Please, allow me to make amends now."

He listened intently as she explained, everything making sense now. Renee laid a hand on his arm. "It's all right. I'll watch over her."

Damian turned to the phone. "I'll meet you. Where?"

Raphael rattled off a place. Damian hung up, pocketed the cell.

He glanced at Renee. "Don't let anyone in. When Jamie wakes up, don't let her leave the house."

"Go meet with your friend. Be careful. Terrible darkness has taken over the city." The woman looked deeply troubled.

Though he trusted few outside his pack and his adopted family, and was frugal with his emotions, Damian hugged her. Renee looked startled, and then hugged him back. She patted his arm in a motherly gesture.

At the Chartes Street Café, his brother sat at a copper-topped table just inside the doorway. His gleaming Harley waited on the street, a shining chrome and metal horse.

Damian slid into the opposite seat.

"Watch our backs," his brother cautioned, nodding toward the bustling street. He scrutinized Damian's casual clothing. "Damian, *ça va?* Almost didn't recognize you without your Versace socks, *t' frère.*"

The endearment of "little brother" made Damian smile. "I'm trying to blend in."

"You blend in like the wolf blends in the henhouse."

Raphael signaled for a waitress and when she arrived, ordered seafood gumbo and water with lime.

"Just water." Damian grimaced, thinking of the crayfish/Morph. He gave his brother a long, steady look. "Raphael." He reached over and embraced his forearms.

The other Draicon squeezed back. His shoulder-length dark brown hair with its streak of pure white accompanied scuffed boots, faded jeans, black T-shirt and black leather jacket. A tiny gold sword earring hung from his left ear, and a day's growth of dark beard shadowed his hard jaw. The ensemble contrasted with Raphael's classically handsome face. It gave him an intense look, as if an angel had stumbled out of a Bourbon sex shop.

Damian leaned forward, serious. "How bad is it? How many?"

"Bad. Morphs are everywhere. Hard to get a count. Maybe fifty, or hundreds."

"*Dit moula vérité!* Are you serious?" Damian sat back, stunned. "Why are they here?"

"We think it's for the Book of Magick. It's been hidden for seventy years, hasn't it? If a spell isn't used in the next couple of weeks, all the spells will vanish. Including the ones for evil the Morphs want, to make them more powerful."

And the spell for curing Jamie would vanish, as well. Damian felt his insides clench at the thought. "If they get the book first..."

"They'll use the bad magick to kill all Draicon. They're killing machines now, here in town. And when they kill, the bodies they leave... They're targeting the homeless. I've taught my guys to sniff the blood, find and destroy the bodies before the police arrive. We've gotten to most of them in time. We can't risk cops poking into our world, our war."

Damian felt his canines descend with the urge to hunt and destroy. A low growl rumbled from his chest. A passing waitress gave him a startled look. He offered a charming smile, which faded as she walked away.

"Bastards," he muttered.

"Don't fret, *t'frère*. I took out a few. One dared to call me a dog. I showed him the unfriendly side of my blade before popping him." The charming smile Raphael offered didn't meet the hardness of his dark eyes.

Raphael was the Kallan, the only Draicon permitted to terminate the life of another Draicon, even a relative, without consequence. He had died and gone to the Other Realm and received the gift of immortality. Little scared him. Morphs who messed with Raphael lost.

Raphael's gumbo arrived and he dug into it with zest. Damian sipped his water. "My father didn't tell me where he hid it. Only said he entrusted a good friend with the secret until I was older. I wish our ancestors had never handed it down through my family, but it's my responsibility."

"What happened to your father's friend?"

"Morphs killed Jordan when they killed all Father's pack." He stared at a droplet of water sliding down his glass like a tear. "The cure for Jamie is in the book."

"So, tell me about your mate. We researched her. Her friends, her parents dying in that plane crash when she was five, the aunt and uncle who raised her. Hell, we even tracked down info about that bastard who imitated her brother. What's she like?" Raphael asked.

"A killer."

"Pretty?"

"She tried to kill me."

Raphael stared. Damian explained.

Silverware rattled as Raphael slapped a palm on the table. "How the hell can you trust her? She deserves punishment." His hand went to the dagger always tucked into his belt. "Remember our vow? You're my blood brother."

"And she's my mate," Damian said quietly.

"Then, *t' frère,* you have a big problem. If you don't bond with her, you'll turn feral. But how can you mate with a human who wished you into a coffin?"

Damian leaned back, edgy and wanting. A male's draicara pumped up all his testosterone, driving him to prove his strength and sexual prowess. In Alphas, the mating drive tripled, turning males wild and unpredictable. If he didn't mate, he'd be dangerous even to his pack. Would they drive him away as his father's people had?

He wanted only Jamie now, her scent, the taste of her skin, the feel of her soft, naked body beneath his. He couldn't shake off his lust.

"Let it go, Rafe. I can handle her."

"Then do it fast. Sounds like she's running out of time. Sex can slow the porphyry *cunja.* If you trust her not to slam a knife in your back while you mount her." Rafe's jaw tightened.

Sex might be a solution. A Draicon's cells, including blood and semen, contained magick. As a purebred Alpha, his magick was more powerful than other males'.

"Could I cure Jamie by infusing her with my magick when we have sex?"

Rafe raised his gaze to his. Damian tensed against the haunting sorrow swimming there.

"No. Your blood, or coming inside her, will only slow the spell. It can't stop it."

He stared at the big vein on Raphael's neck, throbbing with life. His immortal brother whose blood contained immense energy and power. "Maybe…"

Rafe tensed and looked away. It was forbidden for Rafe, and he knew the consequences would be drastic.

"I have to find the book." Damian ran a hand over his face. "But I can't leave her alone. It's too risky."

"Then let me help. I'll send Adam and Ricky. Keep watch. They'll do anything to keep her from leaving."

"Don't you dare let another male near her." Damian growled, his fingers digging into his napkin. Instinct urged him to stake a claim. Rip apart any male who glanced her way.

"Damian, easy, easy."

Shreds of linen napkin lay on the table. Willing himself to calm, he retracted his claws.

Raphael's wary look said it all. He dug into his gumbo, ate in silence. After a minute, Damian felt his control returning. His brother gave him a mild look.

"So tell me. Is she really dying?"

Raphael cursed in French after Damian told him. "My guys are yours. Take Adam and Ricky. Best warriors, can kick Morph ass from here to Houma. Or any of my other males. There's twenty now, all show promise of being good fighters. Anything to help, *t'frère.*"

Raphael had taken unmated male Draicon with no blood relations, taught them discipline and bonding and formed them into a pack to fight Morphs. Too many wild, frustrated males roved the streets. A grieving and angry Draicon without the close-knit society of a pack was dangerous.

"Merci," he managed. "But I can't risk a pack trailing me. Do your part. Find and kill Morphs, as many as you can."

"It's war," his friend agreed.

Damian narrowed his gaze as his mouth flattened into a ruthless line. *"Laissez les bons temps rouler."* Let the good times roll.

"Damian? This Jamie. She'd better not try anything on you again. Mate or not. You're blood, *t' frère.*" Raphael removed a gold dagger from the sheath hanging on his jeans. Light played over the intricate runes carved into the sacred Scian. He flipped it into the air, catching it by the hilt. His eyes were stone-cold.

"My business, Rafe. Leave it be."

They locked stares, muscles quivering until Raphael sheathed the blade with a small nod.

"What can I do, then?" Rafe asked.

"Be available. I may need help. And fetch my stuff from the hotel, bring it over when I call." A grim smile touched his mouth. "I'm moving in with her."

"Latcr, then." The other Draicon clasped his arm.

Damian left, glanced around the busy sidewalk. His priorities were clear. Get Jamie to trust him and find the book. He'd go back to her, she was probably hungry...

Fresh fruit. Natural fructose might help. He stopped at a small grocery store and purchased peaches.

He retuned to her house, headed upstairs with the bag. Jamie sat on the couch as she typed on a laptop. Damian nearly dropped the fruit. Elongated purple elfin ears stuck comically out of either side of her head.

She glanced up as he set the peaches down on

the coffee table. A question in his eyes, Damian sat beside her and playfully tweaked an ear.

"I'm a warrior Night Elf," she said, yawning. "I'm too tired to wear the rest of the outfit. Cosplay makes me feel better. It's comforting."

"I thought women liked dressing in old T-shirts and sweats to get comfortable."

Her mouth turned down. "When I cosplay, I am Celyndra, my elf. She's a tough fighter, courageous and doesn't fear much."

"Ah, she's your alter ego," he said softly in understanding. A frown puckered his forehead. "Such an imagination. Where did you get the idea?"

She grinned at his expression. "Haven't you ever heard of WoW?"

"Wow?"

"World of Warcraft. My avatar is a female Night Elf warrior. Some who were in my alliance used to meet at the square Saturday nights to hang out and cosplay."

Jamie's grin deepened. "Don't tell me you never heard of cosplay, either. Everyone knows what it is. What are you, a hundred?"

"Eighty," he muttered, feeling as old as an ancient mage. Merlin, maybe.

"Eighty! You look like you're in your twenties. No wonder you don't know what anything is."

"I know what hanging out is," he said defensively.

"Cosplay is costume play. You dress as a character from a book or game and role play. World of Warcraft is an online video game. You pick a character and fight battles. It's a lot more complicated than that, but…"

"Battles?" he echoed. Damian narrowed his eyes. "You learned to fight and organize an army? This skill you taught the Morphs came from a game?"

"I did learn some skill from it. But that's nothing compared to some guys I know. Former marines, army guys. Friends."

Raphael's pack had checked out all her friends in New Orleans. Jamie had few. A terrible suspicion seized him.

"Guys you know from where?"

"Online. I met them on MyPlace."

Alarms screeched in his head. Jamie was involved in a dangerous world he knew nothing about. "You have a MyPlace page?"

Damian's glance fell to her opened laptop. He picked it up, rapidly surfed through it. He found her page. Jamie Walsh, in lavender, with beautiful illustrations of fairies in the background. If he weren't so furious, he'd admire the intricate artwork and the delicate simplicity of the winged creatures. Damian scrolled down, shocked at the personal details. She liked fantasy books, alternative music, designed web pages and was a self-professed geek.

People she'd like to meet. "Anyone with real magick because I need magick in my life," she'd written. The sentence sounded a little wistful. He scrolled down to her friends. Her top friends were former military types. But... Damian zipped through the last friends she'd acquired. Names like Wolfeater, Draiconhater.

Online predators. Morphs. "You're an open target with this, Jamie."

"It's my page. My friends are there."

"Friends? Will they come to your aid if you need them? Not these bastards. They used you, Jamie. You don't need friends. You're my mate and you have a pack, my pack and my family here, as well. They're much more important. Family will always be there when you need help." Reining in his emotions, Damian kept his face expressionless.

"Delete it," he ordered.

"No. And I don't need your pack. I do just fine on my own. Go to hell." Defiance flashed in her gray eyes.

Damian stared at her as his hands slowly crushed the laptop, splintering it in half. Her jaw dropped as the crumbled pieces fell to the floor. A strangled squeak arose from her throat.

"You won't do that again. Try defying me and I'll break every single computer you have. Your enemies, and mine, on that page. Who do you think infected you with this spell? You're turning to stone, Jamie. From the inside out."

"Kane had no reason for it," she protested, but her voice shook considerably.

"You're my draicara, my mate. Reason enough. He used you to try to kill me. He used a safeguard, as well. A slow-working spell to eliminate you."

"All I wanted was to learn magick," she said, looking crestfallen. "It's something I wanted my whole life. Is that so wrong?"

Damian cupped her chin in one strong hand. "Then look, little one. Look and learn. I will teach you magick. Good magick."

Releasing her, he waved his hand, summoning a ball of white light. Iridescent sparks glimmered from it. It hovered in the air, danced as Damian created patterns with his palm. Jamie gasped in delight. A wide smile touched her face. Damn, he'd do anything to keep her looking like that. Happy. Young. Carefree.

She leaned forward to study the orb, her slender arm stretching out. Her expression turned to awed wonder as she touched the ball with one finger. The light flashed, turned gray, then black.

Before his astounded eyes, it shriveled, then vanished.

"Oh! Oh...I killed it," she whispered.

Her mouth wobbled precariously. Jamie seemed to shrink inside herself. Moving closer to her, he clasped her hand in his. Cold, so damn cold. Like blue ice.

"It's not you. It's what's inside of you," he said very gently. "When the dark magick is gone, the light won't vanish from your touch."

A tremulous smile touched her mouth. "I wish I could believe you."

I wish you would, as well. He picked up the bag of peaches. "Eat. You need your strength." Damian frowned as he glanced around. "When did Renee leave? I asked her to stay with you."

"Said she had to get back to the shop." Jamie dug into the bag and withdrew a peach. "Thanks. I'm so hungry, I could eat an orchard."

She brightened, a smile touching her pixie face. The sight lifted his own spirits. He steeled against the temptation to kiss her again. "Why did Renee go back?"

Jamie went into the kitchen. Her voice trailed out to the living room. "You should know. She said you'd called, asked her to bring another *gris-gris* to the house."

Damian went utterly still, the hair on the nape

of his neck rising. "I'll be right back. Don't move from here," he ordered.

A horrible suspicion crested over him. He raced out of the house. Sprinting down the street, he reached the voodoo shop.

The door was ajar. Cautiously he stepped inside. The scent slammed into him with the force of a hurricane. Blood. Death. Lacing through it was the faint scent of honeysuckle.

A black cat greeted him, mewling pitifully. Damian crossed the room, started for the back and ground to a halt. Anguish spilled through him like acid.

"Oh, damn. Damn, I'm sorry," he said softly.

Mama Renee lay in the corner, her eyes wide open in terror. Blood splashed over the pretty flowered dress, splattered the walls.

Someone had torn her heart out. Morphs. They reserved the right to lick up each last drop of fear.

Grief and rage twined together. Damian closed his eyes. Renee had been a last connection to his parents. How many more of his people must die, sliced down by evil? His parents, brothers and sister. Members of his pack back in New Mexico. How could he ever hope to stop this and protect those who looked to him to keep them safe?

He pushed aside sorrow. Grief was for later.

The stench of death made him gag. Damian murmured the ancient Draicon blessing for a departed soul. He spotted the altar to the voodoo priestess, Marie Laveau.

Darkness had extinguished the candles.

The police would question, snoop around. Couldn't risk them finding out about his world. He needed a motive. A hate crime, and robbery. Damian withdrew all the money from the cash register and stuffed it into his pocket to later burn. He left the drawer open. He glanced around, found a permanent marker and scrawled on the wall.

DEVIL WORSHIPPER.

The mewling at his legs grew louder. The cat held the scent of an ordinary feline. Picking it up, he studied the animal. "You already used one of your nine lives. Let's get you somewhere safe."

Tucking the cat in his arms, he looked around. Waving his hand, he dispelled all evidence of his fingerprints. The cops would question Jamie, though, and...

Jamie. He'd left her alone.

Damian tore down the street, frantic with fear for his draicara. He unlocked the gate, banged it shut behind him. Releasing the cat, he took the stairs two at a time.

She was sitting on the couch. His knees went weak with relief.

Then he took a closer look. Terror shaded her expression as she stared at her hand. Seeing him,

Jamie thrust out her palm at him. It trembled violently.

"Damian, look at me. Look at me. Oh God, what's wrong with me? I can't bleed. I can't bleed!"

Shock filled him as he looked at her hand. A knife and fruit slices lay on the coffee table. She'd been cutting a peach. Then the knife had slipped and hurt her.

Peaches scented the air, but he smelled no coppery scent of blood. A shallow laceration on her palm showed no crimson. Instead, a sluggish gray matter leaked out.

Gray, like granite.

She was turning to stone before his horrified eyes.

Chapter 4

I'm dying. It couldn't be happening. It wasn't real. Couldn't be real.

Jamie thrust out her wrist at the Draicon she hated, the Draicon who'd warned her this was happening. A hysterical whisper bubbled up.

"Don't let me die."

It was her punishment. In trying to kill Damian, she'd succeeded in killing herself. It didn't hurt. Painless, just this sluggish lethargy as if her limbs were turning to stone. She wanted to feel something, not this horrid draining as if she were already dead.

In her computer world, Celyndra possessed incredible strength and health. Jamie regenerated fast in cyberspace. Now, her body failed.

Damian sank down onto the couch. He seized her wrist, bound it with gauze on the table. Two strong arms pulled her to him. He muttered something she couldn't understand, brushed her hair back. Jamie caught a glimpse of long canine teeth descending. Sharp. Dangerous.

Damian bent his head, nuzzled her neck as if kissing her skin.

He bit her.

Sizzling pain screeched along her nerves. Her scream was cut short by a slow, almost erotic scrape as his tongue traced the wound. Strength fled as she collapsed, sagging like a rag doll.

Damn you, Draicon, I was already dying, she thought fuzzily before darkness claimed her.

She mustn't die. No. Not again. He couldn't watch her die, lose her like he'd lost his family, little Annie...

He'd acted on instinct. Knowing his bite infused her with good magick. Knowing it would save her.

Very gently Damian cradled her as she fell limp. Her pallor grayish, her hysteria abated. He felt her forehead. Cold but no longer icy. He waited a minute, frantic with worry, then checked her wound. Watery crimson leaked out. Blood.

Relief filled him, so intense he shook. Damian licked her laceration with his healing saliva. He fetched a blanket from the bedroom, covered Jamie to keep her body temperature warm. He punched a number on his cell phone and explained what happened.

When Raphael arrived, Damian's duffel bag slung over his shoulder and carrying a paper sack, Damian led him upstairs. Rafe dumped the items and gently picked up Jamie's wrist. "The spell starts working from the inside out on the extremities, then spreads to the vital organs, clogging the blood supply. The fingernails and hair usually turn gray before it gets to this point. *Mon Dieu*, I've never heard of it accelerating this fast. When did she get bit?"

"Kane infected her six weeks ago. Why is it spreading like this? She's human and it shouldn't affect her as much."

A frown puckered Raphael's forehead as he put down Jamie's hand. "Humans. She's your draicara. No Alpha Draicon ever had a human mate. Maybe she's not human."

Stunned, Damian sank onto the couch. He held Jamie's hand, reassured at the warmth spreading through it, the pulse beating slow but steadily. "For now, we have to assume she's human. What else can I give her?"

Raphael dumped the bag on the kitchen table. "I called Paw Paw and got the recipe for a potion. Should help for a while."

"I hope so. By the way, I need you to dispose of a body. Ma Petite Voodoo Maison. Morphs got to her."

Blood drained from Raphael's face. "Renee?"

His brother raced down the stairs. When Raphael returned, he looked grim. "Too late. There's people in front of the shop. She's been found."

Worry riddled him. He pushed it aside, concentrating on Jamie. She came first.

Someone pressed a cup to her lips. "Drink," the deep voice commanded. "It will help you, Jamie."

Still confused, her mind muzzy, she opened her mouth and obeyed. The liquid smelled coppery and tasted faintly of something salty, warm and rich. She gagged and glanced down at the cup. Red liquid sloshed inside.

"Again," the voice insisted.

Jamie shook her head, but instead of the exhaustion she'd felt, energy poured through her. Real energy, as if she were awakening from a spell.

"What is that?" she croaked.

"A magick potion with herbs and spices and nothing that will harm you."

Her mind processed the information. A potion aiding her. A fierce desire surfaced to live, to fight whatever had crippled her.

The cup was put to her mouth again. Jamie grabbed the glass and drank, resisting the reflexive instinct to gag.

More energy filled her. Wary of pushing it, she slowly sat up, flexed her fingers. Jamie stared at the now-healed cut on her hand.

Seeing the question in her eyes, Damian nodded. "You bleed red now, Jamie. I bit you to infuse you with my magick, but it's not permanent. For now, it will help. The tired feeling you had should be gone. It was the spell."

A shiver snaked down her spine. "How long will I feel better?"

"Without more magick, a week, perhaps, maybe a little longer. I'm not certain. I don't have experience with this."

He took her palm, stroked it. "How are you feeling?"

Stronger. Better. Perplexed. "Why did you do that?"

Damian squeezed her palm. "*Chère,* don't you understand? I'm trying to save you."

"Why? I tried to kill you. I'm not the kind of mate you want."

"Want has nothing to do with it. Call it biology. Laws of the pack. You need me, and I need you." His fingers trailed over her palm.

Damn, this was mighty confusing. His brusque statement contrasted with the gentle stroke of his fingers across her chilled skin. It broke down the black-and-white areas into patches of gray. She didn't like gray. Black-and-white was much easier, like computer coding.

I have to survive. And if he's the means, then I'll think about the other stuff later. Like I always have. "I need to see Mama Renee. She has lots of experience with potions. She'll have answers."

Damian exchanged glances with someone standing silently in the doorway. A strip of pure white hair streaked through the man's shoulder-length dark hair. About four inches taller than Damian, he had the face of an angel and dressed like a biker. Jamie blinked in vague recognition. She'd seen him somewhere before. "Who are you?"

Introducing her, Damian explained Raphael was his brother. Oh God. Memories ate her guts like a horde of angry ants. Jamie swallowed hard. One of the Draicon who'd joined Damian in killing Mark. Tearing her brother to pieces, as he screamed…

"Another Draicon? How many stray dogs are there in this city?" Jamie shot out.

Raphael's mouth thinned to a tight slash. He didn't appear to like her any more than she liked him.

"*Dai,* I'm headed out. Call me if you need me." Raphael gave her a hard look and left.

The Draicon slammed the door behind him. Jamie set down the glass and pushed off the couch, relieved to find her limbs functioning normally.

"Where are you going?" Damian demanded.

"Mama Renee's, just a few doors down. Maybe she can... What?"

Damian stood and went to her, putting his hands on her shoulders.

"Stay here, Jamie. There's something you should know...."

Through her thin T-shirt, she felt his hands' warmth. Jamie resisted the urge to collapse and absorb his strength. It had been so long since she'd leaned on anyone. The only person she could trust was herself.

But damn, just for once, it would be nice to have someone truly on her side.

"If you don't know enough, then I have to find someone who does," she muttered.

A loud buzz warned someone was at the front gate. Shrugging off his hands, Jamie trounced downstairs, Damian following close behind. A man in a rumpled black suit with a tired face stood outside. "I'm Detective Robert Ryan. Do you know the woman who lives two doors down, a Mrs. Renee St. Clair?"

"Renee's a good friend."

"I'm sorry to tell you this, but...we believe Mrs. St. Clair has been killed."

Her heart raced as she shrank back. "There's some mistake."

"Perhaps," the detective said evenly. "Does she have any relatives living in the city?"

"She has a daughter in North Carolina, and her son was killed in a car wreck a while back."

"Could you come with us and identify the body, Miss Walsh?"

I can't, she thought with sickening dread. But she had to see for herself. Had to know...that the one woman she felt friendship with was gone. It simply couldn't be real.

Jamie nodded. Damian took her elbow and gave the detective a hard look. "Just a minute. I'm going with her and we need to lock up."

He pulled her inside the gate, out of earshot. "Renee was not here with you. Understand? Otherwise you're a suspect."

Her stomach twisted in knots. They left the house, following the detective. Police cars crammed the narrow street, blue and red lights bouncing off the buildings, yellow tape being unfurled and plastered across a perimeter of the sidewalk. All stuff she'd seen countless times on television crime shows.

Only this time it was real. Too real.

The familiar interior of the voodoo shop looked normal, though a horrid, coppery stench filled the air. Her instincts knew the smell. Blood and violence. Cops milled about, dusting the shelves with black fingerprint powder, taking photos.

"She's back here." The detective walked toward the back room.

She pulled free of Damian and went to a yellow plastic sheet covering something on the floor. Detective Ryan's face remained expressionless. "Ready?"

Jamie drew in a deep breath and nodded, barely feeling Damian's strong hands on her shoulders. The cop pulled back the sheet to show a face.

A face she knew and didn't. Lips pulled back into a silent scream, warm brown eyes dulled and glazed with horror.

A strangled moan arose in her throat. Jamie jerked her head forward. "It's her, but how…" She had to know, even though she knew what she would find would be horrible.

Trembling fingers clutched the sheet's edge, ripped it from the startled detective's grip. Jamie pulled the sheet back with a vicious yank, exposing the body. Dark bruises ringed Renee's neck. Blood splattered the pretty flowered dress and a ragged hole showed where… Her heart. Her big, generous heart. Gone.

Jamie gagged, clapped a hand over her mouth. Oh God, her friend…died in pain, horribly. A boulder the size of Louisiana compressed her chest. Her bottom lip wobbled precariously as the burning rose in her throat.

Her parents. Mark. Would the streak of deaths ever end? Maybe the Grim Reaper was only a happy camper when he kept slaughtering everyone in her life.

She ignored the tightness in her throat. No grief. She tried to speak past the cotton dryness in her mouth. Damian put a hand on her shoulder, squeezed gently. His fingers trailed over her nape, stroking in soothing motions as if he tried calming her.

"Wh-who could have done this?"

"Someone with a great deal of strength." The cop swept her with an even gaze. She guessed his thoughts. Small, slender hands, barely enough strength to rip open a cereal-box top.

But who did possess such strength? Draicon did.

"When did you last see her, Miss Walsh?"

Menace and anger rolled from Damian in thick, violent waves. He gave the cop a look cool enough to freeze burning coal. "She's not up to answering questions now."

"It's okay," she told Damian, then looked at the detective. "This morning, we had tea, and then she got customers."

Each question tossed at her she answered steadily, her mind sharpening, her emotions dulled. Her mind raced. Who could want Renee dead? The woman had no enemies, nothing much of value to steal... The laptop. Jamie's gaze darted over to the side table where Renee had last placed it. Gone.

"May I go into the back rooms, Detective? She was a good friend and I can tell you if anything is missing."

"I'll go with you," Ryan said.

In the kitchen, the shiny new blue notebook sat on the table with a wireless Internet card tucked into the slot. Black fingerprint powder covered the surface.

"Nice notebook." Ryan gestured to it. "Odd the killer took only the cash from the register and not this. She used it to send an e-mail to her granddaughter today."

A chill fell over Jamie. She glanced up at Damian's stoic expression.

"Maybe the killer didn't want it tracked back to him," Jamie said softly. She glanced around. "Where is Renee's cat?"

Ryan frowned. "We found no cat."

Archimedes must have escaped. He was a survivor, and probably out roaming the streets. The least of her worries now.

"Detective, is her diamond pendant missing? She loved it and it should be in her jewelry box upstairs. I'll stay here. I'm feeling faint."

Jamie slipped into the chair before the laptop, burying her face in her hands. No lie, for she was feeling sick. She waited until he left the kitchen, then lifted her head.

Damian leaned over the table. "I need to get you out of here."

"No, wait, I have to check this out." She glanced around. "Make sure no one comes in here, 'kay?"

She powered up the laptop, scanned the files. An e-mail to Renee's grandchild, just as the detective had said. Jamie pulled up the browsing history. Erased, of course. No matter.

She went into DOS and typed a program she'd written. A long list of Internet addresses scrolled down. Shocked dismay filled her as Jamie stared at the screen.

"What?"

"The computer," she said dully. "Renee never touched it. Her fingerprints are all over it, but she didn't use it. She didn't know how to use the Internet. And these sites, they list antique shops in the French Quarter."

"Antique shops?"

Jamie caught the note of alarm. Warm breath feathered against her cheek as Damian leaned over her and studied the screen. He muttered something in French. Jamie shut off the machine.

Damian waved his hand. "I just erased your fingerprints. Let's go. I'll tell the police you're ill."

Outside she gulped down lungfuls of fresh air, but Damian didn't let her stop until they reached her house and were safely inside the gate. As Jamie sat in the courtyard, a small black cat darted out of the bushes.

"Archimedes!" Joy filled her as she went to pick him up.

The cat turned his back on her and sat by a dying potted palm. Jamie frowned. Not like him to be so unfriendly.

"I brought him back here for you." Damian sighed.

"What is it? Tell me," she demanded.

He ran a palm over the brick wall as if to assure himself the safeguards were still in place. "That's why they killed her. She knew about the antique shop."

"What shop?"

"The first clue to where the Book of Magick is hidden. It would be in my grandfather's old house, which is now an antique shop." He paced, his hands squeezed into fists.

"Renee knew my grandfather's house held the first clue. My father adored games. He told me that when he hid the book, he planted clues all over the Vieux Carre and the first one was in my grandfather's house. The Morphs must have gotten it out of her. Not the location. Just that it's an antique shop now."

"Renee couldn't know where the book was hidden. She didn't even know who you are. And even if she did, why would the Morphs murder her?"

Damian's fingers relaxed as he stopped to regard her. "She did, Jamie. Renee knew my family well. She was a Draicon. That's why they killed her—to ingest her energy and give them power. The dying fear of a Draicon is much more powerful than a human's death fears."

She sagged into the chair. Impossible. Draicon were evil. Uncaring, brutish werewolves, not sweet, motherly psychics.

"Years ago, Draicon here were outnumbered by Morphs and went into hiding. Renee was among them. I couldn't tell because I didn't recognize her scent. Renee used a chemical compound to disguise her scent from the Morphs. Very clever. Whoever did this must have realized her identity and her association with my family."

Or tortured it out of her. It was too fantastic. Her emotions raced between heartbreaking grief and utter betrayal. "But her grandchild is human. She showed me pictures!"

"Draicon. The parents are from a pack in North Carolina."

Even her friend had been the enemy. Jamie tried sorting it out. As she had with first her parents' deaths and then Mark's, she shoved grief into a dark corner. First came survival.

"I have to find the book. It contains a spell to remove the dark magick, and counteract the spell infecting you. The Morphs know where to start looking now and they won't stop until they find it."

Damian leaned against the wall, crossing his powerful arms across his chest. "I hate leaving you here to search for the book, but I have little choice. I'll send Raphael's guys to guard you."

The hell with that. Damian would find the book and her solution to lifting the binding spell crippling her powers. He would wield it over her, always dominating her with his magick, and she'd be trapped. His, forever.

She gripped the chair's armrests. Damian was the key to finding what she desperately needed. Trusting him was impossible, but for now, she had to join forces with him.

"I'm not staying here. I'm coming with you."

"The hell you are."

"The hell I am. My life is tied up in the book.

Do you think I'll sit here and wait? I'm not the waiting sort."

"Listen to me," he said quietly. "You made choices before, wrong choices, and lived as you pleased. Not anymore. You will do as I say, Jamie. Period."

She glared at him. "You're such an über Alpha."

He knit his eyebrows together. "Über Alpha?"

"An antiquated one who doesn't even know what über is."

"I know what's best for you and how to keep you safe. That's all I need to know."

Her pique faded as she remembered the sluggish gray matter seeping out of her wound. "I wonder if anything can keep me safe. This thing inside me feels like it won't die. Just been pushed back, and it's waiting in the wings," she whispered.

Something flashed into his expression. It might have been the late afternoon sun slanting across his face, but she could have sworn it looked like worry. Ridiculous. Damian would never be afraid for her, the woman who tried to kill him.

The woman he claimed was his mate. He had an ulterior purpose.

He wanted her alive, to make her into something like he was. A wolf, absorbed into his pack like sugar dissolving into hot liquid. Force her to assimilate and change. Her entire life people wanted to shape her to fit their world. Her damn uncle, even Mark couldn't accept her for who she was.

Even Renee… Grief arrowed through her. Renee scolded her for using magick and had only watched over her as befit a Draicon's duty. All this time, she'd been on Damian's side.

I'm better off alone, Jamie thought sadly.

Time to shift tactics. She lifted her shoulders in a casual shrug. "Fine, I'll stay here with those guys you mentioned. Might even be fun. I bet they know how to play World of Warcraft. If they're young enough, maybe I could play other computer games with them."

Fascinated, she watched his nails elongate. Gouges scored in the ancient redbrick as he raked his fingers across the wall.

"No. You're coming with me. But you will do exactly as I say."

She could handle that, Jamie reasoned. Optimism buoyed her. "We could start now."

Damian didn't check his gold Rolex, but glanced at the sinking sun. "The shop's closed. We'll have to start tomorrow morning, when they open. That's when we'll find the first clue."

Chapter 5

As Jamie went upstairs and headed for the bed-room, Damian followed. Archimedes darted past him, bolting inside the apartment.

Her stomach grumbled. Fishing through the fridge, she found her usual grazing fare. Nothing looked appealing, not the leftover tofu or the brick of Swiss cheese.

A craving surfaced for fresh meat. Not even horrified, she entertained the idea of something raw and tasty. "I'm starved," she muttered, slamming the door. "Maybe some fresh crayfish. So fresh they're still crawling."

Blood drained from Damian's face. "How about a tender, juicy steak?"

He picked up the phone, spoke a volley of rapid French.

Minutes later, Raphael came over. He dropped a plastic grocery bag on the kitchen table.

She peeked inside and her mouth watered. "Oh, wow. Raw cube steak!"

Raphael gave Damian a look she couldn't understand.

Jamie ripped away the cellophane. Forget knife and fork. Standing at the table, she grabbed the beef and began tearing off bite-size chunks. One after another, she gobbled them down like candy. Barely pausing to chew, her hunger screaming its demand.

She caught the look they exchanged and glanced down. Blood pooled on the table. Her stomach gave a sickening twist. Jamie clapped a hand to her mouth.

Damian gently pulled it away. "Don't. You're only experiencing a natural human reaction. Your body needs the food."

"I'm a vegetarian." Jamie wrapped her arms around herself. "Oh God, I just ate a cow. What the hell did you do to me, Draicon?"

"I saved you."

"His blood is inside you now. Powerful magick changing your body chemistry and fighting the spell. You should be grateful," Raphael chided.

"Blood? What blood..."

Damian's frown at Raphael warned her. The potion. "You put your blood in that potion?" She fought down the urge to retch.

"Blood from a purebred Alpha male Draicon contains powerful magick," Damian said quietly. "It was the only way of slowing the spell."

She was becoming a damn werewolf. Thanks to Damian, her body had already started changing.

He tipped her chin up with a fingertip. "Relax, and go with it, Jamie. It won't hurt you."

"I don't care if it hurts me. I can't bear to hurt an animal. And now I'm eating them?" She stared at him. "Will I turn into a wolf and hunt?"

"*Non.* But you will feel better."

Think of the immediate. Jamie swallowed hard, forcing down the nausea.

"Okay, okay. I can deal. If it helps keep this thing from growing inside me. I'll do what I have to."

He gave a real smile that lit up his eyes like Christmas bulbs. "You are a *zirondelle.*"

Her eyebrows lifted at his gentle, teasing tone. "Tell me you didn't insult me."

"It's Cajun French for dragonfly. Dragonflies are honored among my people because they can move swiftly through life, see everything from different angles and adapt as needed. A *zirondelle* reflects sunlight off the bayou waters, is passionate, emotional and rides the winds of change as fiercely as she loves life."

No one had ever laid such praise at her feet. The comparison arrowed straight to her heart. How many times had she darted through life, forced to react and change? She longed to be such a creature, with the ability to soar far above pain and sorrow. A lovely iridescent being, who reflected only the light, and shimmered like the sun. In her heart, she knew it was an illusive dream.

"I'm not a *zirondelle*." Jamie stumbled over the unfamiliar word, picking at her faded T-shirt. "They're beautiful creatures of the light, and fearless. That's not me."

Damian kissed her cheek gently. Maybe he meant it as reassurance, but the soft warmth of his mouth on her cool cheek stirred another hunger.

His lips felt like a down quilt, promising snuggling comfort to chase away her body's chill. Suddenly she craved the heat, the closeness of his body pressed against hers. But she had seen his aggression, the testosterone rolling off him in waves.

He slid a hand up her nape, his touch assured and yet so gentle.

"Donnez-moi un petit kiss, *chère,"* he murmured. "Come on, little one. One small kiss."

Jamie lifted her face. One tiny kiss couldn't hurt. Nothing more, nothing further. Her lips parted in invitation as she slid her arms about his waist.

Something shuttered in his green eyes.

His mouth descended on hers swiftly. Damian cradled her head as he kissed her. Desire flared like gasoline poured on a smoldering fire. She kissed him back, her feelings askew, lust making her limbs tremble.

Her mouth opened wide as she flicked her tongue over his lips.

With a low growl, he pulled her to him and crushed her mouth beneath his.

Her mind went to war with her body. Her mind shouting it was a mistake to kiss a Draicon, this Draicon. Her mind screaming to stop this fusing of mouths, the delicious heat he sent into her cold, cold insides.

Her body telling her mind to shut up and just let go.

She let go.

Jamie clutched his wide shoulders. He thrust his tongue inside, stroking the inside of her mouth in an erotic caress. Taking, penetrating her mouth as if staking his claim. She quivered with anticipation, her eyes closed as she imagined him removing her clothing, laying her down and spreading her thighs apart with his strong hands. Then his big, powerful body mounting her as he thrust his cock deep inside, spreading more of that delicious warmth into her, so she'd never be cold again.

Oh God, she needed this so badly she shook with the craving, like an addict needing a fix. Needed to seal herself to him, climb inside his wonderful warmth…

"*Excusez-moi,* but if you two need one, the bedroom's back there."

Raphael jerked a thumb toward the hallway. Jamie wrenched herself free. Oh, she was warm now. An embarrassed flush crept up her neck. To cover her confusion, she glared at Damian.

"Are you finished, wolf?"

"Not quite," he murmured. "But I'll save you for…dessert."

His intent look was a warning. He licked his lips, as if tasting her all over again. The space between her legs throbbed in answer.

She had to stop this. Keep him at a distance; he wasn't safe, couldn't ever be. A Draicon was dangerous.

She'd seen the powerful male aggression. From what she knew of Draicon, they didn't usually destroy their own, but what if…they did? What if one killed Renee?

Renee must have been terrified. God, what a way to die.

Lifting her gaze, she worked up courage. "I don't think I can take much more of this. And how do I know you wouldn't do to me what happened to Renee? You're werewolves. You tear apart animals."

Raphael muttered a low curse. Damian's expression shuttered. "Jamie, we're Draicon. We hunt to eat when we must, but never take the life of innocents. We're not your enemy. I know you've had quite a shock. But you need to pull together all your strength and courage and move forward to survive."

The old Jamie stirred. Her warrior Night Elf wouldn't grow soft. Neither would she.

"You have no idea how many times I've had to move forward."

Oops. Didn't mean to let that slip. He gave her a thoughtful look. Archimedes meowed as he investigated the kitchen. Poor kitty. She imagined the horrifying violence the cat had witnessed. *We have something in common now, Archimedes.*

Jamie scooped the cat up and, against her better judgment, buried her face in his soft fur. Once, a cat had been her only friend. And then... She swallowed the bile rising in her throat.

But Archimedes struggled and hissed until she let him go. He raced away and sat in a corner, watching her.

Damian frowned at the cat.

"He's had a rough day," she said, excusing the feline's behavior.

The Draicon leader studied the cat. "He looks very well fed."

"He's a good mouser. After Katrina hit, we went looking for stranded animals. When Mark and I found him he was surviving on mice and…" Her voice trailed off. She glanced up to see Damian studying her. As if he wanted to pry inside her mind.

"Your brother. He was not as you think." Damian's jaw tightened.

"My brother was everything," she shot out, knowing how defensive she sounded. Jamie wanted to scream at Damian, the wolf who'd brought him down. "He was a very important wildlife biologist and millions watched his television show. *Wild & Wonderful* was a ratings hit."

"It was a good show," Raphael agreed, smiling a little. As if he were human. He wasn't. He was a damn wolf, a beast like Damian.

"The only show Paw Paw ever enjoyed," Raphael continued. "He doesn't have a television, so he told us to record it and he'd watch every Sunday night when he came over for dinner. His favorite was where Mark wrestled with an alligator in Florida."

Reluctant memories surfaced. "He'd just gotten the word the show was syndicated. Mark was amazingly brave. He could encounter any type of wild animal and have a calming effect on it. Even insects. Once he backed up against a nest of hornets. They just swarmed over him like babies, not hurting him. It was fascinating."

"Wasps." Damian's upper lip rose.

Raphael grinned. "*T'frère,* your allergies. Remember when you accidentally stuck your hand in a nest? Your face blew up like someone kicked it."

"If you're so powerful, how can you be allergic?"

Her question brought dead silence. Jamie's gaze whipped from the suddenly tense Raphael to a grim Damian.

"Draicon young are like human children. Until we reach puberty, we're powerless. Alpha purebreds like myself have very vulnerable immune systems until we're five. Someone set loose hornets in my room when I was two." Damian's expression turned hard.

Holy... Jamie wrapped her arms about herself. "It must have hurt like hell."

His mouth was a tight slash. "Enough for me to remember even now. *Maman,* my mother, heard me scream. She saved me, but the residual effects were the allergy. Enough stings and I won't die, but it sure as hell weakens me."

"Oh, Damian." Unexpected pity twisted her

heart. "Why did this person do it? If they wanted you…"

She halted, troubled by the grisly image.

"He wanted me to suffer before I died. There were enough wasps to kill."

Jamie shuddered. "Who did it? Did they catch him?"

The guarded look dropped over his face. "My father…delivered swift justice. It was the relative of a good friend, one we protected. Someone who watched over me when my parents were gone."

"Someone you liked?"

The answer came in his compressed lips and flat eyes. She felt a reluctant ache for a child whose trust was violated. Damian, too, had known betrayal and pain. Then again, he had parents to watch over and protect him, unlike her. Or did he? His past remained murky. He watched her now with hooded eyes. Keeping secrets.

She had secrets, as well. Jamie found herself shutting down.

"Enough of me. Tell me about Mark and your life together," he insisted.

Silent, she stared at the faded blue wallpaper. Sharing information about Mark felt sacrilegious, telling the enemy who relished slaying her brother.

Raphael shifted against the wall. Damian spoke.

"Something about your brother bothers me. After that last episode, the one after Hurricane Katrina, the show ended. I heard rumors about Mark killing an animal and some viewers getting very upset."

Jamie bristled, her hands fisting. "My brother never, ever killed anything."

Damian's cool, assessing look penetrated the fib. She bit her lip.

"Okay. Just once and it wasn't his fault. I think that's why he stopped the show, it upset him so much. He was touring the bayou, showing the effects of Katrina's damage. I went with him to help rescue strays. He heard a dog howling inside an abandoned cabin and went inside. Zane, his producer, insisted he bring the rifle just in case. A sick or wounded animal can be dangerous."

Her voice wobbled. "We heard these awful sounds, like a dog snarling, and Mark was yelling. Then a gunshot. When he came out, he snapped at everyone. It took a while for him to calm down. He seemed different. Said the dog was rabid and he had to kill it."

Damian and Raphael exchanged glances. Jamie hated it, those knowing looks, like those who'd accused Mark afterward of recklessness and other, much darker acts. "He never would have if he hadn't have been certain. Mark loved animals. And those people blathering about him killing… They didn't know him…. Not like I did…"

She hated this, her voice cracking like shattered china.

"I'm sure you're right," Damian murmured. "He sounds like a man who wouldn't ever hurt anything."

Enough said. If Damian suspected she knew he'd killed her brother, how would he react? The Draicon was unpredictable and she was far too weak and vulnerable now.

Troubled, she bent over to stroke Archimedes' back.

The cat hissed. For a moment, its fangs looked lethal. Recoiling, Jamie shrank back.

"Hey," Damian snapped. "Favorite pet of Renee's or not, enough. You will learn manners." He scooped up the cat with one hand and headed for the door.

Raphael gave her a hard look. "Jamie. Listen to Damian and do what he says. He's your dracairon and will take care of you."

"I can take care of myself."

His mouth narrowed to a thin slash. "He'd give his life for you, even though you tried to take away his."

Simmering anger in his voice sent alarm bells clanging. Not one to mess with, any more than Damian. But she never backed away from a confrontation. And wouldn't now. "You don't like me much, do you?"

"I don't need to like you. Damian does. I'm just his brother, and you're his mate." He took a menacing step forward. "But try hurting him again, and you will find out just how strong the bonds of brotherhood are."

Canines gleamed sharp in his mouth as he flashed a wide smile. The door banged shut behind him.

Jamie dismissed the warning. She had bigger problems. Six feet of problem, with broad shoulders and long, muscled limbs. She studied Damian as he returned to the kitchen. A natural leader, he even moved with authority. Her mind raced over the possibilities. He had tremendous power and magick and was her only pathway to the book that would cure her.

She fetched another laptop, placed it on the kitchen table and powered up, clicking onto the Internet. "We need to make a list of all the clues you have, the antique shop, what your father told you about the book."

Damian eyed the computer the same way Renee had. "I thought I destroyed that."

"I had another."

"It's not safe with that thing."

Another one stuck in the Stone Age. "How much do you know about computers?"

"Enough," he asserted. "My last one was a Commodore. Are they still available?"

A sound between a snort and a laugh fled her lips. "On eBay, maybe. Look, you have no idea what technology is like these days. This machine is password protected. No one can break in. I have a dozen ways to block hackers. Including a virus that will wipe out hard drives. I could wipe out yours." She offered him a singularly sweet smile.

His face flattened. "You already tried that once, Jamie. The poison in your kiss was lethal, but defeated. I may not know machines, but I know my enemy and they can counter any protective measures you impose."

Gone was the gentle Damian, replaced by a hardened warrior who would never allow his guard down. Suddenly his hand shot out, captured something. Jamie twisted in the chair. In his cupped palms Damian held a fly.

"Morphs can shift into insects so small you can't hear them. They make perfect spies. Their brains retain intelligence, no matter what the form."

Her breath hitched as she waited for him to crush the fly. Instead he released it out the window.

"Forget the Internet. Let's talk about the search.

You're not leaving me out of this, Draicon. I want all the information you have on the book."

"I told you, my name is Damian. And if you're thinking of finding the book on your own, you can't. The clues are all in French." A hard smile curved his lips. "My father's precaution against outsiders infringing on our business."

The ringing phone interrupted. Fresh anxiety filled her as the caller introduced himself. Her hand shook as she replaced the receiver.

"That was Armand, Renee's son-in-law. He's in town. The police are releasing the body tomorrow and they're holding the funeral the next day."

They set out to find the first clue the next morning. A few clouds scudded across the clear blue sky. Hairs prickled Jamie's nape as Damian accompanied her like a warden escorting a prisoner. She shot him a sideways glance. His profile was taut skin stretched over bone, his green eyes purposeful. The broad shoulders hinted of arrogant authority. Not a werewolf to cross.

Escaping him would prove difficult.

He'd insisted on sleeping in her apartment. Jamie had pointed the way to the guest bedroom. It did no good. She'd spent the night wreathed in lush, erotic dreams. Memories of when Damian had taken her virginity.

Her hands roving over the hard muscle rippling over his wiry body. Imagining him as a wolf, loping over glade and meadow, proudly leading his pack. The hot pleasure he'd brought with his gentle touch, then the pain as he pushed himself inside. More than the burning fullness had been the overwhelming sensation of Damian filling every pore, every cell, invading her with both penis and mind. Losing herself, as Damian overwhelmed her with male force and power as he thrust into her. The hard edge of lust on his face amid her growing need to bond with him because she must obey the compelling feeling to give herself to him, and him only...

She'd awakened from the dream tangled in damp sheets, perspiration soaking her pajamas. The smell of cooking bacon drifted from the kitchen. Jamie had caved in and eaten the breakfast Damian cooked. It was pointless to resist. If Draicon magick kept her alive, she'd cater to her body's needs. Later, when the spell was broken, she could be vegetarian again.

Now, like tourists browsing for treasures, they drifted in and out of shops. At the second stop, her BlackBerry vibrated. Jamie removed it and stole a peek while Damian was scanning bookshelves. Text message from Paul, her online friend, to meet her. In the square, very public.

Jamie texted back. Can't.

Just got a new e-book reader. The latest and greatest.

Oh, wow. Her eyes widened. She nearly salivated. Her forefingers hovered over the keyboard. *God, I'm such a geek.*

Yeah, she was. If Paul had a new electronic toy, she was there.

Jamie responded in the affirmative and pocketed the BlackBerry.

Around noon, she sensed Damian's real purpose.

The two-story brick building they approached featured a charming balcony with wrought-iron gates. Mesh screening barred the old wood door to the antique shop. Antiques cluttered shelves in the window. Someone locked a battered bicycle to one of the crooked balcony posts.

Damian herded Jamie inside. Cramped and musty, the shop had narrow aisles wide enough for one person. She searched the walls, studying the antique rifles hung neatly on pegs, the nude paintings. She studied the glass display cases filled with silver dollars, toy soldiers and jewelry. Silent as a wolf on the prowl, Damian followed her.

He'd told her to examine the back wall. His father's favorite chair had once sat there. Damian paused before bookcases inlaid into the wall. A

CD of 1930s music played softly in the background as the singer warbled "Ain't She Sweet."

Stark melancholy flashed across his face. The hint of vulnerability shocked her. The look vanished, replaced by a cold, analytical one as he caught her staring. "Stop wasting time and start looking for it." Curtness lashed his deep voice.

Jamie examined the wall, glad of his mood shift. It reminded her what an arrogant ass he was.

She scanned shelves crammed with faded dolls, Lionel trains and antique beaded purses. Next to the bookcase was a four-foot section of exposed brick. Dusting off his hands, the proprietor approached, asked if he could help them.

"I'm looking for the words of Andre Marcel. Have you seen such a book?"

The man's face was careworn, but his brown eyes were sharp. They scrutinized Damian as if studying a rare coin. "You followed Andre Marcel?"

"Yes, but not when I was younger. It was only when I became an adult that I realized his wisdom."

The odd exchange warned Jamie of its importance. An approving smile came over the man. He glanced about the shop, then brought over a rickety footstool. After climbing it, he reached for a book at the very top shelf and climbed down.

With a reverent look, he handed it to Damian. "You may find this of interest." Then sorrow flashed into his eyes. "Mr. Marcel was an extraordinary person. Consider this a gift from an admirer."

Damian nodded, hiding his expression as he opened the musty leather-bound book. The proprietor picked up the stool and vanished into a back room.

Jamie craned her neck to read over Damian's shoulder. Her eyebrows shot up. "*The Strange Case of Dr. Jekyll and Mr. Hyde?*"

A wry smile touched his mouth. "Father told me there was truth even in fiction. Men often show two faces. He was always teaching a lesson."

On the next-to-last page was a cryptic note, a penciled drawing of a wolf's head. Beside it was scribbled something in French.

"Gentleman buccaneer imbibes," Damian murmured.

Dust motes drifted outward as he snapped the book shut. Damian tucked it beneath his black T-shirt, then grabbed Jamie's hand.

"What's wrong?" she asked.

His mouth thinned. "*Allons.* Come on, let's get back."

Outside, she blinked at the bright sunshine. People strolled the streets, pushed past them. Haunting sadness flickered in Damian's eyes as he glanced at the storefront. Jamie shifted her feet.

This six-foot male with his muscled body in the tight jeans and the hands that could snap her neck in half was a ruthless, arrogant killer. Yet now he looked like a lost little boy. Damian whirled around, caught her looking at him. She knew all about loss, and memories and regrets. And the blast of sorrow he emitted engulfed her, amplified her own sense of loss.

Chapter 6

A short while later, Damian sat before the brick fireplace in her bedroom, feeding a fire. Flames licked at the leather-bound book. He'd explained to her the importance of burning the book so it would be destroyed and the Morphs wouldn't find the clue.

"What did the clue say?"

"The gentleman buccaneer. My father always added history into everything he did. He meant Jean Lafitte. The bar named after him is on Bourbon. The next clue is there."

"No wonder your father didn't think you were old enough to follow the trail," she observed. "He was waiting until you were of legal age."

"Which was more than sixty years ago," he drawled. "I'm quite legal now."

"When are we going?"

"Tomorrow, after the funeral. I want to provide a diversion to throw Morphs off the trail."

"What kind of diversion?" Jamie's curiosity stirred.

He playfully tapped her nose. "You'll see, little one."

He stood, stretching. Fascinated, she stared at his broad shoulders shifting beneath the tight T-shirt. Damian poked at the dying embers with the toe of one scuffed boot.

"I have things to do, so, against my better judgment, I'm sending two males Rafe trusts to guard you. They're from his pack and have sworn allegiance to me while I'm in town." Damian gave her a level look. "Two males warned against interacting with you. They're stoic and utterly loyal. You'll find them completely boring but you will not leave the house."

A prisoner in her own home? No way. Jamie headed downstairs, taking her backpack, but Damian followed. As she reached the front gate, he snagged her wrist gently.

"I said you're not leaving." His tone was steely.

"And I say you can't keep me here. I'm meeting someone."

Now his gaze grew intent. "Who?"

"NOYB," Jamie taunted. None of Your Business. See if he could understand her slang.

He drew his thick eyebrows together. "Who is this Nob?"

"A guy who knows what NOYB means." She struggled to free herself and glared. "Besides, he's from my world, a geek like me."

He released her and she staggered backward. Damian's big shoulders tensed. His fingers extended, claws grew from the fingertips. He raked a hand over the green wooded gate, scoring marks, growling as if he wanted to carve up the man she mentioned.

She backed up, swallowed hard. With a deep breath, he dropped his hands, the claws retracting. When he spoke, his voice was mild.

"Your world, *chère*. You've left it behind. You can't return to it. You're in my world now, with my blood in you. I know it must be frightening, and confusing. With everything you know turned upside down, you want the familiar and the comfortable. But you must move on, because sometimes the familiar is dangerous."

Jamie's lower lip wobbled. Damian pinpointed all the roller-coaster emotions she'd ridden since the day Mark died. She felt close to crumbling into a ball at his feet. Instead, she scowled. "The familiar is not dangerous. Paul's a friend I met in cyberspace. I did an in-depth background check on him. We've known each other for a year now and we're meeting in a very public place. Perfectly safe. I need to see him."

Long, lean fingers trailed over her cheek. His green gaze burned possessively. "You don't need another male. Or want one."

Sexual heat poured off him. Her own body responded, desire rippling through her like a rock tossed into a tranquil pool. Why did she want him when he'd taken away everything she'd loved?

"You're wrong."

"Jamie, I told you. You're my mate. Our body chemistries are intricately tied together. You can no more resist the desire than I can, and no other man will satisfy you as I will."

"Maybe I should try."

"You will not." Male possessiveness flared in his eyes.

Jamie rolled her eyes.

He wrapped his fingers about her upper arms, holding her, but with absolute gentleness. His deep green eyes searched her face.

"Jamie, listen to me. This male, he could be a predator." A hint of vulnerability flashed over his face. "I can't bear to see you hurt. There's so much out there that can hurt you."

The chest-beating male was gone. Confusion filled her. Why was he acting so protective? No one was interested in her welfare. Mark had been too absorbed in his television show.

She clutched his arms, feeling taut muscles flinch. And kissed him, just a peck, really, like she'd give a good friend.

He groaned and pulled her to him and delivered the real thing. Full body, mouth merging, tongue tangling, let's-have-sex kiss. And wow, it was amazing. His mouth was warm, wet and he tasted like faint spices. Jamie licked the inside of his mouth, nipped his bottom lip.

Damian's eyes closed. Beneath her hands, she felt him quiver like a wild beast straining to be free. Jamie sucked on his tongue, siphoning his arousal, anything he gave her. He pulled her closer, thrust his tongue deep inside, as if trying to crawl inside her.

She opened her mouth wider. She didn't care, as long as she could touch him, feel his body against hers, find a way to ease this awful craving.

Werewolf. Killer. The thought flashed like a movie marquee. *Danger. Warning. Steep grade ahead. Sheer drop. Brake hard. Now.*

She froze. Fear leaked out of her like sweat.

To her surprise, Damian pulled back. His eyes darkened, and he was panting as if running a marathon. He rested his forehead against hers.

"Why did you stop?" she asked.

"You're afraid. I can smell your fear," he said abruptly.

More surprises. She thought Draicon were asses who took what they wanted, regardless of others' feelings. And someone proud as Damian would do as he pleased.

"I need to go," she whispered, torn between wanting to stay and leaving.

"No. It's dangerous out there." He took her palm and pressed a kiss into it. "If anything happens to you like what happened to Renee... I won't let it happen."

He seemed determined to protect her and this felt so confusing. Damian towered over her like a mighty oak shading a tiny sapling. Her gaze dropped to his biceps and smooth, tanned skin. Remembering his naked body moving slowly over hers as they'd made love, she blushed. Jamie dragged her gaze up to his face. His eyes looked haunted.

"Why should you care what happens to me?"

"You're pack now, Jamie. Mine. I always protect my own." He ran a thumb across her cheek. "Next time we'll take it at your pace. I won't push you."

She hesitated, staring at the cords and veins standing out in relief as they mapped his neck. Wondering what he tasted like if she bit his collarbone, ran her tongue along his shoulder. Salty or sweet? The rigid barriers inside her lowered for a minute. No one really gave a damn about her. Her cousins would dance for joy if a meteor dropped on her skull. She knew a few people who might be upset if something happened, but not...

Devastated.

She ran her hands up his arms, feeling the tense muscles, the power. Suddenly having this big, bad wolf watch over her made her feel erotic and wanting. Jamie tugged out his shirt, slid her hands up his flat, ribbed abdomen, feeling him quiver beneath her touch.

"Push all you want." She purred.

His eyes darkened. Damian took her mouth in another drugging kiss. His hips pushed against hers. Jamie slid her hands around his back, squeezed his ass and rubbed herself against him, desperate to relieve the throbbing between her legs.

"I have to taste you," he muttered against her mouth. His hands fumbled with the gray sweat-pants. He tugged them past her hips, slid them down her thighs.

Shame flushed her face as he stared at her white granny panties. But then he hooked his fingers around the waistband, shimmied them down. She realized he didn't care. His purpose was to get them off. Now.

As if watching from someone else's body, she saw her clothing bunch around her ankles. Moisture seeped out of her as she realized what he intended.

"Mine," he said roughly, standing upright again. "No other male will dare touch you and you will not want them. You're mine."

His hands caressed her hips. Damian nuzzled her neck, gave it a slow lick. Pain, sharp and brief, laced her as he nipped her skin. His tongue caressed the wound, replacing pain with erotic pleasure.

"My scent on you, *chère*. Your scent on me," he said hoarsely.

Dropping to his knees, he slid his hands inside her thighs. Drew them apart and put his mouth on her.

Shocked pleasure shot through her. Jamie threw her head back, put out her hands to protest. Instead she grabbed his hair to anchor legs threatening to collapse. His tongue caressed her, lapped her, sliding between her sensitive folds.

Then he stroked the one place aching for his touch. Quick, powerful flicks that drew her taut, made her quiver and moan as she clutched fistfuls of his hair, gasping until she threatened to fall apart, building the sweet tension higher and higher.

With a shrill shriek, she came. Jamie convulsed, crying out his name. Tremors spilled through her. Damian stopped, cupped her bare bottom and stood. She sagged against him, still trembling, her hands sliding weakly down to clutch his waist.

"Remember, Jamie, I'm the only one," he whispered, gently rubbing the pad of one thumb over her kiss-swollen mouth. "The only one you want."

He slid up her clothing. Dazed with languid pleasure, she remained speechless.

The intensity in his gaze deepened. "You're mine, Jamie. You belong to me. There's nowhere you can run, nowhere to hide that I will not find you. I can track your scent a mile away. If another male dares to touch you, I'll shatter his bones."

His expression said what he did not. *You want nothing between us but skin. Soon, I'll have you under me and be inside you as deep as I can go.*

Her feminine core throbbed in response. Jamie put a hand to her trembling mouth and staggered to a chair. Sex with Damian was dangerous. Involvement. Risking her heart with an unpredictable Draicon who turned her boneless with sexual need and made her forget common sense. Keeping him at a distance was wise. Maybe a whole football field would suffice.

She would go meet Paul at Jackson Square.

Just as assurance that she didn't need Damian. She didn't need anyone.

Through hooded eyes, he regarded her. "As soon as Adam and Ricky arrive, I'm leaving, but I'll return soon. Stay here. If you dare to leave, I'll find you. I'll always find you, Jamie."

The hell you will, she silently vowed.

Hands jammed into his pockets, Damian walked around his city, gathering information. He raked each building with his hard gaze. Two men strolling along with hurricanes in hand gave him a wide berth.

He visited a few favorite haunts, eating rare steak and drinking beer, spilling it on his shirt to cloak his scent. The vampires running the bars gave disturbing information. Even they were worried. Morphs hid themselves among the population and successfully disguised themselves. They sprang from lonely, angry, single male Draicon populating the city, who murdered close relatives to gain power.

His thoughts drifted to Jamie. Lone, angry Jamie, who insisted she didn't need anyone. How could he coax her into mating with him and leading his pack females when she preferred to be alone? Was the darkness inside her controlling her every move? He told Jamie to trust him, but hell, could he trust her? She'd tried to kill him, but he doubted she'd try again. No, this time she'd merely leave him.

If she found the book, she'd run away again. He felt it in his bones.

His only solution was to ensure she didn't have the chance.

His steps were sure and quick as he made several detours. As he walked down a deserted side street, Damian stopped.

Instinct slapped him. Someone was following him. Someone without a scent, except for a very faint fragrance of perfume. He whirled.

They came out of the shadows. He counted eight, no, ten. Young men and some women. "Draicon," they whispered.

Damn. How had he been so foolish to let them get the jump on him? How could they track him so easily?

Muscles tensed, he prepared to fight as they rushed forward.

How easy it was to fool these wolves.

With one eye on the game she played, Jamie kept aware of the two werewolves guarding her. Ricky, with a day beard and shoulder-length blond hair, was parked on a chair as he worked on a laptop. Absorbed in a book, Adam sat on the couch. Ordinary, with light brown hair, dark eyes framed by oval glasses and well-shaped features.

Dressed in jeans, a turtleneck and black leather jacket, he looked like a cross between a college professor and a Hell's Angel.

As Jamie manipulated Celyndra to attack a horde of Orcs, she kept an eye on both werewolves. They weren't looking. Abandoning the game, she opened her BlackBerry Pearl and text-messaged Paul, arranging to meet at 4:00 p.m. at Jackson Square.

She logged off the game and looked at the wall clock. "I'm tired of beating up Orcs. I'm taking a break downstairs to work on some coding."

"I'll go with you." Ricky went to shut off his laptop.

"No bother. You're busy and the signal is wobbly downstairs. I'll just be in the courtyard."

Heading downstairs and into the courtyard, she dragged the lounge chair beneath a banana tree. She sat down, unpacked her laptop. Sure enough, Adam appeared on the upstairs porch. She waved and pretended to settle back.

After a minute, she glanced up. He was gone.

Quickly she went to the western door and fished a key from beneath the mat. The house had been subdivided into apartments Mark rented out during Mardi Gras. She'd made good use of one after his death, storing all manner of items that might come in handy someday.

Like now.

Minutes later she emerged from the back apartment toting a life-size CPR dummy. She unlaced her sneakers, removed them and her white socks, and put them on the dummy's feet, then placed it in the lounge chair with the laptop in its lap.

"Have a nice time, Annie," she told the mannequin.

The banana tree's sprawling branches hid all but the dummy's legs from the upstairs window. Unless they came down to check on her, they'd never know.

"Who's the real dummy, Draicon?" she whispered, slipping into her sandals.

Ten against one was very bad odds. The Morphs shape-shifted to their normal form. Hunched over, they had long, greasy hair, black eyes, yellowed fangs and sharp talons. One hissed at him, saliva dripping from its thin mouth. Anticipating a Damian sandwich for lunch. Not likely.

"Beg for your life, Draicon," it rasped.

"I never beg. Ever," he said pleasantly, and leaped forward.

Ten minutes into the fight, he was totally bemused. These Morphs fought like such wusses his patience was grinding down.

He'd killed one, but injuries to the others were

superficial. Each time one charged, it attacked from a different angle. But instead of aiming for his heart, they merely raked him with their talons. Drawing blood, they'd howl with triumph, then retreat backward.

Enough. Bored and irritated, Damian focused on the tallest male and started for him. Daggers at the ready, he charged.

One Morph shape-shifted into a wasp and flew at his face. Caught off guard, Damian staggered, swatted at the little bastard.

It stung him on the cheek. He winced, smacked it. Flicked it off even as the sting began to puff up like an inflated balloon.

Damn allergies. He directed healing thoughts at the sting. The swelling went down. Damian went to charge his enemies again.

But instead of fighting, the Morphs ran away. Took off as if he were the devil himself, coming to drag them back to hell.

They vanished into an alleyway. Damian leaned over, wiping blood off his chin.

Morphs never ran. They relished the kill, and fed off the victim's terror. If they managed to terrorize a Draicon, the power rush trebled.

His mind calculated the possibilities. They had fought like a pack of wild dogs, launching at him and then retreating, looking for his weak spot as if to…

Test him. See how much power he held.

Like animals rushing up to test an electrically charged fence, they had attacked from all angles, looking for a weak side. Then retreated. To fight again later?

Why not finish him now?

"Because they want me to find the book first," he mused aloud. "Then kill me. And next time there won't be only ten."

Twenty. Or thirty. Or maybe even a hundred.

The city was in trouble. Big trouble. And he and his mate were in the thick of it.

He headed toward Raphael's house on Esplanade. Raphael wasn't home, but the keys to his Harley were on a peg inside the garage. Damian snagged them. His hand trembled as he brushed it up against the concrete wall.

Memories poured into him like smoke. Blood, screams. Terror. He shuddered, fought them off.

Damian took a gleaming black helmet, started the bike and roared off to inspect the city on wheels. He headed toward Jackson Square, stopped by the light by Café du Monde. Then caught a familiar, intoxicating scent.

Jamie walked past with a tall, young male. Ordinary, college age. Damian's fury bloomed, the scent sharp and heady.

The male put his hand on her shoulder as they

paused to cross Dumaine Street. His blood froze as Damian saw the talons emerge.

Morph.

Jamie remained blissfully unaware she was walking to her death. They crossed the street, headed up the steps leading toward the Moon Walk. Damian roared toward her, but they cleared the tracks just as the gates came down. He sat, trapped by the train as it lumbered past.

Beneath the black leather jacket, his skin grew cold as he thought of how easily the Morph could take her down. Rip her to shreds, leaving nothing but blood…

A bloodied stuffed animal, under the bed. His sister hadn't a damn chance.

Had to get to Jamie. Now.

When the last railroad tanker finally cleared the crossing, he roared past the tracks, parked the bike at the foot of the steps. And ran like hell, praying he wasn't too late.

Soft, slow jazz drifted from the saxophone played by a street musician. A cool river breeze rustled tree leaves in a nearby planter. Jamie walked on Moon Walk with Paul, following the redbrick pavement toward the direction of the French Market and the charred wharfs destroyed during Katrina.

Paul was tall and wore jeans too baggy for his

long legs, and an olive T-shirt far too big for his thin chest. He had chestnut curls and deep blue eyes. He was a Level 60 in World of Warcraft, and liked eating Fritos while he designed Web pages for corporations. But he acted far different in real life than in cyberspace.

Distant, almost cold.

She tried to make small talk with him about everything they'd chatted about online, but he made one-syllable answers.

Maybe this wasn't such a good idea. Instinct hummed like a live tension wire. Her sneakers shuffled along the red brick. Jamie glanced around. Unease pricked her spine. A single living soul was yet to be seen. She ground to a halt, went to turn around. "I'd better go."

He shoved his hands into the front pockets of his jeans, looked hurt. "Don't you want to see my e-book reader?"

The load roar of a motorcycle drew her attention away. She glanced at the biker shutting off the engine and pulling a black helmet off. He stalked toward her direction like a predator.

Paul's eyes narrowed. "Who's that?" he demanded.

"My elderly uncle Damian," Jamie said weakly.

"Elderly uncle?"

"He's older than he looks."

Wearing a black T-shirt, leather jacket, faded jeans and scuffed biker boots, the Draicon climbed the stairs and headed for them. Jamie sighed. "I'd better…"

She stared at the hand Paul held out. Talons extended from his fingertips. Jamie trembled, blinked hard and looked up.

"Jamie. Don't you know…never trust strangers."

The creature grinned at her, saliva dripping from its yellowed fangs. A scream died in her throat. She turned, ran, but it snatched a fistful of her shirt. Pulled back, its strong arms reeling her in as if she were a minnow.

The Morph raised its hand, razor-sharp talons hovering near. "You're going to die anyway, but not before I shred your pretty face to the marrow."

Jamie drew back with a sneer. "And I'll still look better than your bony ass."

Giving a hard, sudden twist, she yanked, kicking at the same time. Living among the Morphs when they took their natural form taught her a little about their soft spots.

Like the fronts of their spindly knees.

The Morph grunted, reeled back, loosening its grip. She wrenched free, ran and saw Damian barreling it. His eyes fierce, his concentration was absolute.

Damian launched himself at the thing in a flying leap, a dagger suddenly materializing in his hand. An earsplitting snarl rumbled as the Draicon tackled the Morph.

His dagger sank straight into the creature's chest. The Morph reeled backward, arms pinwheeling. It collapsed to the pavement, and turned to ash.

Her hands shook violently. She drew in a breath, tried to calm herself. Hysteria just wasn't her thing, but damn…

Damian came back to her, slid an arm about her quivering body. "Let's go," he murmured.

He handed her the helmet as she climbed onto the Harley. In a few minutes, they were inside her gate. As Damian parked the bike to one side, Jamie pulled off the helmet, placed it on the seat. Adam came downstairs. He stared at her and then saw Damian's fury. Ricky, just behind him, skidded to a halt.

"Oh crap," Adam said softly.

His words turned to a strangled moan as Damian shoved him up against the gate, his hand on Adam's throat. "You failed in your duty," he said, the softness of his voice making him even more menacing.

"You, as well." Damian turned his head and growled at Ricky as if he wanted to carve him up and serve a Ricky roast.

A chill shivered down her spine at his ruthless expression. "It's not their fault. I put a decoy in place," she protested.

"This is pack business, Jamie. There are rules. Discipline is necessary. When I give an order I expect complete obedience." He didn't look at her, but narrowed his eyes at Adam. "Everyone in the pack knows the consequences. The rules are there for a reason, to protect the pack."

He released Adam, who fell with a gasp, rubbing his throat. Damian crooked a finger at Ricky, who swallowed hard and stumbled forward, eyes cast downward.

Jamie bit back a gasp at the ferocity of Damian's punch. Ricky reeled backward, but made no sound.

"Sorry," Adam rasped, holding up his hands. "Really sorry, man. I looked down and saw the sneakers, and she said she was downstairs, so I thought…"

"Me, too," Ricky echoed.

"Don't. Think. Just leave. Now." Damian flicked a thumb at the gate.

The two Draicon obeyed, the gate banging shut behind him. Damian stalked to it, locked it and returned to her. She glanced at him warily. Would he discipline her, as well?

He said nothing. Didn't lecture her, didn't

shoot her an accusing look. He merely stroked his thumb soothingly over her cheek.

Damian didn't need to scold her. She was too busy talking to the few brain cells still functioning, admitting what ten kinds of fool she was. She hadn't trusted Damian, only trusted herself. Not even herself anymore. This stint proved her poor judgment. And it sickened her to realize how blissfully she'd walked into the yawning jaws of an obvious trap.

"You're pale. Did it hurt you?"

"No. I'm okay, but…"

"But what? Jamie, tell me." He slid a hand around her nape, his touch light and reassuring. As if he were a rock to hold her steady.

Her courage resurfaced. Jamie met his worried gaze. "I changed my mind about the e-reader. Think I'll stick to my BlackBerry after all."

Emotion flashed in his jade-green eyes. Damian put his forehead down to touch hers. "You have much strength. I doubt any females in my pack could stand up to a Morph attack and come off it as if they'd done nothing more strenuous than shop."

"That's such a guy remark. Have you ever seen women at an after-Thanksgiving sale? Scary. Very scary."

Damian smiled, released her. She eyed the

stairs with longing. "I'm heading to bed. Enough excitement for today."

She didn't wait for his reply, but took off. In her room, she shut the door and sat on her bed. Jamie buried her face in her hands.

Face it, Damian has better sense and awareness than you do. He knew Morphs could disguise themselves as humans... Oh God. Morphs disguised as humans, and this was the second Damian has taken down. What if, just what if... Mark...that night...

No way. Her brother could not have been a Morph.

But the nagging whisper refused to go away.

Chapter 7

In the morning, they attended the private burial with Renee's family.

In the rented car, Damian drove on Esplanade, his anxiety kicking up a notch. At the St. Louis cemetery, he parked on the street. Tension squeezed his muscles like a wine press. His parents, brothers and Annie were buried here. His father's pack refused to have anything to do with them, so he alone smuggled the bodies into the cemetery. In the dark of night, Damian had used magick to unseal the marble crypt and then bury them. Then he used magick to engrave the names on the marble and pen them into the record book so cemetery officials would not question the new engravings.

He had never gone back, until today.

Renee's family formed a semicircle before the opened crypt. Emotion clogged his throat as Renee's son-in-law murmured the Draicon blessing for a departed relative, and then looked at him with expectation. Damian, the Alpha, who should traditionally say a few words of comfort.

Words stuck in his dry throat like cotton. It was his fault Renee died. He never should have left her to guard Jamie. Renee was too vulnerable.

Another one I've lost. How many more lives will I fail to keep safe?

Jamie glanced at him, and began speaking with touching eloquence about Renee. When she finished, she bent down to address Renee's granddaughter. Gentle compassion radiated from her.

"Marie, your grandmother was a good woman. She loved you very much and always talked about you."

"She's gone. And I'll never see her again. She left me alone," Marie whispered.

Damian's throat tightened.

"She will always live on in your heart." Jamie hugged the little girl. "I promise you this. So you'll never be alone."

She stood, nodding at Renee's family. "Please, go back to my house. I have refreshments."

As she gave directions, Damian stared at the crypt. Jamie handled the situation with dignity, compassion and authority, proving the qualities he knew she possessed.

He jammed his hands into the pockets of his silk trousers. When Jamie looked at him expectantly, he steeled himself. "Go back with them. I'll follow soon."

The labyrinthlike cemetery stretched on endlessly. He finally found it, barely recognized the tall, imposing structure. Damian trudged up the steps and laid a hand on the warm marble. Annie Marcel, age four. Remembered forever in stone. His heart twisted as he read the carved words.

He stared at the white mausoleum. So dark inside, so cold. Damian desperately wanted Annie to have her stuffed toy, but he'd carelessly forgotten it. Just like he'd been careless before she died, not listening to his worried father. If he had stayed instead of chasing rabbits like a *loup fou,* a crazy wolf, Annie would be mated with a clutch of little ones of her own.

Annie, I'm sorry I abandoned you.

Damian traced the letters in Annie's name with a hand that shook like paper tossed in a hurricane. Self-loathing seized him. He had been a stupid, reckless changeling who'd abandoned his family for the chance to run wild and free.

And what was his excuse now?

He abandoned Jamie, too. Should have chained her to his side after taking her virginity. He'd

tried so hard to be gentle, but ah, her scent had
driven him over the edge. It had all been new,
intense and scary for her, a big male invading
her vulnerable, untouched female body. Jamie
needed a day's worth of cuddling, romance and
old-fashioned pampering afterward. Yet instead
of paying attention to her needs, he played Macho
Wolf. Gathering his brothers to hunt the Morph
impersonating her brother. Big Super Stud Hero,
out to slay the evil dragon. Save the princess.

In the meantime, the princess threw herself at
the dragon's even nastier cousin and slid down
into the evil blackness. All because she felt hurt
and betrayed. Smart move, letting her think he'd
loved and left her. Supersmart leaving only a
piece of paper as explanation, easily destroyed
by the Morph calling himself her brother.

He'd failed his family.

He'd failed Jamie.

Damian went rigid as a familiar scent drew
near.

"Your family is here."

Jamie read aloud the names. He glared. "I told
you, go home and leave me alone."

"You should know by now I never listen." She
traced Annie's name. "My God, only four years
old? Who was she? How did she die?"

Damian pulled away her hand. "None of your
business."

"I know what it's like to lose someone. Sorry. Didn't mean to interfere."

Compassion tinged her voice. He was Draicon, a leader, and couldn't afford pity. Pity was for weaklings.

Wordlessly, they headed for the Lexus. Damian drove, tension knitting every muscle. She was his mate. She should know.

"Annie was my sister. She, my brothers and parents died when I was twelve."

He felt the heavy weight of her stare. "I thought Raphael was your brother."

Damian cleared his throat. "Rafe's parents, Remy and Celine, took me into their pack, after. They adopted me. Later, when I grew older, I went west and found distant kin of my father's and formed my own pack. I'm a purebred Alpha and knew I couldn't stay here for good. I'd fight Remy for control of his pack."

No details. Nothing else. He couldn't bring himself to tell the rest. What his father's pack had done. The shame of being outcast riding through the throat-clogging grief. He concentrated on the road.

Silence. He'd expected the usual platitudes, soft murmurs of sympathy. Not what she said next.

"She never had a chance, did she?"

A bicycle pulled out unexpectedly. Damian swore and twisted the wheel. "What?"

"Annie, your little sister." Jamie sighed. "She never had a chance to ride a bike, learn to read, go to her first dance, get her first kiss. So many firsts."

"Never." His hands tightened to white knuckles. Never had a chance against her killers, either.

"Death sucks. But when you're that young, it's cruel, as well."

After a moment he spoke. "I saw you with Renee's grandchild. You're very good."

Her smile was sad. "I know what it's like to feel left out and confused when someone you love dies. I only treated her the way I wished someone had treated me after I lost my parents."

He parked a short distance from her house, cut off the engine. "At least you had your aunt and uncle and cousins to help you through. You had family. Family is everything."

A hard coldness dropped over her gunmetal-gray eyes. "I wish they had dumped me on the street. I was better off living in alleys and picking out of garbage cans."

"What happened?"

A chill draped the air as if she mentally and physically withdrew. "It's in the past and I don't want to drag it out."

They walked to her house in silence. He felt as if he slogged through mud. What the hell had happened to her?

* * *

Soon after, they arrived at Jamie's house. Outside the green gates, Archimedes the cat paced. He meowed madly upon seeing Jamie, and wound around her ankles.

She picked him up. "How did you get out?"

The cat purred in her arms as they went inside. Minutes later they joined Renee's family in the courtyard, eating sandwiches and drinking lemonade. The once-disdainful cat was now friendly and ran up to each guest, rubbing against their ankles as they sat in the courtyard, until little Marie began feeding him tidbits of sandwich.

Armand beckoned to Damian. "Jamie is yours, isn't she? But I can't scent her," Armand said quietly.

"Jamie's mine. But not Draicon."

The man's eyes widened. He shot Jamie a speculative glance. "Fascinating. She's very nurturing and caring. A unique individual."

To his dismay, Armand raised his glass. "To the Marcel pack leader and his mate. May they make many babies!"

Delighted cries filled the air. A sour expression twisted Jamie's mouth.

"Sorry all. That's not going to happen. Not with me."

"But you have to make babies with Damian," Marie cried out. "You're the only one."

Jamie shot Damian a funny look and turned to the girl. "What only one?"

"His draicara. Damian's a purebred Alpha and can only make babies with you because he's your mate. He can't have young with anyone else. Don't you like babies?"

The child's innocent question caused crimson to creep over Jamie's face. Not embarrassment. Fury. Damian met her enraged look with a level one.

"I'm not cut out to be a den mother," Jamie shot back.

Sandra, Marie's mother, stared in amazement. "Jamie, I don't understand. Without you his line dies. You're very privileged because only you can carry his heir."

"There's always adoption. Lots of unwanted wolves around, I'm sure." Jamie pushed off her chair. "I need to get more refreshments."

The little group fell silent as she banged the door behind her. Armand shot Damian a bemused look. "It's the highest honor for a female to bear the young of a powerful Alpha."

Damian suspected Jamie would rather tie his private parts up in a nice, neat knot than participate in said honor. "It's complicated."

"Good luck, sire." Armand's gaze held a measure of respect. "I sense this is a difficult mating, but it may be a sign. Perhaps your mate possesses

powers the Draicon left behind and this is why
you must become one with her. Our Alpha recently said odd things are happening. The coming together of the one again as was foretold. The
halves made whole, and the Draicon regaining
strength to defeat the enemy."

Tension made his jaw rigid as rock. "My people will fight to the end, to our last breath. And
I will die before I let another Morph take one of
my pack."

"It's not your fight alone. We must learn to
fight as one pack, and defeat the evil walking
among us," Armand insisted.

Armand studied Archimedes wending about
his daughter's ankles, meowing loudly as if begging for attention. After Damian told him how it
was Renee's pet, the man gave him a speculative
look.

"Marie has always longed for a cat. If she
doesn't mind, can we take this one with us since
he was Renee's pet? You still have another cat."

Damian frowned. "Two? We don't have two
cats here."

"Then what do you call that?" Armand pointed
at the tangle of bushes in the garden.

Dread filled him as Damian stared at the second black cat silently regarding him. Same size
as Archimedes.

Of course it was just a cat—probably snuck in.

And the house had a shield against Morphs. But magick shields weakened the more times a Draicon performed magick. He'd performed powerful magick since arriving. And failed to reinforce the house shield.

The feline in the bushes blinked. Green eyes showed a soulless black.

At Marie's feet, the other black cat arched his back, hissed and then ran off. The cat in the bushes released a chilling yowl and hissed as it darted out of the bushes toward Marie.

Realization slammed into Damian. The real Archimedes had been outside the gate all this time. This one he had taken from Renee's shop, thinking it was Archimedes, was really...

A Morph.

The cat swiped at Marie's bare calves. The little girl screamed in pain. The cat began twisting. Changing.

"Take your family and run. Now," Damian ordered Armand.

The Draicon didn't need an engraved invitation. He whooshed his little girl into his arms, herded his family out, slamming the gate shut behind them.

Damian turned to face the cat. It contorted, twisted, shifting into its original form.

Morph.

Ugly yellowed fangs showed as it hissed;

greasy hair hung from its skull in strands. The hunched figure was hideous. Then it shifted again. Human this time.

A female human, with big eyes, and a helpless look.

"Please, don't hurt me," it whimpered loudly.

It glanced upward at the house where Jamie was and smiled.

His emotions vanished as if someone pulled a plug. With a hand wave, Damian dispensed his clothing and shifted into wolf with a snarl. He sprang forward to attack.

As his massive jaws opened to rip apart the Morph, he prayed Jamie wouldn't witness this.

What an exhausting way to turn twenty-one.

First the draining emotions of Renee's burial. Then finding out she was destined to bear Damian's children.

"Happy birthday to me," she muttered, shoving a hand through her casual hairstyle. "You get to mother a race of wolves. Don't think so."

Spent, she sagged against the wall. Marie's innocent words bothered the holy hell out of her.

Especially coming on the heels of her mother's conversation. Jamie had realized this was a rare opportunity to get to know a Draicon female better. She'd asked questions. Questions about Alpha males and sex.

Sandra had smiled a little and told her.

Male Draicon were always tender and considerate of their mates, but they were dominating and highly aggressive. It drove them crazy to smell their female's arousal.

"And if he's coming off a fight, where his testosterone is up, he'll instinctively turn all that male aggression toward sexual release." Sandra had said this with a small, secret smile.

The image of Damian, jacked up and hot, did weird things to her body. Jamie felt herself grow soft, wet and wanting. It was biology. Sure. She wanted sex, just sex with Damian, a big, domineering Draicon who wanted her. A wickedly handsome Draicon. Wanted his big maleness and all those hard muscles covering her, thrusting inside her until he'd given her enough orgasms to light up all of New Orleans.

Made perfect sense. Biologically speaking. Now if she could just get her mind to tell her body to get with the program and remind it Damian was a dangerous killer who would destroy anyone who got in his way...

A woman's cry of distress derailed her thoughts.

Jamie scurried for the window. She looked down and saw Damian change into a wolf. Oh God, was that Renee's daughter-in-law there with him?

Damian charged, relentless as a locomotive. His powerful jaws opened, snapped and tore flesh off the woman's leg. Blood splashed over the redbrick walls. The woman's mouth opened in a silent scream.

The Draicon gave no mercy. He went for her throat.

Jamie ran downstairs, her short heels clattering on the wood steps. She flung open the door, shouting for him to stop.

Just as she hit the courtyard, the wolf's jaws locked around the woman's heart. Jamie skidded to a halt, panicking as the wolf bit down.

Her heart thudded a crazy beat as instinct screamed to run. Something shimmered inside her, humming with power. Riding it beneath was a quiet sense of calm, as if this were good.

Good? Damian just killed a woman, a woman, oh God, and...

The woman dissolved into a pile of gray ash. No human woman. Damian had killed a Morph. Just like the crayfish vendor and Paul.

Dumbstruck, she watched the nasty acid burns on the wolf's muzzle slowly scab over. Then it seemed turned toward her. It sniffed the air, jacked up from its powerful kill.

The wolf advanced. It was massive, muscled, gray with black bands about the muzzle. Alpha markings. Jamie shrank back against the wall.

This was Damian, the wolf who ripped her brother to pieces.

In an eyeblink, he shifted into human form. Cruel lust hardened his face. She remembered Sandra's warning about all that male aggressiveness.

Naked, he stalked toward her with an intent look. Her shocked gaze fell downward, caught a glimpse of the steely erection thrusting from his groin. Marie's sweet voice echoed in her mind.

He can only make babies with you.

She was integral to his survival. And he would ensure his line went on, whether she wanted to participate or not.

Reasoning with him might help. But spying the fierce desire darkening his eyes and seeing the tensile strength in his rippling muscles, she knew the truth. She was much shorter, much weaker than the powerful Draicon.

It was hopeless. He wanted her now. And he'd have her.

Aggression poured through Damian. Having vanquished the enemy threatening his mate, he only wanted to rip off Jamie's clothing, push her flat on her back and spread her legs. Thrust deep inside her softness, filling her with his seed. Claim what she'd withheld. His right. His draicara. The mating instinct screamed. Enough stalling. This was his right. *Mine, all mine.*

Jamie made a small noise. "Please," she whispered. "Don't."

One word. Damian ground to a halt. His body shuddered with the effort to control himself. With all his strength, he roped in the raging lust.

She bit down on her plump lower lip. Her full, rosy mouth reminded him of the softness yielding against the hard press of his own. He wanted to take her mouth, stroke his tongue inside her... Damian looked away from the temptation. He inhaled.

Terror glanced off Jamie in huge, spiking waves. Horror darkened her large, gray eyes. Oh *mon Dieu,* she'd seen. Watched him tear the Morph's heart out.

Damian forced his hands to hang limp at his sides. In her eyes, he saw a reflection of himself, ugly and stained with violence.

"I wish you hadn't seen that."

"It...that...was a Morph you attacked... killed..." Her voice faltered, as if seeing the blood splatter.

"Jamie, *chère,* I won't hurt you. Stop looking at me like that," he said quietly.

"What you did...to that...thing..."

"I did it to protect you. It's my nature."

"Your nature. You mean, wolf. Wolves are

ruled by instinct." Her gaze fell to his erection. She wrapped her arms about herself, her gray eyes huge. "You would force me to get what you want. That's what your people do. You take what you want and the hell with all else. You're after me to mate, so what's stopping you?"

He felt as if sandpaper scratched his insides raw. Damn, the way she looked at him, as if he were some two-headed Gorgon. He softened his voice, hoping to reassure her.

"Don't be afraid of me. I would never force you."

"But you're a wolf—you mate, you want to breed."

"For you to become pregnant, we have to achieve a mating lock first. Become equals, exchanging emotions and absorbing each other's powers and magick. It's mutual pleasure, not force that brings us together as one, Jamie."

He had to convince her he wasn't a threat. What would help? The fear shone in her eyes like lights reflecting on glass.

He never humbled himself before another. He was Alpha, powerful, dominating, in control. But this was Jamie, who needed reassurance. Rough brick scraped his bare knees as he sank down, facing Jamie in the least threatening position he knew.

"Look at me, Jamie. I won't hurt you, or ever

force you. I want you so badly I feel like I'm being eaten up inside, but I won't do it. This mating drive, I can't control the wanting, the needing. But I can control myself. I'm a Draicon, yes, but everything in my blood and bones is shouting at me to protect you, not violate you. It's what males of my race do. We cherish and honor our females. We never degrade them."

A heartbeat of silence passed.

"Honor females? Never…degrade them?"

He put a hand over his heart. "To my last breath, I would keep you from all harm. I would die for you before allowing anyone to hurt or humiliate you."

Jamie took a step forward. The fear evaporated from her expression, replaced by wondering awe. "I wish human men were the same. Draicon males could teach them something about gentleness. I wish every man was the same."

They stared at each other across the courtyard in an odd moment of communion. In a flash he saw her barriers drop. It was if he faced her in his physical nakedness and she bared herself inwardly to him.

Given access at last, he merged into her thoughts.

What he saw there made his blood freeze.

Sobbing screams, the pleas, *please stop, don't do this, please don't*…images of a large man, hands big as whole hams, a knife gleaming in the light raised to strike...

Damian pulled out, shocked and horrified.

What the hell had happened to her?

Immediately he scrambled to his feet, driven by the need to comfort her and banish the thoughts hemorrhaging from her. The moment of unity snapped like a cracking branch. Jamie blinked. She shook her head, assuming her usual mask of indifference.

"Okay, then. What now? It's not Mardi Gras yet. Put some pants on. We need to hit the Lafitte Bar tonight and you'll have every woman in the place staring at me in envy."

He angled a smile. But she didn't fool him, because he caught the slight quiver in her voice. Damian waved a hand and clothed himself. Jamie, brave, spitfire Jamie. Could probably face a horde of Morphs and ask them to please step aside, they were blocking her damn sidewalk.

His smile faded as he realized the truth. Beneath the bravado and tough talk, Jamie was running scared. She wasn't afraid of him.

She was terrified of something else.

Her past.

Chapter 8

Jamie combed through her bureau. She clawed through the hateful, waist-high cotton briefs, tossing a handful into the suitcase. Archimedes, the real Archimedes, had gone home with his new owners, Renee's family. Damian did not want to take any more chances with shape-shifting cats who might be Morphs.

Laptop, secure in her backpack. Toothpaste, toothbrush, facial soap...cosmetics? Didn't wear any.

Her fingers paused on the two lacy thongs lying at the drawer's bottom. Jamie fished them out, dangling them from her fingers. How she hated wearing embarrassing granny panties. She stroked the soft silk, staring at the electric blue and green colors. Not for her. Not with her deformity. Jamie shrugged, tossed them into her luggage.

"Rafe sent the car over. Are you ready?"

Damian poked his head into her bedroom. She snapped the suitcase lid shut as he came forward. Tension knotted her stomach.

"I feel just like I did when we evacuated for Katrina. Like I'm never coming back."

"You'll be back. This is just until my brothers can sweep the house with magick and clean out the dirt." Damian gave her a reassuring smile.

"By using magick." At his nod, she sighed. "Magick I lack. Because inside me, there's nothing but blackness. That's why you put the binding spell on me back in New Mexico."

"No." He came forward, cupped her face. "I put the binding spell on you to guard you from harm. If you couldn't use magick, the Morphs wouldn't want you. I didn't know Kane had already infected you with a spell to drain your life."

"I feel like I'm still linked to them," she said in a low voice. "But it's weird because there's something else there, as well."

He went preternaturally still. "Like what?"

"Something struggling against darkness, wanting out. I feel like a loaded gun waiting for the right trigger. Like there's good magick inside me, waiting to be used. But I can't tap it."

An intent look came over him, as if he struggled with a weighty decision. Damian stepped away from her. He lifted his hands and began chanting in a strange tongue. Iridescent sparks swirled around her, dancing in the stray sunbeams.

She felt a curious lifting inside her spirit, then it faded. He dropped his hands.

"You're free. I released the spell binding you from doing magick."

Power hummed inside her. The magick instilled in her through Damian's blood sang like a crackling electrical line. Awe filled her at the trust he'd placed in her. If there was darkness inside her, she could direct it at him with a killing thought.

"Aren't you afraid I'll use it against you?"

"You can't hurt me. My magick is very powerful."

"I could try." She stared at him. "I did before. I nearly killed you."

"With a kiss. Remember? You kissed me. Do you want to try again? Kissing me?"

A knowing smile touched his mouth. He was all control, in power and knew it.

His smile shifted, became speculative. "Why did you try to kill me, Jamie? Someday you'll tell me the truth." Damian reached out, fingered a lock of her hair as if he couldn't bear not to touch her. "I know how much you hurt inside. I've seen your pain, your anguish. You hide something from me, something important. But I still can't read you."

His hand fell. He looked away. "If there is good magick inside you, it's time to release it. But be careful. The more you exercise power, the less the magick I've given you can hold the stone spell at bay."

A haunted look flashed over him. "And if something should happen to me, you can protect yourself. Just in case. I will never again lose anyone like..."

Her heart gave a crazy lurch. "Like what?"

"Nothing. Let's go. This place is too dangerous to linger."

Minutes later, Damian parked the Lexus on the street in front of a mansion on Esplanade. Home, for now. Until it was safe to return to her house.

She wondered if it ever would be safe. If a cat could turn into a Morph and attack a helpless little girl, what else? If Damian hadn't caught and dispatched the Morph, it might have been her that lay in a pool of blood. Just like Renee.

Damian assured her Raphael's home was safe. The mansion welcomed her with quiet warmth. Fragrant honeysuckle and rose bushes scented the property. Painted a soothing ivory, the two-story house boasted Ionic columns and a wide front porch with comfortable white wicker chairs. A wrought-iron fence with lacework grilling guarded the property from the street. Spanish oak trees bearded with moss lined the avenue. The Creole mansions lining the street reflected a more relaxed era.

A time where you could sit on the porch sipping a cool iced tea, never worrying about the friendly cat winding about your legs turning into a demon.

The iron gate had a complicated latch. Damian reached for it, hesitated. He raised his eyes to the majestic house as if in benediction, his expression forlorn and yearning.

Jamie studied the gate. "What's wrong? Is something broken?"

"Mon coeur," he whispered. *"Toujours."*

High school French flashed back. *My heart, always.*

A lump clogged her throat. She touched his arm. Damian looked down at her hand. He flicked up the bolt, opened the gate and ushered her inside the house.

Her sneakers made soft squeaks against the polished hardwood floor as she examined the entrance hall with its antique oak coat stand, gilt mirror and delicate vases and imposing grandfather clock. In her ragged jeans, faded Nirvana

T-shirt and scuffed sneakers, she felt like a hill-billy. Yee-haw.

Yet for all its charm, the house's hushed elegance felt like someone preserved it to seal in the past. The word floated into her mind. *Ghosts.*

Damian watched her. She glanced at him, knowing he expected a reaction.

"It's very beautiful," she managed.

"I hate it."

"Then why bring me here? A hotel is good."

"It's safer here for you. Rafe set up enough safeguards to fry Morphs small as a gnat," he muttered.

She ran a hand over the silk wallpaper. A shiver raced down her spine. Jamie shook her head. "I don't think I should stay. Something happened here. Something bad. Really bad. It's faint, but I still feel it."

Damian's face tightened. "Nothing here will hurt you. The energy you feel is from the past. But it can't—won't—hurt you."

Jamie waited. He set her suitcase down as if it were glass. Then he dragged a worn boot back and forth over the glossy floor. Making scratches, as if raking claws over it. Damian arched his neck, staring at the high ceiling, the carved crown moldings, the artwork hung tastefully on the forest-green wallpaper.

A minute dragged by, rasping like his heel

against the fine-grained wood. Finally he jammed his hands into his jeans pockets.

"My parents' house was once here. When they died, I inherited. Remy, my stepfather, insisted on my rebuilding to honor my heritage."

Damian's home. Not Raphael's. "Why does Raphael live here?"

"I gave it to him as a gift. He sees himself as a caretaker." His eyes took on that haunted, tormented look. "I didn't want anything to do with it."

"What happened to your original home?"

"I torched it after my family died."

Jamie blinked. "You destroyed your own house?"

He shut down like a machine powering off. She knew why. Some things were just too damn painful, like slicing open a healed wound with a knife. But if he wanted her to sleep tonight, she had to know.

"Let's give you a tour." He nodded toward the closest room.

The living room boasted a burgundy Aubusson carpet, oil paintings on beige walls, a mahogany couch and Louis XV upholstered chairs, but an Xbox and PlayStation sat before the wall-length armoire. Jamie pulled open a door. "You scored a copy of Assassin's Creed. Sweet."

Those wide shoulders shrugged. "Rafe and Gabriel play."

"What about you? I hear it teaches good fighting skills," she teased.

"Computer games are a frivolous waste of time."

He looked so serious, his chiseled jaw set like dried concrete, his green eyes stony.

The rest of the downstairs tour went quickly. Damian picked up her suitcase, headed up the stairs. Jamie trotted behind. When they reached the last bedroom at the end of a long hallway, he opened a door with a crystal knob. Jamie gasped in awe. Forest-green and rose carpets added color to the hardwood floor. Hanging on the mint silk wallpaper was a large gilded mirror and two Sargent reproductions. Cut-crystal lamps on a carved walnut dresser cast shadows on the luxurious four-poster. The room boasted a mahogany armoire and a Queen Anne desk. It was all very charming, Creole and elegant.

He set down her suitcase near the bed and jerked a thumb at a side door. "My room is next door, connected through the bathroom. We have the two master suites. My brothers are staying here. The house has five bedrooms, plus a large playroom in the attic with bunk beds, and the old slave quarters in the back are a guesthouse. Rafe stays there."

Despite the room's beauty, an underlying feeling of something bad ran through it. Something horrific, as if it screamed up through the earth, penetrating floorboards and howling through the house.

"Someone was hurt here."

He went still. "How can you tell?"

"I'm sensitive. Always have been." Jamie hugged herself, looking around. "There's nothing evil here anymore. I just feel sad. Very sad, like my heart is breaking."

A muscle twitched in his jaw. Damian went to the window, lifted the lacy curtain with the back of his hand.

"Damian, how did your family die? It was violent, wasn't it?"

For a moment, he said nothing. When he spoke, his voice was low and raspy. "They were killed by Morphs. Slaughtered in our own home. It was…brutal."

Jamie's breath hitched. She joined him, ran a hand over the whitewashed sill. "Killed here, that's why I feel the sadness. Your sister…your little sister, she was only four…"

He drew in a deep breath. "I found her. Under the bed, trying to hide."

Sickening dread punched her chest. Jamie shivered, imagining the little girl's terror, the howling grief Damian felt when he discovered her body.

"And you survived," she marveled.

"I survived only because I learned to fight. And win. Life is nothing but survival for my people. When we cease to fight, we cease to exist."

Something more lay beneath the surface. Damian's muscles tensed. Knowing he'd suffered his family's loss just as she did made the distance between them shrink.

Maybe, just maybe, Mama Renee had been right. Trust those you want to trust the least.

Damian dragged a hand through his short, dark hair. His gaze was haunted. "Go ahead, settle in. I'll be downstairs."

When the door shut behind him, she sat on the high four-poster, swinging her feet back and forth. The itch beneath her skin intensified. A heavy sorrow filled the air, currents of melancholy. Not just the past, but Damian's emotions, as well.

Jamie headed for the shower. She lingered, letting hot water cleanse her skin. When she emerged from the misty bathroom, the intense sadness was worse. She pulled on a black vintage Star Wars T-shirt and jeans, feeling Damian's pain screaming through her veins.

She could go outside, escape, wander the courtyard. She needed fresh air.

Barefoot, she jogged downstairs. In the hallway, the thick sadness nearly suffocated her. Jamie paused before a masculine study with a long English oak bar, Chippendale slant-front desk and white marble fireplace. The twin scents of Damian and alcohol tinged her nostrils.

She ached for space and untainted air, but loathed leaving him alone in his misery. Jamie poked her head into the room. Damian lounged in one of four leather chairs arranged in a circle. On the marble-topped table beside him sat a half-filled bottle. His muscled legs were splayed open. A crystal wineglass with ruby liquid dangled from his long fingers.

Despite the relaxed attitude, his jaw was set like steel. Jamie girded herself.

"Hey, want some company?"

He hedged a minute. Then shrugged.

She snagged a glass from the bar's overhead rack, poured from the opened bottle and sat opposite him, tucking her legs beneath her.

Damian stared at the fireplace as if it divined the world's secrets. Jamie took a bracing sip, running her tongue over the liquid. "Awesome. Hint of smoke, a touch of something sharp, like leather. I'd say it's from the Medoc region."

Surprise widened his eyes. "You know your wines."

"I learned because of Mark. He was an oenophile. In addition to being an audiophile and a biophile. I think he had some other, more refined philes in him, but those were the most prominent."

Her little joke failed to raise a smile. Damian raised his glass, gave it a desultory swirl. "My father drank wine as if it were water. When he and my mother left France just before the Revolution and came here, he packed his habits with him."

"The Revolution. Is that a new Xbox release?" she teased.

"The Revolution was nothing compared to the war we're fighting now."

Finally he raised his green gaze. Jamie stifled a gasp. It was like glimpsing an algae-choked pond. No life. No movement. Nothing. God, he looked like she'd felt after Kane had bitten her and given her magick. Alive and breathing, but dragged under by cloying, impenetrable blackness.

Whatever happened, it sank to his soul. She knew all about that kind of desolation. Seeing this strong, proud and resilient male wrapped in deadness twisted her in knots. Jamie set down the glass, driven by a desperate need to shake it out of him.

Don't do this. Don't let it own you like it did me.

"Tell me, Damian. Tell me about it."

* * *

Damian sipped the Cabernet Franc in his glass. Complex, excellent vintage, but it could be muddy water in his numbed mouth.

She wanted to know about his war. It seemed never-ending, a rolling ribbon of violence.

"My life has been nothing but war. After my family died, I lived with Rafe's family. Remy and Celine took me in, taught me to hunt and survive."

He studied her slender, still body through the dark ruby liquid. Red, like blood.

"The *Fedoighlas,* as they're known in the Old Language, or in English, Morphs, were once Draicon like us. Before the last century, they were few and easier to eliminate. Now they outnumber us. Daggers straight to the heart is the only way to kill them."

"Why do Draicon turn Morph?"

The question was simple as a child's, but he sensed the deeper meaning. Damian dragged himself out of a vat of self-pity. She'd swum in a quicksand of evil darker than anything he'd ever encountered.

"Millennia ago, our race lived in the dimension of the Other Realm. We could move through air, create matter from energy, manipulate objects, shape-shift to any form. But we wanted to learn of Earth, so to do so we willingly split ourselves in half to lessen our powers."

"Makes sense. Can't have omnipotent beings running amok."

A reluctant smile cracked his dry lips. Damian sipped more wine. "The Draicon became wolf shape-shifters, to be closer to the earth's environment. Our missing half, or the genetic descendant, still walks on earth. This is why we constantly search for our mate, so when we join our bodies together, and hearts and emotions, we become one. In the mating lock during sex, we exchange thoughts, emotions and magick, each absorbing the other's powers. But some were too impatient and greedy. They craved power. And found by killing that which is most sacred, blood kin, they could become any animal or human form. Evil gave them power, but they must feed off the fear of dying victims for nutrition."

Blood drained from her face as Jamie hugged herself. "They wanted me to teach them battle maneuvers. I taught them what I knew from the games I played. Sometimes I was afraid of becoming one of them, nothing in me but the stench of rot and death."

Worry stabbed him. Damian set down his glass, leaned his forearms on his opened thighs. "Jamie, you survived it. You're too strong to let them win."

"And you're too strong to let the sad energy in this house and its memories do the same."

Flustered, he reeled back. Talk about a verbal one-two punch. He realized just how clever his draicara was, manipulating him into concern for her, then switching it back to him. Damian tightened his lips. His past, oh no, they were not going there. End of conversation.

He finished his wine, wiped his mouth. "You presume too much. It's my private business, so stay out."

An odd look shifted over her face. "It's not possible. Because this house is screaming with memories and pain. And I sense you're screaming inside most of all."

Damian started as Jamie came over to sit on the wide armrest of his chair. He breathed in her fresh scent of youth and energy. Damn, he needed her, more than he dared to admit. But he wouldn't let her get close. Couldn't let her slide under his skin, make him weak. Weakness and pity were for fools who let their guard down. When he let his guard down, people died. Never again.

She slid her hands on his thick shoulders and squeezed gently. Jamie had never approached him, touched him like this.

"You're too tense. Let me care for you," she murmured.

No one did. He saw to everyone else's needs. They looked to him for leadership, guidance and protection. They looked to him to do everything. Damian, the invincible Super Wolf who did it all.

Muscles in his shoulders stiffened and relaxed as she kneaded, her fingers finding the knots and working them out. The massage soothed, and stirred his blood. Damian's head fell back as his body became caught in a helpless grip of animalistic pleasure. He quivered as she rubbed behind his neck, his body responding instantly with growing arousal. Jamie stopped.

"Is it too hard?"

"Getting there."

Jamie looked at his lap. She reached down and with absolute gentleness, kissed him on the mouth while her hand slipped between his opened thighs.

And stroked.

Damian went hot all over, blood surging thickly in his veins. He let her kiss him, her tongue licking at his, her teeth playfully nipping his bottom lip. Let her take charge. Her show. Jamie's innocent, awkward caresses fueled his arousal like gasoline on a smoldering fire. His cock ached, strained against the tight jeans, wanting out, wanting inside her, wanting...

With a low snarl, he pushed her hand away, broke the kiss.

He shot out of his seat, had her sitting there and her jeans off in a minute. He growled at the white cotton panties, wanting them gone. Fingers curled, claws grew from the tips replacing his nails. He hooked them under the fabric, taking enormous care not to touch her skin, and ripped. Cloth shredded. Damian reached down and snagged her underwear with his teeth, tossing the panties aside. His nostrils flared, catching her scent. She was aroused, wanting.

His goal achieved, the claws retracted. Damian slid his hands along the inside of her thighs, opening them, and then reached for his zipper to free himself. The urge to mate lashed him, eradicating all but need and instinct....

Until he realized she was trembling.

Damian paused, hands resting on her slender, pale legs. He'd forgotten. She was inexperienced, not used to his kind, hell, any male's passion. He looked up, seeing her gunmetal-gray eyes widen.

"Slow," he whispered. "My bad. We'll do this nice and slow."

A small smile curved her mouth, whether from his usage of her lingo or relief at his mood change, he didn't know. He pressed a soft kiss inside her thigh. Her skin tasted like ripe berries.

Jamie shifted, a radiant blush racing over her face like sunrise.

"What do you want, *chère?* Do you want

me…here?" He skimmed a hand up her leg, near her center.

"Yes." Her voice was throaty, a bare whisper. "Please."

Her hips lifted and surged up, an ancient instinctive plea. He smiled.

His head dropped between her opened thighs. Very gently he spread her feminine flesh with his fingers, marveling at the moist pearl pinkness, her secret beauty.

"Ah, damn, you are perfection," he purred, leaning closer, catching another heady whiff of her scent.

He buried his head between her legs and began tonguing her. Slow slides, loving her taste, the rich sweetness of her mixed with tangy spice. She slid down, moaning, clutching fistfuls of his hair. Sweet pain grabbed him as she held on, pulling.

Damian swirled his tongue, harder and faster.

She climaxed violently, her body bucking off the chair.

He gently stayed with her through her convulsions, kissing her softly. Then he reached for his zipper. Beneath his jeans, his cock strained, his balls ached. He needed to be inside her, bad, so bad he shook as he clasped the zipper. Her breath came in ragged pants, but apprehension shone in her eyes.

Apprehension because of him.

Damian cursed softly in French, reached for her panties, realized they were lying in strips on the Oriental rug. He grabbed them with a rueful look, stuffed them into his pocket until he could dispose of them discreetly.

Jamie stared at him. "Why, what are you…"

Leaning over her, he put a finger over her lips. "Hush. This was for you." He smiled at her. "Ah, for me, as well. I enjoyed it, very much."

The rosy flush of arousal darkened. Jamie pushed her hair out of her face and stood. She went to turn around as if hunting for her underwear and stopped.

"Close your eyes," she muttered. "I don't want you to see my butt."

His eyebrows arched. He'd already seen her naked, flat on her back when he'd taken her virginity after they'd first met. Strain showed in her clenched hands. Damian turned his back as she shimmied into her jeans. The zipper rasped and he pivoted.

Only to find her looking down, shuffling her feet. Jamie's hands were on her lower back.

She was ashamed. What had happened to her?

Chapter 9

People packed the Laffite bar. With a hand at the small of her back, Damian guided Jamie to an empty table in view of the bar. His touch sent a shiver through her, knowing what happened earlier. Knowing where his mouth had been, the crazy pleasure he'd selflessly given her...

Moisture gushed between her legs. Oh yeah, she had it bad. This afternoon wasn't enough. More, her hormones growled.

Damian looked down at her, nostrils flaring. A soft smile touched his mouth. He pulled out a chair for her.

"What do you want?" he asked.

You, on top of me, with all that male strength....

A blush raced across her cheeks. "Uh, whatever domestic beer they have on tap."

He returned with two filled plastic cups, handed her one. Damian sat, his keen gaze scanning their surroundings. Always alert, on guard. Intense. Arousal faded, nudged aside by sadness. His family had been slaughtered. He alone survived. What kind of ghosts haunted him?

Jamie knew the feeling. She reached over, laced her fingers with his. He didn't realize it, but his secret forged a small connection. She didn't want it, but it was there.

I understand.

Damian looked up, a smile erasing the deadly warrior look. His thumb made little circles on her skin, making her nerves flare with sensual awareness. As if he sensed it, and knew it wasn't the right time, he slid his hand out.

People crowded the bar, their laughter and talk filling the space around them. She remembered wanting to come here for her birthday, but Mark had been too busy. Last year he'd forgotten it was her birthday.

Jamie had quietly let it pass, reassuring herself her brother was an important man with much more on his mind than her birthday. Birthday celebrations were for children. So what if she'd never had a cake, with pink icing, candles and lots of people singing to her? Did it matter? Such silly dreams were for others, not her.

A lump rose in her throat. Ruthlessly she swallowed it down.

Damian scanned their surroundings. "Stay here. I'll be back."

She watched him walk the room's perimeter, staring at the exposed brick as if studying the centuries-old setting. To the casual observer, he resembled a fascinated bystander examining history. He was searching for the next clue hidden on the brick.

Loud laughter from the bar drew her attention. A slightly overweight man in a red polo shirt talked with a pretty brunette. His loud, obnoxious remarks about animals rankled her nerves. Her thermostat shot up to boiling.

Jamie stared at the man's beer, wishing she could dump it over that smug grin.

Barely had she entertained the thought when the glass slid toward him. Jamie gasped. She rubbed a sore spot blooming on her temples and stared. Beer drinker went to grab it, swiped at empty air. The brunette laughed.

She stared at the beer mug, silently willing it to tip. Seeing it splash all over him, cooling his jets.

A small thunk of glass hitting wood followed.

The man jumped to his feet, sputtering. "What gives?"

The glass lay on the bar, a yellow lake of foam spilling over the side. A small pounding began in her temples. Jamie swallowed convulsively. She had done that.

A college-age male approached, plastic cup in hand. He was tall, with a bristling crew cut, designer jeans, a polo shirt and loafers. Fraternity boy. Crappa Kappa Zappa. She rolled her eyes. He took Damian's empty seat. The smell of vodka clung to him like wet paint.

Jamie gave him an even look.

"Hey there, pretty lady, all alone? Whadda yah having?" He nodded at her glass.

"Peace and quiet until you came along." She leaned forward, gave him a pointed look. "And if you're going to ask my sign next, it's Do Not Disturb."

But he appeared unaffected by her chill. Vodka Breath leaned forward until his knee nearly touched hers. "You're very lovely, very spunky, just the type I like," he said, and it seemed a small growl rumbled in his chest.

Before her astonished gaze he suddenly rose three feet off the ground. Behind him, Damian lifted the chair, spilled the man out like wet laundry. Jamie snickered as the man glared, vodka soaking the front of his preppy shirt. At Damian's level stare and bristling aggression, Vodka Breath scrambled away.

Righting the chair, Damian turned it around and straddled it. "Any more like that and let me know, I'll take care of them, *d'accord?*"

But she was too intrigued by what she'd just accomplished to pay much attention. How did she tip that beer from all the way over here?

Damian gave her a long, thoughtful look. *It appears you have your own magick.*

His soft, deep voice inside her head shocked her speechless. Communicating telepathically? A satisfied smile touched his sensual mouth. He reached for her hand, entwined his long fingers with hers.

You're my draicara. It's normal for us to talk like this. I've been waiting for this moment, Jamie. It means you are finally opening up to me and the dark magick inside you is fading, for now.

Damian invading her mind. Power energized her. Jamie felt as if she'd sucked down a wagonload of caffeine, yet this wasn't accompanied by the troubled guilt when she'd acquired dark magick. This felt different. Natural. Yet instinct said Damian's magick wasn't the cause, but a catalyst. Impossible. She had no natural powers.

Jamie pushed aside a fleeting sorrow that she'd again borrowed someone else's magick. Lowering her voice, she asked him about the clue he'd found.

He answered in that odd mind link, his voice sounding inside her head as clearly as if words came from his lips.

I found the words scratched on the brick— "Natchez *boat water revolution = mark on bust of French failure." It must be the next clue.*

What does it mean?

Think of it. The Natchez *is a paddle-wheel boat, and displaces water with...*

It makes no sense. The Natchez *was built long after your father's death.*

Each revolution of the paddle wheel, she finished. *So the number of revolutions of the paddle wheel is the same as the mark on a French failure?* Jamie frowned. *Who could the French failure be?*

Napoleon. My father always lectured how ego was his greatest downfall, Damian replied in their mind link.

His eyes widened. *Someone else put the clue there.*

Someone else knew where the book was hidden. Yet why had that person left a clue? And why hadn't that person simply taken the book for himself?

"Let's get out of here," Damian said aloud.

They passed tables of patrons laughing and

talking. A few glanced up, nodded at Damian with a respectful look.

"Friends of yours? Draicon?" she asked outside.

"Vampires. They like the nightlife." He winked at her.

"Why is this happening to me? Why now?" Jamie scuffed her sneakers along the cracked sidewalk. "Maybe I came into this power because I just turned twenty-one?"

Damian stopped and turned. "What do you mean, you're twenty-one? You're twenty-five. And your birthday isn't for another two months. Rafe looked up your driver's license and—"

"Oh, that. It's fake. Mark changed a few things around after I came to live with him. He had a way of sneaking into the system and shuffling records. Said I'd be a legal adult much sooner and come into our parents' inheritance, so then our uncle couldn't touch me."

"Your birthday is today?"

Jamie shrugged.

Damian's expression softened. "Happy birthday, *ma petite*. I didn't realize." He pressed a soft kiss into her palm. A shiver of pleasure shot up her spine. "I promise, I will make it up to you. What do you want?"

An absurd joy wriggled up from her stomach as she imagined her dearest wish. It was so stupid. A wide smile broke over his face. "Ah, excellent. Good choice."

This sure was freaky, having someone else peer into her thoughts. She felt invaded, exposed. Maybe she could block him, and she thought of a redbrick wall.

"Do it again. Read my mind," she insisted.

His smile dropped. "It's not necessary," he said curtly. "Just tell me to stay out and I'll stay out. You don't need a gatekeeper."

Damian dropped her hand as they continued walking. She felt a bit ashamed, acting as if he were some pervert, eavesdropping into her thoughts like a peeping Damian.

They turned from Bourbon onto St. Philip, slowly approaching the McDonough school. As they walked, hair rose on the nape of her neck.

Someone's following us.

Blushing again, she realized she'd used their mental communication. Damian only nodded. *Stay ahead of me.* He shuffled so she walked slightly in front.

Suddenly Damian stopped and whirled with a snarl. Oh, great. Wonderful. Jamie sighed with exasperation as she recognized the man who'd hit on her in the bar.

"Hey there, sweetie. Why are you with this loser?" He glowered at Damian.

"Leave us. Now," Damian said, his expression tightening.

"I'm not afraid of you." Vodka Breath raised his chin defiantly. Claws grew from his fingers as he swiped at Damian, who sidestepped.

"Not human, but not pack. Rogue," he said. Putting Jamie behind him in a protective maneuver, he faced the male.

"Give me the female. I need her to breed. She has an aura of power and will make strong young," Vodka Breath snarled. "I challenge you for her."

Shocked disbelief coursed through her as he flashed two very sharp descending canine teeth.

Damian smiled slowly. "Your right. Your mistake. But not on the street. Too many eyes."

He leaped over the low iron gate separating the school from the sidewalk and went into the yard. Shadows covered him. Vodka Breath followed, then shrugged out of his clothing. He stood naked, then faster than she could blink, changed into a wolf. A muscled black wolf with bared fangs.

Damian merely waved his hands. Clothing vanished. Then he shifted, his far more powerful and larger Alpha wolf outweighing the other male by thirty pounds.

Jamie gasped as the two wolves charged, their

bodies smacking together with a dull thud. She climbed the fence, jumping onto the ground.

Frantic fear cresting over her, Jamie reached out, fingers stretched outward. With a mighty thought that sent pain spiking through her brain, she hurled the black wolf backward twelve feet into an alleyway between the school and the brick building next door. The wolf growled, shook its head. Blood droplets from its torn muzzle sprayed the wall. In a brave, suicidal rush he charged Damian, who waited with calculating patience. Damian turned, drew blood on the other's muzzle.

Damian would kill him, she realized with sickening dread. Damian fought for the right to mate and breed with her. And he'd tear apart any male who threatened his authority. She knew the animal world, knew what drove Damian. But she couldn't let him kill this inebriated fool.

Yet she remained motionless, reluctant to test her powers again. The pain had proved too much. Jamie hugged herself as she watched the battle rage.

The black wolf retreated then darted around, tearing at Damian's hindquarters. Blood dripped down his flanks. She cried out. No more. He was hurt.

Ignoring the pain stabbing her temples, she directed all her thoughts.

Just as Damian bared his fangs and sprang for the male's throat, Jamie sent them both flying upward. Knives stabbed her temples. Jamie winced, holding them aloft despite the agony. She only wanted to collapse and scream. With every ounce of her strength, she concentrated.

The large gray wolf suddenly shape-shifted back into Damian. A fully clothed Damian. Slowly she lowered him to the ground. He came to her, his hands framing her face.

"Jamie, put him down. I can feel your pain. *Chère,* what is this?"

Slowly she released the other wolf, letting him drift downward. When all four paws touched the ground, she staggered back and released a low moan. Jamie clutched her pounding head.

The wolf charged, jaws snapping, Jamie in the way of its target. Damian whirled, pulled her aside just as the wolf leaped. Claws skidded on the ground as the wolf attempted to stop, and crashed into the iron fence.

Agony speared her temples. Jamie moaned, sank down to the ground. "My head, it hurts. Just give me a minute, please."

Damian leaned over and gently touched her temples. His fingertips were cool and soothing. Some of the pain fled, bringing intense relief. She struggled to her feet.

He narrowed his gaze at Vodka Breath, who

shifted back into human form, and quickly dressed. "You could have injured her. You're so obsessed with winning her, you forgot the first rule. Protect your mate at all costs. You're brazen for your age, and need to know your place."

"I apologize. I never intended to hurt her." The other male lowered his head as Damian stared him down. Submissive at last.

Damian gave him a level look. "You need a pack, cub. Being alone among humans hasn't taught you manners. You need to be with your own kind." He slid an arm about Jamie and named an address. "Tomorrow, go to that house, ask for Raphael, tell him what happened. He'll accept you if you're humble and tell him I sent you. If I see you on the streets alone again, know this. Your ass is mine."

Looking mortified, the male nodded and mumbled thanks. He shuffled away.

She let herself sag against Damian with a small moan.

Magick always came with a price. And this one felt almost too high to pay.

Jamie's pain radiated through him. He supported her weight. She felt ice-cold. Like death. He had to warm her, get her home fast. Frantic, he checked her pulse. Too slow. Sluggish.

Breath caught in his throat as he glanced down at her fingernails.

Gray. Like stone. Magick had activated the spell.

He lifted her into his arms as if she weighed no more than a sack of cotton candy. The street was deserted. But for the revelry drifting from the Lafitte bar nearby, he heard nothing.

Then footsteps. Slow, purposeful. A threat.

A group of ten walked toward them, their steps determined. Instinct screamed to fight, but he couldn't risk Jamie. Carrying her, he retreated back into the shadows of the schoolyard. He set her down, reached for his phone and speed-dialed Raphael.

"McDonough. Jamie's hurt and I've got company," he muttered, then shut off the phone and pocketed it.

The people suddenly stopped before the schoolyard, turned with exact precision toward him. Military precision.

In an eyeblink, they shifted into a swarm of angry wasps and flew toward him.

No choice. He lowered Jamie to the ground and covered her body with his, turning her face to let her breathe and protecting her head with his arms and hands. The insects buzzed angrily around him, stinging, trying to get at skin. They stung through his thin silk shirt, crawled on the back of his neck. Wasps landed on exposed parts of his face. He just had to outlast them and pray his magick would heal him fast enough before the allergies kicked in. Fighting back the burning pain, he hung on. Several wasps landed on his cheeks, ears and neck. A few crawled toward his eyes. Damian squeezed them shut.

No use. They stung his eyelids. He clenched his teeth.

Minutes later, several motorcycles roared to the curb. Damian heard the thump of heavy boots on concrete, snarls, and felt the power in the air. Eyes closed, he waited, still covering Jamie.

"*T' frère.* Oh, *merde.*" Raphael helped him to his feet. Wasps littered the ground, tiny corpses fried by Rafe's powerful magick.

"Take Jamie home. She's hurting, bad," he mumbled through swollen lips.

His hands looked absurdly like Mickey Mouse's. Raphael picked up Jamie, slid her onto the bike, and then hopped on, supporting her unconscious weight with one strong arm.

Damian's arms and legs burned. He spoke into her mind. *Go with Rafe. He'll get you home safely. I'll be along shortly.*

"I'll take care of her," Raphael promised, and roared off.

Adam stared at him from behind round glasses. "What about you?"

"I'll walk." Damian passed a swollen hand over his equally swollen face.

"Man, you look bad," Adam muttered. "Let me give you a lift."

He mustered strength to shake his head. Damian managed to hold himself aloft. When the bikers roared off, he sank into the shadows. His body felt twice its size. Like a wounded animal, he slunk farther into the schoolyard's darkness. White-hot flames licked his skin.

For a moment he lay curled on the ground. Control. Discipline. When Jamie had infected him with the disease that nearly killed him, he used both to ride through the pain. No one in his pack suspected how he'd hurt. Even as he lay in bed, wasting away, he issued orders. Remained in charge. Worried about his people.

You can do this. It's nothing. Damian clenched his jaw and rode it out.

Fifteen minutes later, he stood, feeling less shaky. His body began healing itself.

He walked back, feeling his skin slowly mend, the swollen stings gradually fade. Magick drained from him rapidly. If more Morphs attacked, he could fight. Barely. *Bring them on.*

They didn't want him dead. Their purpose was only to injure and hurt. The decoys Raphael planned tonight had failed. Someone tracked their moves.

And Jamie's newfound powers presented possibilities and concerns. Inside she was a well of power waiting to be tapped.

She'd tapped it, all right. Like a damn geyser. His magick should only slow the spell, not give Jamie power. More power than he possessed.

Or control. She needed to learn. He could teach her, but too many questions remained unanswered. What was Jamie? A human with powerful psi abilities, the ability to kill with her mind?

He stopped, ignoring the crowds pushing past him. She'd tried to save him when she thought he was in danger. Not the actions of a woman determined to murder her former lover.

The fragile shaping of a bond had begun. He only hoped it would continue.

Before the spell set in for good. Her gray, clammy skin worried him. He shouldered the thought aside, concentrated on centering his thoughts to heal.

Damian headed for Bourbon. In the thick crowd out for drinks and a good time, no one noticed him. His face healed first, then his limbs. He walked for a long while. By the time he reached the end of the strip, he'd healed fully.

Turning, he headed toward Raphael's house. A few minutes later, his cell phone rang, playing Creedence's "Bad Moon Rising." Jamie had changed the ringtone. Little minx.

"She's out cold," Raphael told him. "Guess you figured our plan failed."

"T'me dis pas," he said dryly. "What happened?"

Damian had spread the word he was taking Jamie to the City Park. Two of Raphael's friends shape-shifted into Damian and Jamie's forms. It took incredibly powerful magick assisted by potions. Unfortunately, unlike the Morphs, they couldn't hold the forms long.

"They went to the park, but no one followed. Bastards knew they were decoys. Someone's stalking you, *t'frère.* And I can't figure out how they're doing it."

"I'll find out," Damian told him.

He thumbed off the phone.

A while later, he arrived at the house. Raphael sat in the parlor on the upholstered couch, laptop open before him. He glanced at Damian.

"Raw steak in the fridge. I figured you needed it."

"Not tonight. I need to hunt. Can you watch over her while I'm gone?"

"Sure. Besides, it'll give me time to record this." His brother turned the computer around so Damian could glimpse the intricate Web page with streets, graphic pushpins marking locations.

"Password protected. Every time there's a Morph attack or a murder, we record it on the computer."

"Risky if someone finds out. Or hacks into the system." Something about the computer nagged Damian, but he couldn't pinpoint it.

"Let them try. It's secure. I have guys who are genius with systems and software."

Damian headed out of the room, paused. He spoke over his shoulder. "I never did thank you for all you've done, for me and for all our race, Rafe. So, thanks."

Silently he entered Jamie's bedroom. On the large four-poster, she appeared to sleep, her face smooth of suffering. But her skin was still gray and clammy to his touch.

Unable to resist touching her, he kissed her forehead. "Ah, *chère,* how I wish you would realize I would never hurt you," he whispered.

Damian looked down at her, sorely tempted. So innocent, all her defenses lowered like the barricaded gates to a fortress. So easy it would be to awaken her with soft kisses, raining all over her skin, pulling off her clothing. Sex as a means to slow the stone spell spreading through her veins. She'd be easy and pliable in his arms, and willing.

Not now. He needed to hunt.

He released a frustrated sigh and left. Damian paced down the back steps. Moonlight dappled the trees in the courtyard. He let himself out the back gate and headed for the river.

Where railroad tracks spliced through the land, he raised his head to the waxing moon. She caressed his face with healing light, power.

With a hand wave, his clothing vanished. Bones and muscle lengthened as his body shape-shifted. Wolf now, he slipped into the night. Bounding down the railroad tracks, he followed them east as they curved south. Following the bend of the Mississippi, past the ruined charred remains of the coffee warehouses.

He did not return until the moon receded in the sky like a small nickel. At the Ursuline street-car station, he shifted back and walked to the house.

Damian went upstairs to Jamie's room. Light spilling from the hallway speared the darkened bedroom. She lay fast asleep, her breathing even. But something felt wrong. Dread hammered at his chest with twin fists. He bent down, stared at his destined mate.

Gray streaked her beautiful dark hair. Another sign the stone spell had advanced.

He picked up a strand, rubbed it between his fingers. Damian kissed her chilled forehead and left. He stripped and lay in his bed. Weary, he closed his eyes. But sleep did not come for a long time.

* * *

The nightmare came with swift, punishing precision. Annie was screaming and he couldn't reach her. Sharp claws scudded over the mansion's cool tile floor, drawing nearer. Curling herself into a tight ball beneath the bed, clutching her stuffed wolf for protection. The scampering claws drew nearer. Annie screamed again. Damian tried to run faster, but he was mired in a thick bog. Then the screams shifted and became lower pitched and the face changed.... A woman with a lovely pixie face and beautiful gray eyes...

The Morphs wanted to kill Jamie.

Suddenly the dream split as if a movie screen parted in half. Jamie was there, but no terror etched her expression. Her smile was soft and reassuring as she slid into his arms, murmuring reassurances. Calming peace settled over him. She felt good and he never wanted to let go.

Damian awoke with a soft weight pressed against him. Jamie curled against him, lying peacefully in his arms. Awed, he blinked.

Tonight, she dream-walked with him. Entering his darkest nightmare to soothe him with her presence.

Careful not to awaken her, he stroked her gray hair. What caused her to come to him? Was the bond between them pulling her?

How much power did she have yet to reveal?

Chapter 10

Music mingling with loud male voices dragged her out of a sluggish sleep. Jamie threw an arm across her face, struggled to awaken. Glancing at the ornamental clock on the nightstand, she pushed down a groan. Eleven. She'd crashed the whole night. Had terrible dreams, about Damian, lost, alone, the haunting sadness on his face making her reach out to him, offering what little comfort she could.

And the other. Wasps, hundreds of them, stinging him. The memory slammed into her. Jamie skimmed a hand over her face. She wasn't hurt. Damian had taken the hit, covering her with his body.

She used the bathroom, then picked up the

brush to untangle her hair. The mirror reflected her pale face and her hair....

Oh, dear God.

Gray. All of it. As if she'd aged forty years in eight hours. The brush fell from her opened fingers, clattering on the counter. Jamie glanced down at her hands.

Her nails were gray, as well.

Squeezing her eyes shut, she tried quelling rising panic. Nothing, just nothing. She'd exercised newfound powers and this was the result. Damian could give her more of his magick to slow the spell. Hell, she'd even drink bat's blood.

And what if she didn't have Damian? Who could she rely upon to help her? The mirror reflected her large eyes, gray as her hair. She couldn't go it alone any longer. She needed him. The thought disquieted her. How could she rely on someone else, especially a killer wolf?

Selecting the thickest robe she could find, Jamie belted it on. Terry-cloth armor. At the head of the stairs, she paused to listen. The voices were coming from the living room. Hard rock punched the air. Nickelback.

Someone had good taste.

She crept downstairs, crossed the hallway and hovered outside the room. Jamie stole a peek.

Tucked away in a polished walnut armoire, a wickedly hi-tech stereo blasted the deep bass of

Nickelback's "Fight for All the Wrong Reasons." Lounging about in the fussy chairs and couch were five very big, very badass Draicon. She immediately recognized Damian and Raphael, but the three others were strangers. Yet not. Something familiar about them nagged at her.

Damian sat on the sofa. His socked feet dangled over the armrest. Jamie's heart gave a little jump. Dark shadows lined his eyes. Day beard scuffed his jaw. In a black T-shirt and black jeans, he looked sexy as ever.

Raphael was parked on a chair, scuffed boots propped up on the antique coffee table. The furniture might be expensive, but she liked how they treated it as if it were her flea market stuff. He looked pretty pissed off.

"You, *t'frère,* are in deep. What the hell is going on?"

A hint of menace flashed in Raphael's obsidian eyes. "My guys gave me the full report. Do you know in the bar last night, some humans were talking about how they saw that little stunt Jamie pulled with hurling you and the other Draicon in the air? Gabe had to give them a little mind work-over. Convince them a magic show was in town."

A tall male, his muscled body stuffed into a black Harley Davidson T-shirt, black leather jacket and tight jeans, flicked a finger at Raphael.

His square jaw and full mouth bore a slight re-
semblance to Raphael, but a black cowboy hat
dipped over his brow, hiding his eyes. "Rafe,
easy. It's no problem, man."

"Damian, what is she? She's not human. So
what gives?" Raphael asked.

"I don't know. She's telekinetic and God
knows what else. She turned twenty-one yesterday, so your info is wrong. She's coming into her
power. We need to know more about her parents."

"We know enough about her brother. Took
care of that problem," said a deep voice filled
with menace.

Jamie's heart went still. She craned her neck,
staring fully. Oh God. Now she knew what they
were....

These were all the Draicon who were with
Damian the night he killed Mark. They'd helped
murder her brother.

Her hands shook wildly. Jamie took a step
backward.

Damian's head whipped around, nostrils flaring as if scenting something. Jamie shrank back.

"Come out. I know you're listening, Jamie."

Come inside to the wolves' den. Every bone
in her body cried out against it.

Summoning all her strength, she stepped inside. In addition to Cowboy Hat and Raphael, two
other males lounged in chairs. One was dressed

in jeans and a polo shirt. He had well-trimmed brown hair and kind blue eyes. The other was leaner, his salt-and-pepper hair shoulder length, a whipcord toughness lurking beneath the olive-green denim jacket and camouflage pants. A closely trimmed goatee framed the thin slash of a mouth. The bladelike nose and the pale blue eyes showed someone not to tangle with, unless you enjoyed having your limbs removed and handed back to you on a china platter.

The wolves who killed Mark. Capable of ripping apart a fully muscled, tall man into bits of flesh and bone. She shrank back into her skin.

"Jamie, it's okay."

The quiet, soothing voice shattered her fear. Damian came forward. Hands on lean hips, shoulders wide in the tight black T-shirt, his body was taut with muscle. A dangerous Draicon who killed.

Then she remembered. The wasps. He'd covered her body, protecting her. Jamie reached out and ran her index finger over the smooth skin of his biceps.

"The wasps, did I dream them? They attacked you. You were hurt, badly."

His expression softened further. "I'm fine, Jamie. And it was no dream."

"You threw yourself on top of me, kept me from being stung."

For so long she'd been forced to handle everything herself. The thought of this big male sheltering her with his body, taking blows for her, melted her with tenderness. Jamie glanced at the other Draicon, watching her every move.

Fear still inched along her spine, but Damian wouldn't let anything happen to her. She should just say thanks. Instead, she kept stroking his arm, testing the taut flesh beneath her fingers.

Jamie picked up his hand, brought it to her cheek. She kissed the knuckles, the callused palm. Damian cupped her chin, lifting it to meet his gaze.

"I will always protect you, *chère*. To my last dying breath."

Intensity radiated in his darkening gaze. Her body flared to life. A gush of moisture seeped between her legs, dampening the pink PJ bottoms. Her nipples punched the thin cotton sleep shirt. She ran a wet tongue around her mouth, the wanting suddenly very bad.

Damian's expression shifted. His powerful body trembled, as if he could barely hold himself back. She read the need in his tense muscles, the flaring nostrils and the sudden erection tenting his jeans. He was ready to mate.

So was she. Another wave of heat slammed into her, arousal flooding between her legs.

Expressions on the other males shifted. Their

nostrils flared, as if scenting something very appealing. Damian's hands fisted. The hungry look in his eyes turned darker as he glared at them.

"Whoa," said the one wearing the cowboy hat. "Damn."

"Control yourself, Gabe. I'm warning you." Damian growled deep.

"It's all good, *t'frère*. We know she's yours." Cowboy Hat went to the mantel, picked up a lighter and a slender stick of incense. A blue flame flared and the sweet smell of sandalwood drifted upward. "Helps in difficult situations with other males' mates."

Dragging in a deep breath, Damian took her by the hand, led her to the couch. He pulled her close, his arm securely around her shoulders. He was a muscled barricade of flesh between her and the other Draicon. Heat drained from her, leaving behind a mighty chill at the other males' frank sexual appraisal.

Damian introduced her. Etienne was the one with kind eyes, denim jacket was Alexandre and cowboy hat was Gabriel. His older brothers.

"They're staying here for a while. More protection, and they know more about the Old Ways, and powers our people had before," Damian explained.

"Older brothers? Like in how old?"

"Etienne's the eldest. He's 307."

A werewolf older than the Declaration of Independence. Despite her rapidly pounding heart, she gave the males an icy look. "You can stop staring. I'm not dinner. Or lunch. Or even toast."

Damian's grip tightened as he kissed her temple. She felt him smile against her skin. Etienne grinned. Gabriel released a short bark of laughter as Alexandre and Raphael looked surprised.

"Sharp one, Dai," Gabriel said, touching the brim of his hat. "Pleasure to meet you, Jamie. Must be his match. Unless you make the *cunja* on him."

"She is my match," Damian cut in. "And the spell is on her, not me."

"'Course she is, *t' frère*. That power, it's obvious. So what kind of power do you have?" Etienne asked.

Alexandre with the cold, dead eyes turned to her. "Tell us, pretty little Jamie," he drawled, making her name sound almost obscene. "What powers do you have?"

The pounding beat of Nickelback's "Animals" rapped against her chest. Animals. Wolves. Teeth, muscles, lethal power. She forced herself to look at them. All of them. Five werewolves who had killed her brother. A hysterical laugh bubbled in her throat. The family who kills together stays together. Hairs stood up on the nape of her neck. Damian said they were staying here.

And so was she. Scared as she was of the answer, she must directly confront them.

Even if they lied, she had to ask.

Deep down, she sensed Damian would throw himself at them to keep one hair on her head from being damaged.

Inhaling a lungful of air, she held their gazes. "Just one question before the interrogation starts. Why did you all kill my brother, Mark?"

Five Draicon stared in dumbstruck muteness.

Jamie wanted to laugh. Talk about a conversation stopper. Yeah, that was her, all you needed to grind the party to a dead halt. She waited. Show no emotion. No anger. Nothing. But sharp, pungent fear spilled out of her pores. Seeing their nostrils inhale, she knew they scented it.

She pulled the robe tight around her neck, refused to lower her gaze.

"Ah, Jamie…" Damian braced his forearms on his knees. "How did you—"

"I saw you that night. I was in the empty building by the alley. I looked out the window and saw all of you change…and, Damian, you changed into a wolf and you…"

"Merde," muttered Alexandre.

"Damn," said Gabriel, tilting back his cowboy hat.

Brown eyes, he had brown eyes, dark as the swamp. Dark as her brother's had been. Jamie bit her lip. No emotion. No mental communication. Living among the Morphs had taught her to guard her thoughts.

"Tell me, Damian," she said in a neutral tone.

She stiffened as he took her hands in his. His touch should feel warm and soothing, but she felt only cold, bitter anger.

"Your brother didn't die as the police report said. He died long before. What you thought was Mark was a Morph. I, along with my brothers, hunted him down and killed him."

"Liar. Are you saying I didn't know my own damn brother?"

He gave her a steady look. "No one knew. Mark died at the river cabin when he tried to rescue the dog. The dog was a Morph, who killed Mark and then took his place. I knew the thing masquerading as your brother was a Morph the first night I met you."

"It was Mark, and I was there, you murdering Draicon. I heard you, I heard Mark, he was screaming as all of you tore into him and killed him. You killed him, you lying bastard!"

Unable to contain her fury any longer, she jumped up and paced to the room's entrance. Released like a floodgate, rage poured forth. He stood, watching her. Suddenly objects began hurling across the room at Damian's head. A heavy crystal vase, books, a picture of a smiling family. Not her damn family, she had no family anymore...

Shouts erupted from his brothers. Damian ducked, letting the objects smash into the wall. He made no attempt to restrain her. Just as quickly, her temper died. His brothers jumped up, walked toward her with purpose.

Icy fear raced down her spine. Jamie cringed, remembering what killers they were. Damian stood in front of her and faced them.

"Back off her. Now."

Quiet command radiated in his voice. They resumed their seats. He turned around to face her. Regret darkened his green gaze.

"Jamie, that's why you wanted me dead. It all makes sense now. But I would never hurt an innocent, especially someone you loved."

"Prove it. Oh wait, you can't. You just want me to take your word that it was a Morph and not my brother. It's not true." Weary, her body feeling boneless, she slid into the nearest chair.

"I would never take such drastic action without checking my own instincts against cold facts. Rafe, get the documents."

She closed her eyes, rubbing her face. A moment later, papers dropped onto her lap. "These are authentic," Damian told her.

The legal-size paper was a contract. "Mark would never purchase a hunting lodge. In New

Mexico?" She examined a photograph fallen out from between the pages.

Mark holding up a dead deer's head. Revulsion filled her.

"Mark would never hurt an animal."

"Or purchase a lodge to kill the animals he loved so much. Unless your brother was duping the public with a false image." Damian sank down on his haunches.

"My brother risked his life to save animals." Doubts gnawed at her.

"But a Morph would use Mark's considerable assets to purchase a lodge, a lodge a few miles from my pack, to hunt game. And hunt Draicon. A perfect ruse to destroy my people, and you, if he failed to kill you before we mated."

Blood trickled from the deer's head. Mark sported a dark grin, far from his usual cocky smile. The photo fell from her fingers.

Squatting down beside her, Damian picked it up. "Jamie, I'm sorry you witnessed my killing the Morph. Had I detected your scent, I would have sheltered you from seeing anything. I wish I had known your brother. He seems like an honorable, good person."

Uncertain and confused, she shuffled the papers. Ever since Mark's death, she'd had a clear direction, a purpose fueled by grief and hatred. Now her world tipped upside down.

How could she have lived all those months with an impostor? She'd memorized everything about Mark in her efforts to please him. The cornflakes he liked for breakfast, how he sang while he paid the bills, the way he rose early in the morning to jog along the river...

How he started treating her after that day. His solicitous concern, when he'd never shown any previously. How he started leaving at night. The front door closing. Mark walking inside, the distinct coppery smell filling her nostrils. The tiny fear seizing her that Mark was different. And dismissing it. Because she really hadn't known her brother after all.

The very idea she'd blithely accepted a Morph as Mark stripped away all her confidence. He was her only family. Indifferent, tolerating her with sometimes amusement, sometimes boredom. Stricken, Jamie realized she was better off alone. She felt herself crumble into a thousand tiny, shattered pieces, jagged and sharp, cutting her insides. Damian kept insisting how important family was, how family was everything.

Not to her. Family meant indifferent, greedy bastards who shape-shifted into cruel, horrible creatures.

The skin on her lower back began to itch, as if the long-ago mark placed there by her cousins was fresh. She glanced at Damian. Speculation shadowed his gaze. He was going to probe, ask questions, bring up the past.

No. She lifted her shoulders in a casual shrug. "Mark's gone now. No point in talking about this anymore."

"Why were you in that building so late, Jamie? Did Mark tell you to go there?"

At her nod, he swore softly. "The Morph had to get you out of your house because of the shield prohibiting anyone from performing dark magick. He took you there for a reason, *chère*. He was probably going to kill you."

Her chest felt hollow with panic. Jamie swallowed hard, recognizing the pure logic of his words. She'd trusted her brother, would do anything he said, had been desperate for his approval, hell, anyone's approval, and… Why would he drag her out in the dead of night?

The line blurred between black and white, Damian the murderer and Mark the kindhearted. Her brother was a Morph. Damian killed it to save her skin. She'd lived with evil for months, never seeing it clearly. Not until she willingly embraced it herself.

The consequences of her actions slammed into her like a cannonball. Had she not acted impulsively, propelled by emotion to run away after Mark's death instead of stopping to question, she wouldn't be in this predicament. But she sought revenge, turned to evil and darkness, and now suffered from a spell threatening to turn her into stone, living but dead.

Panic and disbelief burned through her. Jamie stood, blinded by grief, rage and self-disgust. She bolted out of the room, racing through the hallway, out the back door. In the courtyard, she collapsed onto a chair, hung her head.

Tears did not come. Instead, she held herself, rocking back and forth. Heard the back door slam, sensed Damian draw near.

"Get away from me," she said dully. "Just go away. There's nothing good about me you could want. Just, please, let me go."

"I will never let you go. You're my life now." Damian drew up a chair, faced her. "You acted out of grief and loyalty, just as I would. I wish I had found you sooner, to spare you all this. Maybe if I had searched harder, wanted more, I could have."

All the blame rested with her, yet he blamed himself. Sorrow etched his expression. Stricken by his unguarded emotion and her own tumultuous feelings, Jamie examined her gray fingernails.

"I'm going to die, aren't I? Because of what I did, what I let happen to me."

A matter-of-fact statement, black-and-white. Damian's mouth thinned. "Not if we can help it. We'll find a way, I promise, we will find the book and a way out. But your powers… We have to discuss this, Jamie. You have extraordinary abilities, one reason you're probably my mate. But using these powers, they're expediting the spell."

"Then let's talk. Maybe your brothers know why this is happening to me."

Back inside, the brothers acted as if her outburst never happened. Jamie settled onto the couch, Damian beside her. His presence felt reassuring, a sturdy rock in her windswept sea of emotions. She looked them all over.

"Okay, you have knowledge I don't. Can you tell me why I'm getting these abilities all of the sudden? I'm human."

Alexandre lounged in his chair, his eyes sharp, calculating. "Maybe not. You could be a throwback to the original race, before our kind divided in half to lessen our powers."

"Tell me something." Her gaze raked over all of them. "How did those Morphs track us last night? It seems like they're trailing Damian's every move."

Raphael frowned. "I've been thinking the same. My guys have tracked their every move on the computer and there's a pattern. Wherever Damian shows up, they're there. It's like you have a GPS chip implanted in you, *t' frère*."

"Or a Morph chip." Alexandre's sulky gaze landed on her.

Suspicion etched their expressions. She'd tried killing their brother, lived among evil. A likely target. "If it were me, I'd sense them. I could before ingesting Damian's magick. Now I can't tell what's a Morph anymore."

Briefly Damian explained about her ability to spot them.

"Maybe they have a sophisticated system in place. You do." She pointed at Raphael. "So why wouldn't they use technology? Or use yours against you?"

"Our system is hack-proof," Raphael said tightly.

"Nothing is hack-proof. But leave that for later. I want to show you something first."

Jamie went upstairs to her bedroom, fetched her laptop and went back. Sitting beside Damian, she powered up.

He glanced over her shoulder. "You're tracking down something," he guessed, frowning at the text on the screen. "Is this computer code?"

"Yeah. When I was on Renee's laptop, I made a mental note of the browsing history. There was one Web page that caught my eye, in addition to the sites listing antique shops. A MyPlace page."

She brought up the page. Against the black background were scrolling photos of music celebrities, video showing a popular rap star. The site belonged to someone called "Rocker 21 NOW." It resembled a typical page for a music-obsessed teen.

"This Web page is actually a means of communicating in code with others who know the key to the code." Jamie glanced at him. "Someone you know is tracking our moves. Someone is receiving covert direct orders. Someone familiar with computer technology."

Damian looked at her screen. "How can you tell?"

"Each Web page is written in computer code, like HTML or Java. Anyone familiar with programming can understand the code. But I checked this page's computer code and there is encrypted text, like a secret message—symbols I can't decipher. I think this is how the intruder is communicating, and giving directions on what to do next."

"Damn," Raphael said softly.

"Which means we have a spy." Alexandre withdrew a knife from a sheath at his waist. The blade reflected the hard edges of his sharp profile. His gaze flicked to her. "When we catch him, leave him…or her…to me. Whoever it is will pay."

Blood drained from her face as she stared at the knife and his fierce expression.

Damian lifted her chin with his fingers, his touch light and reassuring. She breathed in his delicious scent, blocking out all else. "Jamie, pay no attention. I won't let anyone hurt you." He shot Alexandre a warning look.

The other Draicon sheathed the blade. The brothers bid them goodbye and left.

When the door shut, she breathed a little easier, shut off the laptop. Damian leaned back, his thighs spilling open, his arms splayed over the couch's back. He looked in control, sexy as hell and confident. But emotion flashed in his eyes as he gazed at her gray hair.

"Get dressed. We need to find the next clue. We'll pick up breakfast and coffee on the way."

Chapter 11

They found the number of paddle-wheel revolutions on the *Natchez,* then returned to the house later that afternoon. When he gave her another mysterious cocktail, she knew it was his blood, but drank it. Grayness fled her nails, but not her hair. Damian insisted on her resting. He had to leave for a while with his brother Etienne, but Etienne's wife, Cindy, and their children would be in the house. She'd be perfectly safe as nothing unwanted could get inside, Damian assured her.

Then he'd told her his family dined formally at seven. Jamie felt a yawning pit open in her stomach. Family dinners. No way.

She fell instantly asleep on the soft, acre-wide

feather bed. What seemed like hours later, something tickled her nose.

Blinking, she slowly awakened, feeling more energetic. A small, delicate face came into focus. Lips were pursed and blowing air toward her.

"Ana, stop it. You're gonna wake her up and it's her naptime," warned a childish, somewhat stern voice.

"But she looks like fun and I wanna play."

Jamie sat up, rubbing her eyes.

"Now you've done it," the other scolded.

Clustered around her bed were four very curious children, including twins with blond hair hanging in ponytails.

"Hi. Welcoming committee? Or room service?"

Giggles spilled out of them. "I'm Ana," the angelic pixie piped up. "And you're Aunt Jamie, Uncle Damian's mate. I'm five. I just had a birthday with a cake with pink icing and lots of presents."

Jamie smiled. "I just had a birthday, too. I love cake with pink icing."

"Well, you can have some of mine 'cause Mama had leftmovers."

"Leftovers," the stern voice said. A male with thick brown hair, calm blue eyes and a steady look thrust out his hand. "I'm Michael. I'm eight and I'm the oldest. I told Ana not to bother you."

"It's all right," Jamie reassured him. She sat up, hugging her knees, studying the twins. "And you guys are? Sisters maybe?"

The girls giggled and introduced themselves. Sophie and Sandy were seven. They began chattering about the house, their move here, their sleeping quarters.

Ana. Damian's young sister had been named Annie. Her heart pounded. The little girl with her angelic, blond beauty and waifish air tugged at her. This Ana would never get hurt, she suspected. Uncle Damian would throw himself on a dagger before it happened. This Ana was what childhood was supposed to be, smiles, laughter, teasing and plenty of loving arms to hush and soothe when she skinned a knee.

A lump rose to her throat. Jamie hoped Ana would never know the darkness of her own childhood.

Damian walked through the front door, alarmed by the loud shouts and insistent thumping upstairs. He glanced up. Attached to the wall across the second-floor railing was a makeshift hoop made from what looked like aluminum foil. What the...

Jamie raced into view on the upstairs landing, chasing a blond little girl dribbling a basketball with both hands. Ana. Jamie picked up the child and then leaped over the railing.

He froze. His blood pressure plummeted.

"Ana," Etienne said hoarsely. The groceries in his hands fell to the floor with a loud clatter.

Jamie grabbed the crystal chandelier. Fifteen feet above the floor, she dangled little Anna in one arm and held tight to her precarious perch with the other.

"Shoot," Jamie cried out.

Damian stared, sweat gathering on his brow. Ana went to toss an underhand throw. And then Jamie's hand slipped from the chandelier. Both he and Etienne shouted, ran and positioned themselves beneath the light fixture to catch them both.

Jamie *floated* toward the basketball hoop, lifting Ana, who dropped in the ball.

"Score," she cried as the ball banged onto the floor below.

Ana giggled. A deep, full-bodied, sultry gurgle of joy spilled out of Jamie, reminding him of rich red wine and smoke. Dumbstruck, he stared. Dear God, he'd never heard her laugh before.

Etienne's face blanched. He lifted his arms. "Ana," he said thickly. "Come to Daddy."

Damian's heart leaped to his throat as Jamie floated downward holding Etienne's daughter.

"Let's do it again, Jamie!" Ana cried out as Jamie's feet touched the ground.

She released Ana. "Later. Your dad's looking a little white."

Etienne scooped the little girl into his arms. The look he shot Jamie as he marched away was cold enough to freeze hot coals. Damian braced his hands on his hips.

"What the hell are you thinking?" he lashed out.

"I wasn't thinking, I was playing. The kids wanted some fun, so why not? It was fantastic."

"You could have dropped her. Did you think about that? She's my niece and I won't see anything happen to her. Understand? You're new to your magick and you could have slipped. Damn it, why are you so irresponsible?" He picked up her hands. Gray. Damian resisted the urge to shake sense into her.

"You will not practice magick again, Jamie. Every time you do you speed up the stone spell. My magick can't keep it at bay forever. Why do you keep risking it?"

"I've gone without magick for so long. If I am going to die, I want to at least experience life, and live," she said quietly.

"You're not going to die. I won't let it happen."

Jamie mopped her face with a corner of her sweatshirt, showing a patch of smooth ivory skin on her flat stomach. The glimpse of soft flesh raised his ire more, stirring his sex.

She was uncontrollable, distant and his mate. Each day he got a little crazier from wanting her. When would she surrender to what they both craved and needed?

"And I'd cut out my own heart before ever letting anything happen to a child." She folded her arms across her chest, looking wounded.

"Ana is just a little girl. She might have been hurt."

Jamie ran a hand through her gray hair. "Damian, you act like you're five hundred, not eighty. Life's about risk. You can't put kids in a cage and keep them from every little bump and bruise. What about the young in your pack?"

"The children in my pack are seldom allowed outdoors. It's not safe. Our compound was constantly attacked by Morphs. I won't lose any more little ones. I refuse to let it happen."

"Don't you ever let them have fun, run around like kids?"

He went mute. Her gray eyes widened. "You don't. I bet you don't, either. Do you ever do anything just to relax?"

Stricken, he reeled back on his heels. With Morphs trying to wipe them off the planet, fun had become a foreign concept. He tried to remember when he last enjoyed himself. As a boy roaming the bayou, he liked collecting dragon-flies in jelly jars, watching them beat their beautiful wings as they tried to escape their glass cages. Then he'd release them, the air stirring as they darted away, free once more.

Images popped into his head, dancing to Cajun music at the old cabin in the bayou, blowing off frustration among restless pack males with a hard game of football, cultivating the flowers in the garden with quiet pride as he watched them thrive and grow…fishing in the creek near his home.

Like a gentle breath, he felt Jamie enter his mind, share the scenes. Felt her examine them like books on shelves, marveling and putting each one down.

Once he enjoyed life. But now the music was silent. The laughter dimmed, the football abandoned in the field after Morphs attacked and killed during a game. Flowers drew bees that shifted into the enemy, fish could morph into poisonous water snakes, even the dragonflies could be death waiting to attack and eradicate those he loved.

Nothing was as important as family and pack. Family was everything. He filled his head with images of this instead, his undying need to keep his people safe, including her. He felt a flutter of disappointment from her as she slipped out of his mind.

Irritated, he narrowed his eyes. "I have a pack to lead. They're my responsibility, just as you are. My *joie de vivre* is not losing any more of my people."

Jamie sagged against the staircase, her color blanching. She'd expended too much energy. But her voice was filled with spirit and passion.

"You think everyone is out to get your people. Maybe fate steered me to infect you with that disease and make you so sick because for the first time, you were lost. You were helpless and couldn't beat it, if not for Nicolas healing you. Sometimes you need to give up everything to get back your life."

Her accusations stung worse than the wasps. Damian glared at her. "I never give up."

"You never take risks, either. Life is about challenge and adventure, not just danger and hurt." She took a deep breath. "I know all about how life can spin you around like a crazy carnival ride until you just want to scream, but it doesn't stop. So you have to hang on for the moment, and then when it slows and you're finally able to get off, laugh and find your joy again because if you don't you'll end up like I was."

Her voice dropped to the barest whisper. "In

the shadows, alive but really dead, like I was with the Morphs."

He was silent for a moment, then spoke in a deep, weary voice. "Sometimes there is nothing but shadows."

"What happened, Damian? What happened to you that you forgot how to live?"

Annie died. I held her body in my arms and realized the damn consequences of my actions, my neglect.

Damian gave her a long, cool look. "I've lived, Jamie. I've lived through attacks on my people, through watching people I've known, even loved, turn evil and seeing blood and violence and death. I've done so for eighty years so don't lecture me about living."

He stiffened as she drew near. Jamie took his hand, running her fingers over his knuckles. "Oh, Damian," she said softly. "That's life. But that isn't living."

His eyes closed, and a shudder went through him as she gently stroked. He wanted to crush her against him, kiss her senseless then lower her to the floor and put his mouth on her.

Make her come, again and again. Then finally open his trousers and free his erection, and mount her. Making her his at last.

"It's my life. It suits me fine," he said tightly.

"Of course you're too old to change." Challenge shone in her gray eyes.

"I'm not that old," he muttered.

"Prove it. Come out with me tonight. We'll hit bars, whatever hits your fancy and mine. Be spontaneous."

He placed his palm over hers, covering her hand as if trapping a winged insect. "You're not going out."

"Are you saying you, the big bad wolf who would give his life for his people, can't protect me from the dangers of Bourbon Street?"

Caught. And but good. Challenging him like this, daring him. Her hand still entrapped, she lifted both of his to her lips, gave his right knuckles a long, slow lick. He stifled a moan, feeling his groin tighten.

"Come on, Damian," she purred in a sultry tone. "Let's go out and live for the moment."

"After dinner. We're all eating together tonight. As a family."

He didn't miss her wary look. It shifted into a sultry pout. "Please, just you and me? I just want us to go out on the town."

Jamie ran a hand up his arm, her touch igniting him inside. Warmth nudged aside intense sexual heat, layering it with a deeper, more tender affection. He savored her touch.

"You truly want this?"
She nodded.

Damian sang a Cajun tune softly as he scraped
the heavy beard off his cheeks. Steam misted
the air from the shower. With a towel about his
waist, he stared pensively into the mirror. Full
moon approaching. He could shave every hour
and still sport dark bristle an hour later.

Sensing a presence, he turned and saw Jamie
gawking through the open doorway. Her fascinated gaze dropped from the hair covering his
chest, down to the towel tied tightly about his
midsection. A knowing smile touched his mouth
as he toyed with the knot.

"Get dressed, Jamie."

"I don't need to get dressed up for Bourbon
Street."

"Fine. I'll go like this."

He pulled the towel free. She gasped and
scampered away as it dropped to the floor. His
soft laughter followed as she ran into the bedroom.

Twenty minutes later, he joined her downstairs. Her knee-length red dress billowed
out with her graceful pivot. The neckline was
V-shaped, with long sleeves. She clutched a small
red purse covered with sequins, her gray hands

covered with smart lacy black gloves. Breath caught in his throat.

"You're lovely," he managed to say.

"You look very handsome," she said, sounding shy.

Damian grinned, rolling his shoulders beneath the black Armani jacket. He held out his arm in a courtly gesture. "Shall we?"

As they walked on the sidewalk, he tried to relax. If this would make Jamie happy, and help her learn to trust him, he'd do it.

When they reached Ursuline and Royal, Jamie paused. A group huddled together before the Ursuline Convent. The soft glow of a flickering lantern illuminated their fascinated expressions.

"Vampire tour," she realized. "Let's tag along. I love these things. People have the strangest reactions sometimes to the stories." She squeezed his arm playfully. "Some even believe in ghosts."

"Flakes," he muttered.

They eased behind the group of about fifteen people. Enthralled with the tour guide's hushed narration, no one noticed them. The guide was explaining the local legend. "When the convent was a school, girls from France arrived with large, mysterious trunks. It was later thought vampires were transported in those trunks."

"Vampires from France, traveling in cheap trunks. Everyone knows vampires wouldn't be caught dead in anything but Gucci," Damian muttered.

"Hush, I'm trying to hear," she whispered.

"I'm trying to make a spontaneous joke," he whispered back.

An adorable half smile lit her face. He dissolved into pure longing, wanting nothing more than to kiss her. Grimly he thought of the ugliest Morph to pare down his lust.

The tour guide gestured to the dormer windows. "And the girls, it's said, became vampires after the trunks were stored in the attic. The nuns closed it off, and never allowed anyone up there, fearing to unleash the evil inside...."

Damian gave a low, deep growl. A woman clutched her companion's arm and shrieked. "Did you hear that? Wolves!"

Damian grinned. Jamie was right. This was fun.

"Sometimes they say if the shutters are open on the dormer windows, someone will die."

He released a long, musical howl. The group screamed and bolted, nearly plowing down the confused tour guide. Clutching her lantern, she scurried after them.

Jamie laughed. Doubled over, chortling laughter. Damian watched her, and felt something bubble up from deep inside.

Laughter rolled out of him, a ribbon of pure

amusement. They leaned against the convent wall, holding their stomachs.

"Today's the first day I've heard you really laugh," he observed suddenly.

"The is the first time I heard you really laugh, too."

They studied each other with delighted smiles, like naughty children discovering new mischief. "Come on, let's do something adventurous for a thrill," she dared him.

He pondered the risk. "Aren't you afraid of taking chances?"

"If I let that hold me back from everything there is out there, I'll never live." A shadow chased over her face. "And knowing I might die makes it even more important."

She threw her head back and stared at the sky, exposing the lovely line of her slender throat. "It's like my longing for magick. You were born with magick, you probably take it for granted. Snap your fingers and create this beautiful, amazing ball of light. I've wanted that all my life."

Drawing closer, he backed her up until she was pressed flat against the wall. Damian bracketed her with his arms. "Why, Jamie? Why does it mean so much?"

Her lower lip wobbled tremulously. "I sup-pose…after losing so much, I thought if I had magick, I would feel special for once, and not helpless anymore."

She swallowed. "Do you know what it feels like to watch everything in your life slide away and there's not a damn thing you can do to stop it?"

"I do," he said quietly and slid his palm into hers. They strolled, talking of his family, growing up in a Cajun household on the bayou. He asked her pointed, intelligent questions about her computer work and building Web sites.

He took her to Acme Oyster House where they downed shellfish and Tabasco.

Now as they walked down Bourbon Street, his gaze scanned the street. His body tense, ready to leap forward and defend his mate, he barely noticed Jamie's heavy sigh. She stopped and gave him a look beneath her long, dark lashes.

"Damian, not everyone is the enemy."

He turned and lifted her chin with the tip of one finger. His gaze bored into hers, commanding her attention. "Yes. Not everyone is the enemy. And neither am I, *ma petite*. When will you trust me?"

Contact between them sizzled. The sensuality of her full, rosy lips would tempt a monk. "Will you, then? Trust me?"

"Maybe. If you'll let go and relax."

"I can let go of everything. Except you," he said softly, drawing her into his arms.

Jamie's mouth parted. Damian couldn't resist. He kissed her. Her mouth tasted like sweet honey, and he wanted more. A tiny sigh of surrender wafted from her. He fisted his hand in her hair and took more. Ravaging her mouth, his tongue plundering and conquering. Jamie clutched the lapels of his jacket. Her tiny, excited whimpers threatened to loosen the wild beast.

But part of him sensed her reluctance, her mind battling with her body's eagerness.

Damian drew away, touched her cheek gently. This wasn't merely the prelude to sex. He'd had sex with more females than he could remember. Hot, hard, fast sex to relieve his body's needs; sex to replenish energy lost performing magick; tender, gentle sex if the woman liked it slow. This was something deeper, as if he'd tasted all her longings, fears and the tiny hope fluttering inside her.

He would do anything for her, including leash his own desperate need. Drawing his arm firmly about Jamie, he smiled down at her.

"Where to now?"

She licked her kiss-swollen lips, looking a little dazed as if being kissed well and hard on Bourbon Street were a new experience. Well, he had plenty of others to share. And he'd enjoy teaching her every single one.

They headed inside a jazz bar blaring out good

tunes. Damian signaled for a bartender, looked at Jamie expectantly.

"Chocolate martini."

Interesting. He ordered one and a draft beer. They leaned against a wall, sipping and listening. The music was good, slow and sultry. He found his shoulders easing, the tension fleeing. To his shock he realized he was enjoying himself.

Jamie was right. He did need to relax, let go and have fun.

There was nothing wrong with it. Damian glanced at Jamie, his interest shifting.

The heady scent of her teased his nostrils. Light from a wall sconce showed her soft profile. Her high, refined cheekbones, the lush, full mouth and pert, stubborn thrust of her chin. She was a fascinating contrast, tensile steel strength, layered with vulnerability.

Jamie licked chocolate off the glass, her tongue tracing the overflow. Damian stared at each delicate whorl, the slow strokes. *Mon Dieu,* what she could do to him with that perfect mouth of hers...

He *needed* her in his arms. Soft, seductive jazz music began. Damian turned to Jamie, taking their drinks and setting them on the bar. He held out a hand.

"Dance with me."

Chapter 12

The command was a husky whisper. His palm was warm, his fingers long with neatly pared nails, the fingertips callused. Jamie slid into his arms, barely clearing his chin. She rested her cheek against his broad shoulder. Damian's body heat radiated through the silk shirt. Beard stubble shadowed his jaw. He'd shaved. She knew because she'd seen him do so. But now he clearly looked...

A little wilder. Jamie swallowed hard. His scent invaded her senses. Would he surrender to instinct and finally claim her? The power in his muscled body warned her how strong he was. What would stop him from taking her? She couldn't.

Damian stopped, looked down at her.

"Hey," he said softly. "Remember what I said? I will never force you. You have nothing to fear from me."

"Except you stepping on my toes," she replied lightly.

He laughed and slipped his arms about her midsection, hard against his body. Jamie felt her feet leave the ground. She glanced down in amusement as he set her down.

"So much for that fear."

There were many layers to this Draicon, like an oyster building a protective flesh and hiding a beautiful, rare pearl. She was peeling them away slowly. It scared her, because the more she peeled, the more iridescent and glowing the pearl became. He was strong, fiercely loyal, courageous and would knock out his own teeth before harming her.

All things that scared the holy hell out of her. She didn't want a pearl. Her own agenda was set in stone. Literally. Damian was necessary to finding the book, and once she cured herself, she'd be gone. No ties, no regrets, no heartache as if she'd run away from the one person who could reach past her loneliness and pull her free.

Damian held her with practiced ease, his steps light as he guided her. Jamie felt his body's wiry, tensile strength. The tailored clothing hid the steely male within.

The singer stopped, mopped his shiny forehead. A button pressed and canned music rang out through the room. Patrons resumed their loud chatter. Beer bottles clinked, while the street outside roared with revelry.

He drew her close and bent his head next to her ear.

"Give in, *chère*. You asked me to let go. It's your turn now." His deep whisper sent a delightful shiver coursing down her spine.

The promise of sex gleamed in his dark green gaze. Her body hummed instinctively to the sultry call of his demand.

"I need to go powder my nose."

"Hurry." Damian playfully tapped her nose.

She grabbed the little jeweled purse, pushed through to the ladies' room. Anticipation raced through her as she stared at herself in the mirror. Rosy face, pulse racing, pupils dilated. Jamie ran water on a paper towel, dabbed her hot face. Arousal suffused her entire body. Her phone rang. Jamie fished it out of her purse, flipped it open.

Opening the phone, she shivered upon reading the message.

MUSM. I want U. U will b mine. 2nite. DAMIAN.

Miss you so much. I want you. You will be mine. Tonight.

She thrilled to the challenge. Jamie shut the phone, dropped it into her purse and returned to the bar. Damian leaned against the counter, a small smile on his lips as he palmed his phone. She tilted her head.

"Not bad. Not bad at all."

He pocketed the cell, touched her mouth. "KOL." Kiss on the lips. Damian didn't wait for her answer. His mouth on hers was teasing, light. He flicked his tongue lightly over her bottom lip.

Jamie pulled back, trembling, hot. Needing him.

Satisfaction gleamed in his gaze. Damian's long, strong fingers curled possessively about hers. He tugged her out into the street and the chilled night air. Two college-age boys staggered past, foamy beer splashing over their cups like seawater spilling from a ship's deck. Sights and smells assaulted her heightened senses. The scent of sour sweat, the stench of stale beer and Damian's delicious, curiously refreshing scent. He looked far too urbane and sophisticated for the Quarter's decadent revelry. Yet an air of natural authority clung to him, as if he ruled these streets, and with a flick of a finger could command all to do his bidding.

The more she pulled back his layers, the more

exposed she felt, and the more dangerously she teetered toward something more lasting and permanent. Like that four-letter word.

Love.

Love was scary. People professed it and then twisted it into something dark and sinister. All she'd ever wanted was a family who accepted and loved her for herself, but they all tried shaping her into their image of the perfect Jamie. Her parents molding her into a good daughter. Her uncle beating her into a meek niece. Mark dismissing her into an approval-seeking sister. Renee chiding her into a safe neighbor who didn't practice magick.

Damian gently squeezed her palm. "What's wrong?"

Jamie offered a brave smile. "Just pensive."

He stopped and pulled her to the side, letting pedestrians pass. Damian sheltered her with his big body.

"Tell me," he insisted.

The tenderness in his voice undid her. "I can't," she whispered. She leaned against him. For once, she just wanted someone else to take charge, someone else to take over and protect her from all the fears rimming her mind.

He slid a palm around the back of her neck. Instead of soothing, it stirred all her senses. Her nerves screamed to life. He leaned close enough for her to count the dark stubble shadowing his jaw. She felt open, wet and aching. His touch lingered over her neck, featherlight, erotic as he stroked her skin. Damian's gaze scanned the crowd streaming past them.

"Let's go home. Too many eyes," he said authoritatively.

They turned a corner. As they went to pass a dark, narrow alley, her hackles rose. Damian ground to an abrupt halt, thrusting her behind him.

"Damn it," he muttered. "I knew we shouldn't have come out. Too dangerous." He glanced at her, looking torn. His gaze then landed on the door of a locked business. He herded her toward it, waved his hand, unlocking the door and pulling her inside as he handed her his cell phone.

"Stay here. Morphs are in the alley. If you see one approach, punch number one. It's my signal for Rafe. He'll respond instantly."

"Damian, let me help you. I have powers now."

He shot her a warning look. "Stay here," he growled, then shut the glass door behind him as he left.

With a wave of his hand, his clothing vanished. Barely had she registered the sleek, smooth muscles of his long legs and taut ass, than he shape-shifted into a large gray wolf. The wolf raced toward the alley.

The hell with this. She wasn't some helpless woman in need of rescue. Jamie wriggled her fingers, feeling the power rise up. She went outside, cautiously approaching the alley.

Her vision sharpened as moonlight speared the inky black alley. Blood splattered the wall nearby. She recognized Adam, the Draicon admonished by Damian for letting her escape. Four hulking creatures with thin, wispy hair and yellowed fangs attacked. Morphs. They slashed his arms and legs, snarling as sharp talons raked over his chest. Her stomach gave a sickening lurch.

From the back of the alley, a lone figure charged forward, a dagger in his hands.

"Ricky," Adam yelled. "Watch my back!"

But instead, Ricky kept running. The Morphs dropped back, didn't attack him. He ran out of the alley, nearly colliding with her.

She watched Damian attack and kill most of the Morphs, but one got away. Ricky stepped before her. His breath came in short, stabbing pants as he dropped the dagger.

Stretching out her hands, Jamie aimed a surge of energy at the dropped dagger. The snarling Morph leaped at her as Damian sank sharp fangs into its hindquarters. She sent the dagger hurling straight into the Morph's heart.

The Morph exploded into a shower of gray ash, covering Jamie, Damian the wolf, the brick walls.

Shocked, she stared at her hands. Gray streaked up her arms now. Her head pounded again.

Burns marked Damian's muzzle. He shape-shifted back to his human form, waved a hand and clothed himself again. Adam shifted back, as well, shrugged into his clothing then joined them.

Blood streamed down his side even as the vicious cuts on Damian's arms began healing. A violent trembling affected his hands as he wiped gray ash from her face.

"Did it hurt you?" he demanded.

She couldn't speak. Damian gripped her shoulders. "Jamie, tell me."

"I'm okay," she managed.

Damian flipped open his cell phone, barked an order. In a few minutes, Raphael and Gabriel appeared on their motorcycles, Rafe abandoning his to ride with Gabriel. Damian took over Raphael's bike and motioned for her to join him.

She went, knowing it was pointless to argue, and logical to leave.

When they arrived at his house, Damian

herded her upstairs. In her room, he closed the door. Turning, he loosened his tie, pulled it off, removed his jacket and tossed it aside. Fury sparked his eyes. His big body tensed as he removed her gloves. Her nails, wrists and part of her forearms had turned the color of a leaden sky.

Jamie lifted her chin, ready to duel.

"I told you to stay put. You could have been killed, Jamie."

"And I knew how to protect myself. Everything's cool." She drew in a breath. "It's no big deal."

His mouth flattened. "No big deal? Those were Morphs, ready to rip you to pieces, Jamie. You know what they do, but you seem to forget. They won't stop until you lie there, broken and bleeding and dying. You can cry out for mercy and beg someone, anyone to rescue you, and they'll keep slashing at you until you pray for death. And then they'll drink your terror, relish it and watch as you bleed out, whimpering in agony. They kill anyone, anything, women, little girls… *Dieu,* she never had a chance…"

Damian cut off his words. Torment flashed across his face as he ran a hand through his sweat-dampened hair. "I should never have agreed to let you come out tonight. Too much of a risk. I swore I'd never use such poor judgment again."

She bit back the bitter disappointment. "The attack could have happened anywhere. And you had fun," she protested.

Intensity radiated from him. He fisted his hands. "Fun? What the hell point is it when you could have been killed? You talk of enjoying yourself when there's danger at every corner and your life is at stake. I should have paid better attention to my instincts. I let down my guard and you were almost hurt. It's not worth it."

"And me? I'm not worth it?" she cried out.

A muscle ticed in his strong jawline. "You're worth every single breath I take to protect you, Jamie. It's my duty to keep you safe. With every last drop of blood in my body I will do it, but no more taking risks. It's too dangerous and life is too precious to be so damn foolhardy. I won't ever make that mistake again."

This was a side of Damian she hadn't seen. He was blaming himself, his anger directed inward. Not at her. What the hell had happened to him that he couldn't forgive himself?

"If you were so intent on keeping me safe, why did you help Ricky and Adam? It was their battle, let them fight on their own."

"Because they're pack. Rafe put them under me and I take care of my own. That's what family is, Jamie. You step in when it's needed. Teamwork. Don't you understand the value of a strong family?" His voice softened. "Surely your brother did the same for you at some point."

Never. Mark was more interested in his career than her needs. Pack, family. She was a lone wolf. No one ever helped her, so she learned to go it alone and it was a direction she was happy to take. Or had been. Thinking about what she'd never had grieved her so much she lashed out.

"It's only important to you because you see yourself in charge of everything and everyone. You can't let go. You have to have control, always. It's an obsession with you."

His eyes glittered with intent as he stepped forward. "*Chère,* you wouldn't want to see me lose control."

Power radiated from his big body, the muscles tense, his green eyes locked onto her like a laser. Her body responded to the overwhelming masculinity, aching and yearning, the space between her legs throbbing.

Something inside snapped, sexual frustration boiling over like a volcano. "Try me," she taunted. "I can handle it." Jamie stared him down. "But I doubt you can."

No chance to bite back the words, change her mind. Damian cupped the back of her head and crushed his mouth against hers. It was no gentle, teasing kiss, but one of pure possession, staking his claim. His tongue boldly thrust past her lips, tasting her, exploring the wet cavern of her mouth. Jamie moaned and clutched fistfuls of his shirt. Her knees threatened to give out as she sagged against him.

He kept at it, exquisite sensual torture, the tension simmering just below the surface. As if his life depended on her, his next breath, instinct hammering at him.

Heat and masculine lust radiated from him. A tiny shiver skated down her spine. He nipped her bottom lip, then licked it in a lingering caress. Boldness overcame her as Jamie cupped his erection, squeezed.

She opened her eyes, startled at his hot, intent look. It warned she'd pushed him too far.

"Right now," he spoke against her mouth. "I will have you. I won't wait any longer."

A low growl ripped from him. Damian felt desperate to get inside her. His body tensed with the crazed need to mount and sexually dominate.

A rose flush tinted her porcelain skin; Jamie's full mouth begged to be kissed again. He stroked and soothed as her hands clutched his wrists. Jamie's soft breasts pressed against his hard torso. The intoxicating smell of her flooded his senses, the floral shampoo she'd used mixing with her own delicious scent.

His hands slid down her hips to pull her forward then he cupped her sweet little ass, sliding farther up to explore…

The scent of her arousal hit him like a sledgehammer. His body tightened painfully, his balls aching, his cock hardening to solid steel. Damian stepped back, kicked off his shoes, pulled at his shirt. Buttons popped with the force of champagne corks, clattered to the floor. Desire and apprehension flashed across Jamie's face as he shed his trousers.

He divested her of the plain cotton briefs in a minute, pulled up her dress and tipped her backward onto the bed. Instinct roared, his body primed to penetrate, claim and conquer. The wolf inside snarled for the right to mate. He mounted her, letting her feel his immense strength, his power and prowess. Proving he was worthy of breeding with her. Pinning her wrists to the mattress, he dragged in a deep lungful of her arousal.

Wide gray eyes stared up at him. A quiver went through her body.

Damn, what the hell was he doing? Turning feral, letting the moon ride him.

With all his control, he leashed himself and released her wrists. *Don't scare her.* Slow. He braced his hands on either side of her body. The kiss he gave her was gentle, tender.

Jamie pushed back farther on the bed as he climbed over her.

His hands explored, drifted over her slender hips, spanned her narrow waist. She seemed so fragile, yet beneath was enormous strength. A survivalist who endured losing so much and faced challenge with courage and spirit. A woman who was more than equal to him. She was life and adventure and laughter.

She was his. He would make certain no other male would dare touch her again. For all his crazed yearning, his touch was tender as he grazed her cheek with his fingers.

Jamie sat up, hugging herself, eyes big as dinner plates. He pushed her down, gently.

"Lie back and let me care for you," he purred. Damian parted her slender legs with his hands.

He stared at her cleft, wet and glistening. His erection strained to the point of bursting.

"You're beautiful, so damn beautiful," he said softly, dragging in a lungful of her scent. Ah, so sweet, aroused and feminine.

He'd die if he couldn't taste her.

Jamie couldn't let him control her. Pleasure her. It was a power play, and if he took charge, she'd be hopelessly lost. Giving in meant more than surrendering to his sexual dominance.

It meant forging an even deeper physical link between them, a tie that terrified her. Sex presented an intimacy she emotionally could not control.

Damian would trap her in his world, tying her to him.

Resistance to his tender, erotic caresses seemed futile, but Jamie summoned all her inner strength. She tensed and was reluctant to respond to his touch.

And then he lowered his head and put his mouth between her legs.

Licking her, lapping her in long, expert strokes between her cleft, feasting on her sweetness. Damian's tongue on the aching flesh between her legs did crazy, erotic things to her. Every stroke and whorl drew air from her body until she felt herself strained with the need to breathe, to burst out of her skin. He licked, swallowed, the rough bristle from his bearded cheeks abrading her thighs. Tension heightened, spiraling her upward and upward until she stiffened, and gave a keening wail, her body thrashing as she climaxed. The orgasm exploded out of her so fiercely, she almost blanked out.

When she lifted her head, the hint of untamed danger lurked deep in the depths of his jade-green eyes. A wolf, his beast, barely held at bay. But held at bay, all because of her.

In silent surrender, she pulled off her dress and removed her bra. Jamie lay back, holding out her arms to him. Scared as she was of being dragged into his pack, his family, she instinctively knew he would never hurt her. Her body tingled with arousal, hungering for the contact between them.

Damian leaned back on his haunches, wiped his mouth with the back of his hand. His cock ached with the need to penetrate. Mounting her, he felt the enormous strain of his muscles tensing as he tried to keep himself in check. He kissed her again, his mouth drifting down to nip at her throat. Her breasts were like apples, perfectly shaped with rosy, taut nipples.

He kissed one very gently, then ran his tongue around it. She whimpered, her hips rising and falling off the mattress, driven by instincts of her own.

"Soon," he soothed her. Damian took her nipple in his mouth and gently suckled. She clutched his shoulders, her body twisting.

He released her nipple with a small popping sound.

"Give in, *ma petite*," he whispered. "Let me inside. It's time. You belong to me."

He rose on his forearms, afraid of crushing her. She was so tiny and fragile, the delicate exterior camouflaging a tough steel core. The heart of a true warrior beat inside Jamie, someone dragged to hell who clawed her way back to the light.

No one would ever send her downward again. He'd make sure of it. Any person who tried, he'd strip the skin from their bones.

Damian took her mouth, a deep kiss. Over and over, his tongue stroking her inside, imitating what was to come. Nudging his hips between her legs, he braced himself on his hands.

"Look at me," he commanded. "Jamie, look at me."

Slowly he pushed inside her, so slowly, gritting his teeth. Looking at her, her wide, gray eyes filled with trust. Sweet mercy, her wet, tight core felt like a hot fist clenching his cock.

Must take it slow. She deserved tenderness and good loving. Damian strained with the effort to hold back. He withdrew, thrust again slowly.

He nuzzled her neck, blew into her ear. She shivered delicately, her nipples hardening into tight little cherry buds.

With a slow grace, an exquisite smoothness, he pushed into her. Damian laced his fingers through hers, pinning them to the bed, and thrust forward.

Jamie writhed a little, trying to find some ease as his thickness penetrated her fully. She sucked in a breath, and relaxed, opening to him, feeling blunt pressure filling her. Making them one. He pulled back, and began to stroke inside her, his penis rubbing against her sensitive tissues, the friction creating a delicious heat that began from her center. His muscles contracted as he thrust, powerful shoulders flexing and back arching.

Damian consumed her, chased the evil darkness inside her with gentle light. Silky chest hair rubbed against her aching breasts, his hard six-pack sliding against her soft abdomen. She arched to meet his rhythm.

Wonder came over her face as she watched him. His mouth parted on a gasp, lips trembling. The bed beneath her felt soft as down, the male pressing her backward onto it solid muscle. It felt as if he locked her spirit in his, a closeness she'd never experienced.

His thrusts became more urgent, harder, until his flesh slapped against hers. Jamie's legs lifted as her hips pummeled upward in need. Close, so close...she writhed and reached for it, the tension growing until she felt ready to explode.

Screaming his name on her lips, she climaxed, her sheath squeezing him as she shattered, her back arching. He growled in satisfaction, gave one last thrust and threw his head back with a hoarse shout. Hot seed jettisoned inside her, filling her with warmth. Damian collapsed atop her, his face pillowed beside her, his breathing ragged. She bore his weight, welcoming it, but then he eased out of her and rolled over, pulling her into his arms.

Jamie gasped and clutched him, feeling something else.

Magick. Good, strong, pure magick, racing through her body, pushing back the drenching darkness left there by the Morphs. White light streaking along her veins, humming with power.

Frightened, she wriggled, trying to free herself of his embrace. He cupped her face in his hands.

"Let it happen, *ma petite*. It's my magick inside you, countering the darkness. Just relax and let go."

Quivering, she forced herself to lie still, feeling the tinge of power filling her body. Damian stroked her hair, murmuring reassurances until the last of the magick faded, leaving her tired, yet buzzed, as if she'd sipped a very strong cocktail.

She nuzzled her cheek against his sweat-slicked shoulder. His hand stroked her hair in a tender caress. "Don't run away from me like you did in New Mexico, Jamie. Promise not to leave me. Whatever problems you face, we can work them out together."

Jamie listened to his heart thud as she rested her cheek on his muscular chest. A huge step, making that kind of promise. It meant tying herself to him, strengthening the bond already forged in the flesh and...

Her heart. She stirred, troubled by the idea, testing it over in her mind. He was so good to her, so gentle and tender. What woman wouldn't want this?

He caged her with the seductive lure of sex. And she'd willingly walked inside. But filling this cage were wild wolves, a pack who could destroy her.

She buried her face in his shoulder. "I promise to try." It was all she could offer.

Silence dripped between them a minute. Then he raised himself on an elbow, his fingers brushing against her cheek. "Try hard," he said softly. "And I promise if you do run from me again, I will catch you."

His eyes gleamed with that wild, frightening look, a wolf secure in knowing it had caught its prey. "Because I won't let you go. Ever."

Chapter 13

They hunted for the next clue in antique shops the following afternoon, searching for a bust of Napoleon with the marking 111. The number was the same as the revolutions on the *Natchez*. Lemon polish scented the enormous antique shop. Jamie gazed upward at chandeliers dangling crystal teardrops. Oriental rugs covered the original wood floors. Heavy oak and mahogany tables and chairs arranged in discreet settings gave the interior an elegant look.

Somewhere had to be a Napoleon bust. It was the last shop they explored. Before they'd left the house, Damian agreed to her suggestion to signal the others upon finding the statue and returning later to purchase it and defray suspicion.

She had steeled herself against the temptation to remain in Damian's arms last night and let his immense strength support her. Instead, she'd slipped away, sleeping downstairs. Each day she grew dangerously close to letting him into her heart and luring her into his pack and his purpose.

Jamie turned back to the small shelf in a corner. She glanced at her hands. Damian's lovemaking had turned her hands pale white again, but the nails remained gray. All the more reason for her to find the next clue.

A small white bust caught her eye. It was chipped. She picked it up, excitement thrumming inside her. Turning it over, she saw the small mark. 111. The number of revolutions on the *Natchez*'s paddlewheel.

Jamie set Napoleon down. If she hid the bust and returned later to purchase it, she could find the last clue and the book. Cure herself and leave Damian behind. She didn't need him anymore.

Her hands hovered over the bust. Didn't need him? Who was she fooling?

He'd protected her, shown her a tenderness she'd never experienced. Given her magick to slow the spell, and sworn to her it was the two of them together in this. Maybe it was time for her to step out in trust. Jamie went to Damian.

"There's not much here. Let's go." She murmured the code words, signaling she'd found the statue.

Brimming with excitement, Jamie held his hand as they left. Later, they would return and... Damian nodded to a man lounging against a light pole. Alexandre nodded back, and headed directly for the shop.

Her heart dropped to her stomach. So much for trust. Damian studied her mutinous expression.

"He'll buy the statue and bring it back."

"Why are you bringing your family into this? It was supposed to be just us."

"Alex is an expert on antiques. His purchase will be less suspicious than if I bought it. My family wants to help, Jamie." He regarded her evenly. "Help cure you, Jamie."

"You make so much of family, family, family. Being part of a group is way overrated. I wouldn't want someone telling me what to do, where to go, how to live."

"Someone to be there when you need them."

"I don't need them. I do better on my own. Even with Mark, he didn't care..."

She bit her lip, looked away, aware she'd already said too much. Jamie flinched at his soft look of dawning comprehension.

"So that's it, Jamie. The Morph wasn't your brother but it was exactly what you wanted. The Morph played the part of the big, protective brother he thought Mark was. Only Mark really didn't care what you did, no matter how you tried to please him. All he cared about was his career, and as long as you stayed out of the way, he was fine with you."

Physical pain squeezed her chest. "He was my only brother. I always had enough food, clothes, everything I needed."

"Everything but someone to love you. You were living with a roommate, not a brother."

"I don't need love or a family. And I don't need you, either," she snapped.

"You need me more than you realize," he said quietly. "You're my mate and part of my family now. Tonight we're dining with them. You won't put them off any longer."

Her stomach tangled in knots. Jamie said nothing. She walked home, not caring that he walked beside her. She'd trusted him for once, and he'd let her down.

Families? Who needed them?

Not her.

When they returned to the house, she went straight to her room. Jamie ditched the pretty white blouse and plaid skirt for sweatpants and a fleece sweatshirt. Laughter and conversation floated upstairs, making her feel more isolated than ever. Legs tucked beneath her, she perched on a chair before the antique desk and opened the laptop. A family dinner? Her eyes closed as she tried to imagine them passing plates, talking, reconnecting those strong bonds.

Instead she saw only mocking smiles, heard the sneering tones.

Jamie powered up the computer, determined to crack the code on the MyPlace page. After working for two hours, she stopped and logged on to World of Warcraft. Going solo, her Night Elf solemnly engaged in a quest to find spider eggs.

Even on the Net, she was alone. Maybe it was better like this.

Loneliness engulfed her. Jamie powered off, dug into her suitcase and withdrew her purple elf ears. She put them on. Cosplay always made her feel better. But it didn't work now. Too much reality had stormed into her life.

She was not Celyndra, her warrior Night Elf. She was plain Jamie, who possessed scary powers of her own, magick she couldn't control. And memories of a childhood no games could ever erase.

She threw the elf ears into a steel wastebasket.

Soon after came a soft knock on the door. When she called out to enter, Damian came in with his usual grace. Jamie recognized the natural elegance, the innate sense of style. Damian was resplendent in a burgundy cashmere turtle-neck, black wool trousers and polished loafers.

He lounged against the wall. "Dinner is downstairs. The children have already eaten and are in bed."

"Not hungry."

"You need energy. You'll eat. Even if I must drag you downstairs."

"Try shoveling it in my mouth."

Damian came over, bracketing his arms on either side of her. "Jamie, they're my brothers, my sister-in-law. Your family, as well. They want to know you better, *chère*." He dipped his head down to meet her gaze, warm breath feathering over her chilled cheek. She basked in the heat he emitted.

"I'm staying here."

"Then they'll come up after dinner. You can't put them off forever."

Her resolve wavered. Damian seemed determined to make her mix with them. Couldn't put it off any longer. She plucked at her worn Tulane sweatshirt. "I'm not dressed."

"You look beautiful," he said softly. "But if you wish, you can change. But not for me. Or them, either."

Wearing different clothing wouldn't matter. Now or never. Sooner or later, she'd have to face them. How could anyone understand?

Her mouth was dry, her hands clammy as she went with him downstairs.

In the dining room, with the lead-crystal chandelier spilling muted light over the ecru walls, a table big as a football field was set with lace cloth, damask napkins and heavy silverware. All four brothers rose politely when she entered. Her nervousness flowered. She saw a blur of silk trousers, dress shirts, hell, even that biker rogue Raphael was decked out in a pinstriped black suit and white shirt, with French cuffs and gold links. Cindy wore a string of freshwater pearls around her slim neck, a black silk dress setting off her long blond hair to perfection. She gave Jamie a warm smile, but it did nothing to erase the cold pit in her stomach.

Numbly, she slid into the chair Damian pulled out for her. Jamie stared at the table as he sat beside her. Wedgwood bone china. Cut-glass tumblers. On a oval platter were raw steaks. Another serving dish held a mountain of rice, one was stacked high with okra and steam misted from a gravy boat. A smaller platter held slices of rare roast beef, and another was topped with two steaks, grilled. Two quart-size bottles of Tabasco looked out of place among the elegance.

"I wasn't certain what you liked, so Raphael prepared and grilled the beef for you," Cindy explained.

Her blue eyes radiated kindness, and Jamie forced a smile. "Thank you."

The meal began unwinding in slow, agonizing tendrils of time. As she tentatively reached for her water glass, Damian served her a cooked steak and rice.

Jamie thanked him. She sliced off the smallest piece, watching a rivulet of blood trickle. Talk flowed around her like water streaming past a river rock.

The steak was tender and juicy. She swallowed, reached for her water and drank deeply. Not bad. Maybe she could do this, after all. It was only meat.

"So, Jamie, you're a computer geek."

This from Gabriel. All eyes turned to her, riveted as if Gabriel announced she was a plump, juicy rabbit they wanted to hunt. Oh God, the attention—now what?

She blurted out the first thing that came to mind. "I prefer the term *goddess*."

Laughter broke out around the table. They were mocking her, just as her family had. Humiliated, she dropped her gaze to the plate. What a mistake this was, thinking she could fit in.

They should just kick her under the table, salt her milk, spit in her food like her cousins did. Then finally drive her away, give her a plate with scraps to eat on the cold, cold back porch. No one would care.

Ashamed, she wanted to fling down her napkin and flee. Run upstairs, bang shut the door and never come out. But she wasn't a child and couldn't let them know how upset she was.

Silence hung in the room, but for the clinking of silverware against china. Then Gabriel winked. "Good. Rafe is a total loser at playing Doom. I could use a challenge. Maybe you could even teach Damian."

Warmth covered her palm as Damian slid his hand over hers. "I'm sure she will. I could use a diversion and a video game sounds excellent. I'd like to learn."

They weren't mocking her. Jamie relaxed as talk resumed. Gabriel asked her questions about her computer expertise. She eased into the conversational waters, then began to swim with confidence.

"This is good," she told Raphael. "All this needs is a little more greenery. Spinach and kale add color and vitamins."

"Vegetables?" Damian shuddered.

"You can hunt down a tomato or two in a garden." She set down her fork, swept them with a thoughtful look. "You can garden in your human form, and then if rabbits invade the garden, shape-shift into a wolf and chase them away.

Ecologically and environmentally sound farming. Vegans would sing your praises."

She bit her lip, hoping she hadn't crossed some invisible line of werewolf protocol. Oh God, what if she had and they all did something like growl or snarl or snap…

Alexandre's lips worked violently. Suddenly he burst into laughter. His brothers stared a moment, then joined in. Damian looked emotional as he squeezed her palm.

"You are amazing," he said in a low voice. "I haven't heard Alex laugh like that in years. Thank you."

His adoring look erased all tension. Tears she never thought she'd never shed suddenly clogged her throat. Jamie forced them down, concentrated on his hand gently stroking hers.

"Does this mean you'll get me a whole-wheat pizza with extra gorgonzola, pesto and tomato for dinner tomorrow?" she asked hopefully.

Damian made a sound suspiciously like a smothered laugh. Gabriel guffawed. "Are you from California?" His accent pronounced the word with a slow slur.

"New York. Just as bad, only with better water and transportation."

"New York isn't bad. The tourists are very good for dinner," Raphael drawled.

"Not as much as Florida snowbirds in season.

Ça c'est bon." Damian kissed his fingers in an exaggerated manner.

This was followed by a heated discussion on repulsive foods.

"The only food I refuse to touch is a black cat on Halloween night. Bad luck," Alexandre ventured. He grinned and reached for another steak.

Jamie's smile slipped. The meat she'd successfully downed turned to vinegar. She tried, oh, she tried, but suddenly time flashed back. Her stomach pitched and rolled. Fresh air, she needed fresh air. She was going to...

Bolting from the table, she clapped a hand over her mouth. Running down the hall, for the kitchen and the back door, praying, please, not here. Not going to make it, not going to make it, no, no...

She had barely dashed through the back door when she began retching into the garden. On her hands and knees, she emptied her stomach, her whole body shaking.

The back door banged. She didn't look up, only scrubbed her tears away. If someone came along and kicked her in the abdomen, she couldn't feel worse.

A pair of polished loafers came into view. Jamie wiped her mouth with the back of her hand. Ashamed, she slowly stood.

Silently Damian handed her a small, clean towel. She scrubbed her mouth, wishing she could cover herself with the cloth and vanish, like a magician's rabbit.

A soothing stroke of reassurance entered her mind, like arms holding her. But the images she held there, the memories...

Too late, Jamie tried slamming Damian out. Shock glazed his eyes.

"Jamie, what did those bastards do?" he asked hoarsely. He gripped her upper arms gently, holding her steady.

Dropping the towel, Jamie dully let him guide her to a small wrought-iron chair, and collapsed onto it.

"Please, tell me. There's nothing you can't share with me." He pulled up a chair, sat and brushed back her sweat-dampened hair from her forehead. "Is this why you refused to eat with my family?"

Gulping down a breath, she nodded. He'd already seen the graphic horror. She didn't look at him.

"When my parents died, my aunt Miranda and uncle Clement took me in. They were my only relatives besides Mark, and he was off on some African expedition and didn't want me. Not until he realized he needed me to secure all our parents' inheritance. Uncle Clement was my mother's brother. He never liked her. Said she was the devil's child."

Oh God, this was so difficult. She struggled for words never told to anyone, not even Mark, who knew how cruel they were.

"I was five and different from my cousins. Refused to do what they liked—play with dolls or games. So they picked on me. Did stuff at the dinner table, salted my food, nasty kid stuff until my uncle got fed up and just fed me out on the porch, a plate on the floor, like the family dog. My cousins said it was because I wasn't fit company. I was...a witch. Just like my mother."

Damian kept stroking her head. She plucked up courage. "My best friend was a black cat. I loved Mercedes. She kept me company when no one else would play with me. I was terrified my cousins would find out. I hid Mercedes in the barn. But my cousins found her. They said only witches had black cats. The cat was evil. My uncle...he...he..."

Jamie wrapped her arms around herself and met his steady gaze. "He killed Mercedes. He...he...cut off her head and made me watch. That night, for the first time, they let me eat at the dinner table. They gave me a special plate. I thought...oh God, I thought they were being nice for once."

Horror tinged his expression, as if he anticipated her next words.

"I ate the meat. It tasted a little funny, but I was so hungry…and then they started laughing at me. My cousin Ronnie told me what I was eating…. They'd cooked Mercedes…. I was eating my own damn cat…."

Damian bit out a rich curse.

"I never ate meat again." She gulped down a breath. "Until the other day, when I ate the cube steak."

Acid rose in her throat. No tears. She couldn't cry, hadn't in years. Even then. Not one tear shed over losing the only real friend she had. And now, here in the quiet safety of the courtyard, she wanted to cry. Couldn't. Her eyes were drier than the Sahara, grief kept at bay like metal doors holding back howling dogs.

"Jamie," Damian said thickly.

Working up her courage, she glanced up. And saw to her dumbfounded shock something clear and wet glistening on his face.

A single tear dripped down Damian's cheek.

A single tear, just like the one she had wept over him as he'd lain dying.

Marveling, she touched the droplet. Brought it to her mouth, tasting it. Salty. Pure. *This is what grief tastes like.*

Jamie brought her hands to his face like a

blind person, tracing over his cheeks, his solemn mouth, the anguished eyes. She wiped his tear away with her palm, her heart turning over as he opened his arms to her.

Curling up in his lap, she clutched fistfuls of his sweater as he held her. After a moment, she pressed a kiss into the strong muscles of his neck.

"I'll avenge you," he promised.

"Too late. I saw his obit a few years ago. Liver trouble."

His eyes darkened to swirls of furious green, like the sea churned by a violent hurricane. Damian cupped her face. "Never again will anyone or anything hurt you. So long as there is breath in my body I will see to it. Do you understand?"

His ferocity scared her a little, until she realized his anger was directed at her past. Jamie smiled, placing her hands over his.

Damian leaned down, his forehead touching hers. "You amaze me, *ma belle petite.* You are a beautiful, ever-changing *zirondelle.*"

When the back door slammed, they looked up to see Raphael amble down the steps. Jamie scrambled to her feet. He gave her a long, thoughtful look. "If the steak isn't sitting well, we have chicken. But you must eat. Tell me what you want, and I'll prepare it."

His thoughtfulness surprised her. "I'm really okay."

"You need to keep up your strength or the spell will start spreading again." This from Damian, who came behind her, rested his hands on her shoulders. "Rafe, how is she doing?"

The Draicon leaned forward, reaching out for her face with his hand. Jamie shrank back.

"It's okay, Jamie. Let Rafe look at you. He's our Kallan, an immortal, and the only one who can dispatch the life of another Draicon without consequence. He can see into the eyes and discern a person's future. Let him examine you and he can see if the spell is accelerating," Damian said quietly.

Jamie blinked, wondering if she wanted this kind of power this close. But Damian was behind her, supporting her.

With a small start, she realized she trusted Damian.

She nodded. Raphael took her face in one hand. With the other, he gently opened her right eye wide. Jamie's gaze locked on his, drawn to the odd whiteness spreading over his pupil, turning it into brilliance—like fog—like looking into a yawning chasm of forever.

Her own death stared back at her.

Stifling a scream, she yanked away. Raphael released her, stepped back, shoving his hands into the pockets of his Armani jacket. Would ruin the lines, she thought dimly.

"Your magick is holding the spell at bay, Damian, but it'll begin spreading soon. Don't exercise any of your powers, Jamie, or it will accelerate," he said in an authoritative voice. "You need protein. I'll warm up some chicken for you."

Accelerate. Spreading poison in her system, turning her to granite, a living hellish death...

"I need a few. I'll be back at the table in ten."

She ran upstairs, took a quick shower, brushed her teeth, willing herself to stop shaking.

I will not die.

Jamie dressed in a lavender silk blouse and a floral skirt with kick pleats, slipped her feet into a pair of flat pumps. When she returned, conversation continued as if she'd never left. Damian gave her a soft, welcoming smile as she began eating the cooked chicken on her plate. His brothers and Cindy talked with her, joked, acting as if nothing had happened. As families went, they weren't bad.

After, she went with them to the courtyard. Etienne brought out a tray with wine and glasses as they settled around the wrought-iron table. Someone lit the wood sitting in the fire pit. Wind whipped the flame as the homey smell of smoke permeated the air.

She took Damian's hand as they strolled near the night-blooming jasmine beside a shed at the courtyard's far wall. He leaned down, brushed a soft kiss against her lips.

Her heart raced with anticipation. She slipped her arms around his narrow waist, feeling power and tensile strength in his body.

Slowly he kissed her again, small, delicate kisses that stirred her hunger. Little kisses, teasing, coaxing her mouth to open. Jamie made a little moan against his lips.

"Damian?"

"Mmm," he said lazily, not stopping his kisses.

Jamie pulled free, blew into his ear, enjoying the shudder running through his powerful body. "I want you. Now."

Damian cocked his head. "That's good." He gazed down at her, his eyes smoky with passion. "That's very, very good."

He tugged her hand toward the shed, and whisked her inside. As he shut the door and leaned against it, she backed against a wood table stacked with bags of potting soil.

"They're right outside," she whispered.

"So you'll have to be very quiet." He advanced, his expression intent and determined.

Oh, he was wicked, and this was so naughty, it heated her blood as much as the sultry promise of hot sex in his eyes.

The earthy smell inside the shed mingled with his rich, masculine scent of spices. Outside, laughter rang out in the courtyard. Jamie focused on Damian as he came forward. His mouth landed on hers, their tongues tangled in a desperate duet.

His hands pulled up her skirt, wrenched down her panties. Jamie pulled away, removed her underwear as he unzipped his trousers and yanked down his black silk boxers. His penis jutted out, bobbing under its heavy weight. Her feminine core ached, empty and yearning for him to fill her.

She scooted up on the heavy table, legs spread open, wet and ready for him. Damian smiled wickedly, stepped between her thighs and leaned over her, bracing his hands on either side of her.

He entered her in a single deep thrust. She shuddered from the raw power as he clasped her hips. The smooth tactile sensation of his hard cock rubbing against her sensitive inner tissues sent blood surging through her veins. Jamie swirled her hips, feeling his penis jerk violently inside her. A long, sultry purr rippled from her open mouth. Damian softly moaned, his muscles locking.

"You are driving me *fou, fou,* female." He pulled back, then began thrusting faster.

Damian rode her hard, making the table rock. His body strained and slid over her. Their mingled, frantic breaths and the sounds of flesh slapping against hers thundered in the small enclosure. Jamie bit her lip to keep from crying out. The tension built higher and higher. Damian leaned down, kissed her mouth, feathered his lips over her cheek and then bit her neck. Sharp, erotic pain flooded her, then he chased it with a soothing swirl of his tongue.

As she began to climax, she reached up and bit his shoulder, latching her teeth onto the cashmere to muffle her cries. He clenched his teeth, head thrown back, eyes closed and breath hammering out of his lungs. His penis twitched violently as he came, Damian's jaw working back and forth in a silent roar. Draped across her body, he breathed in great, ragged pants, then kissed the side of her neck. He pulled out, arranged himself and zipped up, helping her back into her panties and rearranging her rumpled skirt.

His grin was filled with masculine pride as he touched the small bite mark on her neck. She read his thoughts. His mark, his mate.

Chapter 14

Pride filled Damian as he studied his female after the loving, her hair mussed, her body limp with dazed pleasure as he helped her slide off the table. He pictured her at six, with cute pigtails tied with red ribbons, maybe a baseball cap to counter the girly-girl image. Jamie, hugging her cat, her gray eyes innocent and then clouding over with horror as her uncle took away her only friend. A deep growl rumbled from his chest. If the bastard wasn't dead, he'd hunt him down and serve him his ass on a platter. With a sprig of parsley as garnish.

They left the shed discreetly, but Gabriel glanced up. He grinned, poked Etienne.

"Interesting place, that potting shed. More

than flowers have been planted there," Etienne remarked, sliding a hand around Cindy's nape. She looked at him, blushed.

Damian tucked Jamie's hand into his, murmured an excuse about retiring. When they were inside, Jamie stopped and plucked at his sweater.

"It's not just sex, is it? Or is it, because I'm the only one you can breed with? I feel like it's so much more, and it's a little scary."

Serious conversation time, when he only wanted to usher her upstairs, strip off all her clothing and start on certain parts of her body he'd neglected in the shed. Damian touched her cheek. Reassurance might convince her to see his view. They'd forged a bond in the flesh, and connected telepathically. His family had welcomed her and surely she would accept and understand her role as his mate, and the need to stick close to his side.

He kept his thoughts guarded from Jamie, startled by the depth of his burgeoning emotions. Love was a double-edged sword that could swing back and hit him. He couldn't risk love. He was committed to his pack, his people, but always guarded his heart should something happen and he lost another.

He didn't want to love her. Love turned strong males weak and vulnerable, and made them weep at the suffering inflicted on innocent little girls with cruel uncles.

"It's not just sex, *ma petite*. It's deeper, more real and lasting. Yes, I need an heir, but that can wait and it's not half as important to me as making you smile again. If I could, I'd take back all your past misery. All I can do is try to make it better for you and give you a new family who will treat you the way you deserve. You belong with my people now."

Hope shining in her eyes turned to dismay. Damian recognized the stubborn tilt of her chin. He touched her mind and found a brick wall barricading her thoughts.

"It isn't just the sex, it's the whole package, then? Not just you, but a horde of werewolves. I told you I don't do the group thing, especially not with a group of Draicon."

"We are your new family. My brothers, my parents and my pack in New Mexico are nothing like what you experienced in your family. They'll be everything your family was not, Jamie."

"Oh, they'll love me and make me feel like I'm one of you. I'm not and I'll never fit in. I'm a black sheep in a pack of wolves, and we both know what wolves do to sheep."

"Jamie, have my brothers ever made you feel anything but safe? You are one of us." He compressed his lips, roping in his impatience, need-

ing her to see his point and finally accept him
and his people. It was like trying to capture a
beautiful, elusive dragonfly.

"I'll never be one of you," she whispered, putting a hand to her cheek. "Stop trying to make
me into something I'm not. You can't hold on to
me. Or stop this spell from spreading. It's beyond
your control."

"I can and will." Anger flooded him. She had
no faith in him, and assumed he'd let her down.
His gaze fell to her hand and then he forgot his
anger.

Damian picked up her wrist and held her fingernails up for inspection. "They're no longer
gray. When did this happen?"

She wrinkled her brow. "I guess eating the
meat helped. It doesn't matter. Everything we're
doing is just a stopgap. I need the book, Damian,
and we'd better find it, soon."

He stood staring after her as she trudged up
the stairs. Normal fingernails. Something nagged
at him about that. But he couldn't quite place it.

Inside the voodoo shop, Jamie fidgeted as she
waited for Damian to pay at the cash register.
They had found the final clue. The Napoleon
statue had revealed it was in a painting featuring
a wolf in the bayou. Alexandre had seen such a
painting in the shop while searching the Quarter.

Damian clutched the framed painting covered with paper with one hand and with the other steered her outside. Dark clouds fat with raindrops scudded across the sky. Pedestrians brushed past, their cheerful expressions contrasting sharply with her misery.

Damian glanced down at his parcel with a frown.

"Someone selling art across from Jackson Square painted a wolf in a bayou. But it can't be the right painting, because this one is an antique. Alex confirmed it," he mused aloud. "Then again, it is New Orleans. Bayous and werewolves are common as crayfish."

She said nothing, refusing to talk with him since the fight yesterday. Jamie didn't want his tenderness, the caring or his people. If she joined with them, she'd only end up being hurt again because they'd reject her just as her uncle and brother had when she failed to meet their expectations.

Better to be alone and never know the love and warmth of family than lose something she'd secretly longed for all her life.

"Learn to let go, Damian. Because you can't hold on to me." Jamie pulled away from his loose clasp.

"I told you, *chère,* you're my mate, pack. Pack

sticks together and I will never let you go. You need me, and us."

In minutes, they approached Pirate's Alley. Shrouded by shadows, it looked uncomfortably menacing. Damian went to enter. Jamie balked. Something wasn't right. A very faint foulness polluted the air.

He looked at her. "What is it?"

Don't go down there. Ridiculous. Just an alley.

"Nothing. Let's go."

When they were halfway through, a child stepped out of the shadows. The little girl clutched a stuffed animal marred with a rusty stain. Jamie's stomach gave a sickening twist.

Damian ground to an abrupt halt. Horror etched his face in frozen shock.

"Damian?" The child's voice was sweet. But underneath was a grating ugliness, like teeth gnashing and whirring. Didn't he hear it?

A clatter sounded as the painting fell to the pavement from Damian's loosened grip. The stark anguish shadowing his eyes hit her like a baseball bat to the knees. This was someone he knew. Someone he cared about…

"Damian? You left me and they came, they killed Mommy and Daddy and Ritchie and Pierre. They found me. I tried so hard to hide and I was calling for you. Why didn't you hear me? Damian, you promised to protect me, you promised! They dragged me out and they hurt me, and I kept screaming for you and you never came!"

Shocked, Jamie watched Damian step forward. "Annie. Please, I'm so sorry. I ran, I ran hard and fast but I couldn't reach you—"

"I died because of you!"

Steel threaded through that tone. Jamie blinked hard at the little girl. Summoned the darkness still nestling deep inside. She gasped.

Instead of a little girl stood a gnarled figure with yellowed fangs, talons glistening in the moonlight and greasy hair. Morph.

Jamie tugged at his arm. "Damian, it's a Morph tricking you!"

He wrenched free of her grasp.

"Damian, if you truly love me, help me. Come here, I need you," the apparition begged.

He took another step forward. The Morph gave a sickening smile. It raised a hand, and a sharp dagger appeared.

Using their telepathic link, she entered Damian's mind. But the howling pain screaming there lashed her with such violence, she cried out. Jamie tried one attempt to soothe him. Her weak efforts felt like holding back a tsunami using a bucket.

She escaped his mind.

God, she had to do something now, or he'd

walk straight to his death and let the thing stab him, probably welcome it because she knew the pain he faced now, a pain so screeching and agonizing anything to vanquish it would be blessed relief. Even death.

He walked toward the Morph. Damian couldn't see the rows of sharp, pointed yellow teeth, the saliva dripping from its crooked slash of a red mouth.

It was drooling, anticipating a Damian meal. A powerful Alpha, whose agonizing death would feed it energy for months.

Jamie planted herself in front of Damian. She took his face into her hands, forcing him to confront her. Her touch seemed to shake him free a little of the spell.

"Look at me, Damian. Me. Not her. Can't you trust me?"

At the word *trust,* his gaze snapped to hers. The dark torment in his eyes slowly faded.

"Look hard at her, Damian. She's dead, Annie's dead. She loved you, Damian. Annie would never hurt you like this."

He peered around her shoulder. Confusion and doubts twisted his face. Damian hesitated. The Morph twisted the stuffed animal, claws making a dull ripping sound on the fabric. It whimpered.

"Damian, please, I need you. It's so dark, so cold where I am. Come play with me, I'm so lonely. Please, Damian, if you love me, come to me and I'll forgive you."

Those three last words sounded like a thunderclap. It snapped something inside him. Damian wrenched free. Jamie made a grab for him, and failed. God, the pain he had, what he suffered, the horror... The images circled in her head until everything before her went blurry and the lump clawing up her throat took hold.

Something wet trickled down her cheeks. Jamie reached out, grasped his jacket sleeve like a lifeline. Miracle of miracles, he turned and saw her face.

"Oh, Damian, what did they do to you? My wonderful, brave warrior, it's not your fault. Annie's dead. Please, listen to me because I'm so scared right now and I need you to see this thing for what it is. It's a killer. I need you to trust me now."

"Jamie," he said hoarsely. He reached up, touched a tear hovering on her chin. "Oh, Jamie. You're crying."

"For you," she whispered.

Then he turned, pushing her behind him in a protective stance. Damian waved his hands. Two steel daggers materialized in his palms.

"I see Annie only, but I trust Jamie. You're not my sister. Want to play? I play rough."

The Morph roared. It raced forward, dagger

outstretched. Damian snarled and charged. An outraged howl split the air as his dagger sank into the creature's chest. It collapsed, dissolved into gray ash.

Trembling, she hugged herself as the daggers vanished and he ran back to her. He cupped her face and gently kissed away her tears.

Damian crushed her against him, tunneling his fingers through her hair. Fat raindrops fell, running in rivulets down their faces. "She's dead, buried and never coming back. Ever," he said brokenly.

Jamie stroked his head. They clung to each other. Then Damian lifted his face, the familiar, watchful look back.

"*Allons.* Let's go to your house. It's closer."

Soaked and shivering, they arrived at her house. Damian put the painting on the kitchen table, then joined her in the bedroom as they stripped off their wet clothing. Jamie shrugged into a sweatshirt and sweatpants. She fetched a terry-cloth robe that had been Mark's, and returned to the bedroom.

He stood there, head hanging down, his muscled body quaking. Gently she draped the robe over his shoulders. Damian belted it on and sat.

"Jamie, I need to tell you something."

She waited.

Damian's mouth went dry. Jamie deserved the

truth, but memories lashed at him like a barbed whip. Big powerful Draicon. No, coward. Weak. Outcast. He summoned all his strength to force the words out.

"When I was twelve and experienced my first change to wolf, Morphs attacked my father's mansion. This house. I was hunting in the bayou, against my father's wishes, instead of staying home to help protect my family. Annie died because of me."

Jamie made a murmur of protest. He ignored it, dragged a hand through his damp hair.

"My pack, my father's people, rejected me after. They'd just lost their Alpha, and were terrified."

"They were all you had left and they kicked you out?"

Five feet, five inches of spitfire stared at him. Jamie's lips curled into a snarl. She looked as if she wanted to claw his former pack to ribbons.

"Sit." He patted a space. She sat, swinging her legs, her feet kicking in the embroidered bedspread.

"My pack was French, proud of their undiluted blood. They thought Rafe's family, the Cajuns, were trash. When they came to Vieux Carre to buy supplies, we used to call them names. Mock them, calling them...dogs. Everyone did but my father. I did, too, until my father found out. He whupped my ass good, told me the Cajuns were as noble as our blood was."

"I would have liked your father."

He ran a thumb over the delicate bones beneath her soft skin. "He would have liked you, as well. He was a brave, honorable male admired and deeply respected by many. Like me, he was the firstborn son of a pureblood Alpha, with powers greater than most Draicon."

"Then why didn't your pack want you, Damian?"

"I was too young to rule, too green... And a target for Morphs."

He fell silent, feeling the shame creep over him. The powerful pack Alpha proven weak. A small squeeze of her hand startled him. Damian glanced at her.

"Please, tell me. I understand more than you think. I know, Damian."

Jamie's quiet sincerity fed him courage. "They said shame covered me because I failed to protect my family. I begged to stay, but they kicked me until I ran and then they chased me...like a stray they were driving out of their territory. All the way to the bayou. Until I couldn't stand. So I crawled away. I was so damn hungry and weak. When Rafe and his brothers found me, I was nearly naked and cold. But most of all, ashamed. The Alpha Draicon, the blueblood who mocked them, was an outcast. I almost wished they'd let me die."

He didn't dare look at her. Silence hovered between them for a minute.

"They took you in instead," she said softly.

"Brought me home, cleaned me up, fed me. And taught me how to survive. They were honorable, like my father said. And braver than my pack." A heartbeat of silence fell, then he spoke again. "Braver than me."

"No, Damian." She shook her head, making her hair fly back and forth. "Not braver than you, as brave as you. You blame yourself for your family's deaths. How, Damian? How could you have saved them? If you were there, you'd have been killed, as well. And your father's pack... they were the weak ones. Not you."

Tension eased as he considered her words. "I found out later the Morphs found them, killed them all."

"What happened to the Morphs who killed your family?"

"Rafe and his family destroyed most. One may have escaped."

Jamie squeezed his palm. The compassionate gesture comforted more than words. Sometimes words weren't needed. For a moment he simply relished the comfort she freely offered. Damian closed his eyes, basking in the consolation of her touch. Intimacy wasn't something he'd ever craved. Hell, he'd kept a small distance even from his adopted family. But he found himself longing for it now with Jamie.

This was what having a mate meant. Not merely a physical closeness, but someone with you to share your most painful secrets, who didn't condemn you for them.

She drew him into her arms, giving herself as she kissed him. He took, gladly. Their lovemaking was slow and tender. Afterward, he held her close, his hand running up and down her smooth skin, savoring the feel of her. Running his fingers through her hair…

Her hair, sweet mercy… Damian fingered a lock. "*Mon Dieu,* it's black again."

Jamie bolted out of bed, ran to the mirror and stared. "Is it your magick, when we make love?"

"I don't know," he admitted.

"But I still have dark magick inside me. That's what enabled me to see the Morph disguised as your sister." She sat on the bed, twisting a lock of hair around her index finger.

"How did the Morph find us in the alley? It's like they know where you are at all times."

"They're forming a battle plan, to test my strengths and weaknesses. Annie is a weakness." He looked away, his firm jaw clenching. "So is anyone else I lo…care for."

Anguish twisted Jamie's heart as she studied her lover. She sensed exactly how much it cost this proud Draicon to admit what had happened. Damian saw his role as leader to protect his people, but had lost many. They had more in common than she'd thought. They were separate, alone. But combining their strengths, they might defeat the enemy. Opening herself up to him, she shared the thoughts telepathically.

Awareness dawned in his eyes. "We can, Jamie. You have technological skills I lack. I know the enemy, but there's some tool they're using that's evading me. Tell me what you think."

Buoyed by his confidence in her, Jamie thought hard. "It's like a game, like World of Warcraft. You build strength with your tasks, and you go on quests. They're finding a way past your barriers, so when they do come at you with all their forces, they'll know exactly how to hit you. And they know where you are, when you'll be there... But how? It's like a tracking system, a GPS...."

"Rafe has a tracking system," he said slowly.

Jamie raced for her laptop. "Oh my God! That MyPlace page I found, the one with the encrypted text that is a secret message? I've been trying to crack the code to decipher the words. Your brother Rafe, he's the only immortal Draicon. That must be the keyword to breaking the code!"

She powered up. "I have a new software program designed to help me break the code," Jamie explained as she typed some commands. She typed the word *immortal*. Damian blinked in confusion as her fingers flew over the keyboard, pulling up the MyPlace page. She typed some more.

"I got it! The encrypted text is a command to get to a locked Web page accessible only to those who have the keyword. Look."

Jamie typed in another command, pulling up a Web page. It was a page detailing an exact reverse of Raphael's tracking map. Only on this page, every move Damian had made, every place he had gone was registered. Every move since he'd bitten her, giving her his magick.

Horror-struck, she stared at the screen. "It's my fault. When you bit me to give me your magick, the Morph blood inside me spilled into you, so now they can track you just like they can track me. It's like a damn GPS chip in you."

Damian cupped her face. "I can handle them. I worry about you, *ma petite*. You're so pale— you've been through so much."

Her hands curled about his wrists. "I can handle myself."

He kissed her mouth gently. "I'm proud of you

for cracking their code. You are extraordinary. And I want my entire adopted family to meet you."

Her smile slipped.

"There's not too many—only about fifty." His thumb lingered over her mouth.

Old fears raced through her. Would his family turn out to be the vicious killers she'd dreaded in the past?

Chapter 15

Wind whipped her hair as she clung to Damian on the back of the Harley. Fields gave way to a dense canopy of hardwoods, cypress and live oak. Beside the one-lane road ran a winding ribbon of murky water. The smell of fresh water teased her senses. She buried her head against Damian's broad back.

With his art expertise in antiques, Alexandre was combing over the painting, but still hadn't found the next clue. Damian's frustration was apparent, but today he'd set it aside for the family gathering.

Finally they turned onto a dirt road. They rode for about two miles until reaching the end. A clearing about seven acres wide and long, peppered with trees, opened before them. On one side was the bayou. In the middle of the clearing was a charming two-story gray house with white shutters and a wide porch.

Damian brought the bike to a stop before the house and parked amid a cluster of cars and motorcycles. Jamie dismounted and pulled off the helmet. She smoothed down her wool pants, straightened the collar of her red cashmere sweater. The familiar barricades against families went up. No more emotional pain. She couldn't risk it. Another disappointment, more abandonment, or worse. She had tried to kill Damian by infecting him with the lethal virus. For that crime, Damian's adopted family might turn on her as her own family had. Only, his family had fangs and claws and were dangerous.

"Hey," he said softly. "You have nothing to worry about."

Anxiety clenched her stomach. Would they gawk, whisper? Shun her?

Herding her up the steps, he seemed carefree. Panic raced in her veins at the sound of a large group inside. Damian opened the screen door and whistled. "She's here!"

Conversation ground to a halt. A blush heated her face. Wonderful, here she went again, a real showstopper, maybe they wouldn't stare…

They entered a large dining room. Around a

simple oak table were at least sixty people. Jamie gulped. And then they parted, and she saw what was on the table.

The cake was almost the size of a small desk. In childish letters was scrawled *Happy Birthday Jamie*. The group broke out into a loud chorus of "Happy Birthday, Jamie."

A surprise party for her. A big cake with lots of people wishing her well, and they were grinning at her. A lump rose in her throat.

Something tugged at her pant leg. She glanced down to see cherubic Ana, her blond hair done in pigtails.

"I helped with the icing," she chirped. "You said you liked pink, so we got you pink."

Twenty-one candles burned. Her vision blurred. This was what family should be, what she'd longed for always, the generous, all-encompassing warmth that sheltered you like a blanket, forgave you for stupid things you did and just accepted you for what you were. She swallowed back the tears and smiled.

Jamie scooped Ana into her arms. "I need help blowing all these out. That or a fire extinguisher."

"No," someone said in a thick accent. "That'd be Paw Paw. Nearly two thousand candles and we'd make the bayou dry."

Everyone laughed and then she and Ana blew

the candles out. Damian introduced her in a blur
of names and faces. His adopted parents, Remy
and Celine, had dark eyes and dark hair. They
enveloped her in a hug.

"Paw Paw's out back. I'll introduce you in a
minute. Said his bones are too tired to stand for
long. But first, I want you to meet Indigo. He
doesn't live with the family, but we consider him
our brother. He's half vampire, half Draicon."
Damian drew her over toward a man towering
over the crowd.

Jamie stared in awe at the colossal giant with
black curls parted down the middle, spilling
down his back. Six feet seven inches tall, body
built like a tank, shoulders wide as a doorway. A
close-cropped black beard darkened his face. His
skin was coffee with a generous dose of cream,
his origin, maybe Native American mixed with
Polynesian.

His hand swallowed hers as he shook it very
quickly, then dropped it. Indigo quietly wished
her a happy birthday and walked away. The floor
shook beneath his footsteps.

There were presents, lots of them. Little,
thoughtful gifts like flash drives for her laptop,
a handwoven silk scarf from Damian's adopted
parents and a gold watch from his brothers. A
new laptop from Damian, state-of-the-art. A
sheepish grin touched his mouth.

"It's all I could do, after breaking yours," he told her.

Then the women cut the cake, setting large slices on paper plates. Her emotions teetered wildly as she clutched Damian's arm. "You threw this party just for me."

Tenderness shone in his gaze as he rubbed his thumb over her wobbly lower lip. "It's about time someone celebrated your life." He kissed the corner of her mouth.

They ate the cake and went outside. Insects hummed in the nearby trees. Brilliant sunshine chased away November's chill. In a rocking chair on the back porch sat an elderly icon. In overalls and a simple plaid shirt, he had white hair, a craggy face that resembled a well-worn road map. Wisdom and life shone in his watery blue eyes.

Reverence tinged Damian's voice as he introduced her. The man smelled like spices and pine forest. He sat up, beckoning for her hand. He took her palm gently, turned it over. Rheumy blue eyes widened. A muttering of rapid Cajun followed.

"That doesn't sound good." Jamie glanced at Damian.

Paw Paw squeezed her hand, his grip surprisingly strong. "You are a *Maihaigh*. In our old language, one who brings healing strength to our people. Your kind is extremely rare, with magick once all Draicon possessed."

Healing strength? When she'd tried to kill Damian? Jamie shook her head. "Maggie, in Damian's pack, is the one who heals. I...destroy," she whispered.

"Your strength will help bring us together as one and your powers will restore what was lost to our people. It's inside you, this power, but first, you must forgive yourself."

More tears blurred her vision. She scrubbed them away as she listened to him list her newfound powers. Telepathy. Traveling through space and reappearing in another place. Levitation. Magick she'd craved all her life, yet the possibilities scared her.

"What if I can't control it? I don't want to hurt anyone."

"Damian will teach you. This is why he's your dracairon. He has learned his whole life to control his magick. You've been adrift your whole life and now you've found your direction."

Hope soared inside her. This was meant to be. Damian, someone who cared despite all her shortcomings, and knew exactly what she needed to survive. But did he love her? And could she dare to risk loving him, becoming absorbed into his world and all that went with it?

Damian pulled her upward, gathered her into

his arms. "He's right. I'll be your direction, for now and always," he said softly.

For always. For as long as she lived, what time she had left. Jamie rested her head on his shoulder. No, she wouldn't think of that. Not today. Today was her birthday celebration.

A few of the pack formed an impromptu band on the porch with a fiddle, guitar and an accordion. After some coaxing, Gabriel joined them on the fiddle, singing in Cajun French.

The dancing started. Damian held her in a light grip as they did a two-step. Soon after, everyone took a break. When Jamie saw the females drift toward the kitchen and the males amble away, she put an immediate halt to it. She organized both genders into an efficient cleanup crew, making sure the males did their part. Then as she helped finish, Damian's brothers, even Indigo, started a game of football, laughing and jostling each other.

Jamie set down the plate she was drying, peered through the kitchen window. Damian held himself apart, looking with longing at the others roughhousing.

A gentle hand on her shoulder drew her attention away. Celine followed her gaze.

"Have I told you how happy we are that Damian found you? You make him feel young again.

My son, he is young in age, but his spirit is ancient and weary."

"But I'm not Draicon. How can you just accept me without really knowing who I am?" The confession fled her lips and Jamie wished she could capture the words and stuff them back into her mouth.

Celine gave her an understanding smile. "It doesn't matter who you are, Jamie. We accept you for everything you are and aren't because you are Damian's mate. That's what family is about. You needn't worry about conforming or pleasing us. I can see how Damian looks at you and how the light returns to his eyes when he does. He needs you and that is enough."

No one had ever needed her before. "Go to him, Jamie," Celine told her. "Do what your heart tells you is true. He has been walking in darkness for too long. Be his light."

His light. His hope. After seeing the darkness tormenting him over his family's death, she understood. Jamie plucked at her pretty sweater. "Do you have any spare clothing? Something good for playing football?"

Minutes later, she emerged on the porch. Dressed in a sweatshirt two sizes too big, baggy sweatpants and sneakers stuffed with paper to make them fit, she headed for Damian.

He leaned against a sturdy oak. The familiar searching, wary look was back. Reluctant to relax, always on guard.

When the game broke up, the players clapped each other on the shoulder and sat on the grass, drinking tall glasses of lemonade. The abandoned football lay within reach. Jamie scooped it up, handed it to Damian.

"Here. Let me see how fast you can run, wolf. Throw it."

He stared at the pigskin as if she'd handed him a snake. She backed up, held out her hands. He tossed her a wimpy pass a day-old infant could catch.

Jamie zinged it back to him, the ball smacking him in the chest. Surprise widened his eyes. "Harder," she yelled.

A small smile touched his mouth. He sent it back, putting just the right spin. The ball increased velocity as it sailed toward her. Jamie missed.

She saw his brothers watching. Jamie jerked her head toward Damian. Mouthed a sentence, then tossed him back the ball.

Suddenly a wild yell split the air. Raphael barreled toward him with the relentless force of a charging… *Wham!* He tackled Damian, tumbling him to the ground.

And just like that, the game was on again. Jamie grinned, shoved her hair out of her face and sat on the picnic table to watch. After a few minutes, her mate—yes, her mate, the word sounded good—tugged his T-shirt over his head, and tossed it aside.

Sweat glistened on his brow, caught in the dark hairs feathering his powerful chest. Fascinated, she stared at the smooth muscles rippling beneath golden skin. His wide shoulders seemed strong enough to carry a log. His jeans rode low on his lean hips, hugged his taut ass as he ran past.

The game ended. Warmth filled her at the sight of Damian's cheerful, wide grin. She tilted her head up to catch the sun. This was a great day. Maybe even the best day of her life.

Damian shrugged the shirt back on and grabbed her hand. "Jamie, come here. My brothers want to show you something."

He led her to where they sat. Damian nodded, turned her around so her back was to them.

When he turned her again, five gray wolves lay on the grass. One had black bands about his muzzle. Etienne, Alpha markings. Another had a distinctive white streak. Raphael. Indigo, the largest and most menacing, outweighed the others by a good fifty pounds. Terror clogged her throat, remembering that night...

"Sit." Damian gently guided her downward. "They would never harm you."

Gathering her courage, she watched them warily. They rose, one playfully butting the other against the buttocks. One by one they approached, crawling toward her. And submissively, lowered their heads as they lay at her feet.

"Go ahead, touch them. It's all right," he told her.

She reached out in wonder, scratched the first one's ears. He gave her a big wolfish grin. "That's Gabriel. Turns to mush when you do that," Damian drawled.

Jamie closed her eyes, fear slipping away on four paws. When she opened them again, Damian's brothers were dressed and in human form.

Her fingers curled as she tugged on her sweatshirt. "Thanks, for all you did, in getting rid of that...thing that killed my brother."

Etienne gave a gentle smile. The others looked at her with solemn faces. Alexandre cleared his throat. Harsh lines on his face softened. He almost looked...wistful.

"We would do anything for the mate of our brother, to safeguard you from danger." A deep, wrenching sadness shone in his eyes, then he blinked, the emotion gone.

The others, Raphael included, all nodded. Even Indigo, that scary mammoth who looked as if he could crush cars with his fists. They would give their lives to keep her safe, she realized. The thought tightened her throat even more. They weren't wild beasts, but noble, proud males. Brothers. A real brother, not just a roommate as Mark had been.

The thought jolted her. She had never really known what family was all about, until meeting Damian. But could she assimilate into his world and dare to join in after being alone for so long? What if they changed their minds, turned on her as her uncle's family had?

To guard her thoughts, she broke the tension by standing and tossing the nearby football. Gabriel caught it one-handed.

"I think you're better in wolf form. You must be very fast when you're wolf." She grinned. "Faster than when you play football. Because you know what? You run like old ladies."

"Hey, I'm only a hundred and ninety," Gabriel protested cheerfully.

"I bet I can beat you in a race. You're all *much* older than me." Not giving them a chance to respond, she took off.

"Get her," Damian yelled playfully.

Laughing, they raced after her, their long legs effortlessly eating up the space between them. Jamie grinned and ran faster, feeling a hand reach out, brush her lower back.

Panic exploded. Her back...

Suddenly time flipped back. She was seven

years old again, running from her yelling cousins, a mob of frenzied anger. Adrenaline kicked
in, making her legs pump harder until her thighs
burned, screamed with pain. Jamie sobbed for
breath, snagged her sweatpants on a branch.

Caught off balance, she went down, pants
jerking down past her hips. Her panties, oh no,
she'd worn the pretty silk thong just because she
wanted to feel sexy.

The ground felt cold against her face. She
struggled to stand, but someone grabbed her
wrists, kept her pinned.

"Hold her," a deep male voice ordered, laughing. "Don't let her get away. Damian's afraid
she'll run away again from him. Damn, you're
fast, girl."

Jamie screamed, struggling against the hands
trapping her, the harsh masculine laughter...
Caught again. She writhed and fought.

"Stop it," Rafe said sharply. "You're scaring
her."

"Get off," Damian ordered in a tense voice.
"This isn't play anymore."

Freed, she heard the hush of shock descending.
Someone muttered, "Oh my good Lord. What the
hell is that?"

Shame filled her. She turned her head, saw
Damian kneel down behind her. Felt him stroke
the part of her no one ever saw, not even him

when they'd made love. His fingertip gently traced the mark burned into her lower back.

"Jamie, oh, my beautiful Jamie, what did they do to you?" he whispered.

She closed her eyes, knowing what he saw. The crooked, ugly blue scars as stark as a scarlet letter, written in a childish hand. Carved into her skin by her cousins.

Witch.

As soon as Damian pulled to a stop before the house on Esplanade, she ran inside, fleeing for the refuge of her room. Bad enough for him to have seen her shameful branding, but his brothers? She felt like a victim of the Salem trials.

After she'd struggled to her feet, the shocked pity on their faces had shamed her. Damian knew how she'd gotten the mark. He'd slipped into her mind, seen the past sliding by like film images.

Jamie went to the bureau, fingering the big cotton briefs. They felt heavy in her trembling hands. Instead she dug through the layers, found a turquoise blue thong. It was lacy, feminine and delicate. She stood there, staring at it, wishing, oh how she wished…

Strong, lean fingers took the thong, set it down on the dresser.

"I wanted to wear it…to look pretty for you. As a surprise." Jamie laughed, slamming the drawer shut so hard the dresser shook. "Some surprise."

Damian cupped her face in his hands. "Look at me," he ordered quietly. "Jamie, look at me." When she did, he exhaled a long breath. "You are beautiful and nothing, no mark or scar, will ever mar my perception of you. Understand?"

Something eased inside her chest. "I hate it. I wish I could get rid of it. It makes me feel so ugly."

His thumb brushed over her dry cheek. "What about a tattoo? Indigo runs a shop. It's very clean, and safe. And I'll be with you the whole time."

A tattoo. Damian dropped a kiss on her nose. "Anything you want. But I have to warn you, it will hurt."

"Nothing can hurt as much as…what they did."

He kissed the corner of her mouth tenderly. "Let me call him, and we'll go right away."

The tattoo parlor just outside the French Quarter resembled an upscale beauty salon more than an ink shop. Lots of soft overhead lighting, chrome, glass and green ferns in potted planters. Tasteful charcoal sketches of dragons, werewolves and fairies adorned the powder-blue walls.

"All Indigo's art," Damian said, as she looked around. "He's very talented."

The woman behind the glass-and-chrome desk looked up from her computer. She beamed. "Go in the back, he's expecting you."

Sweat blossomed on her forehead as they entered the room. In the center was a examination table covered with a clean white cloth, arranged so the person could sit upright. A large gooseneck floor lamp and backless stool stood beside it. Metal shelving held bottles of ink, instruments, and the black counters were spotless. A small sink was in one corner, with a soap dispenser and paper towels. Very clean and orderly. She relaxed a little.

Indigo came out from behind a curtain, and smiled. He nodded his head in a gesture of respect.

Damian thrust out a hand, which Indigo shook very briefly as if fearing some offense. "Thanks for doing this, *frère*. Appreciate the short notice."

Jamie's gaze dropped to the small steel tray holding an assortment of thimble-size cups with ink, the mechanical needle. Like a dentist's drill. Her heart pounded so loudly it sounded like it would slam out of her chest.

Damian regarded her with his steady gaze. *You all right?* he spoke gently into her mind. *Are you certain?*

I have to do this, she told him telepathically.

Indigo sat on the stool. "What would you like, Jamie?"

She went to the big male, reached up on tiptoe even though he sat, and whispered into his ear.

Surprise and pleasure flashed on his face. Indigo nodded. "Definitely," he said in his thick Cajun accent. "I'll do a sketch first. Then draw it on your skin so I have an outline to follow."

While he drew on tracing paper, she sat beside Damian, examining the sample book. The artwork was astounding, playful and leaped off the page.

"Ready over here." Paper rustled.

She drew off her sweater, placed it on a chair. Jamie unbuttoned her jeans, shimmied them and her underwear down past her hips.

Indigo snapped on a pair of sterile gloves, the sound sharp as gunfire. She sat on the table, resting her face against it. A shudder stroked her spine, but she forced herself to lie still.

Damian pulled up a chair to her side, clutched her hand. Sensations flooded her: Damian's delicious scent, the feel of paper against her lower back as Indigo traced his drawing, the iron taste of fear in her mouth. Jamie gritted her teeth as the burning began, as if someone pressed a hot iron against her skin. The needle's whir roared in her ears.

She dimly heard Damian murmuring soothing words. Her eyes closed as she focused on his deep voice. Finally the buzzing stopped.

"He's done, *ma petite*."

Jamie's eyes flew open. She sat up, wincing, and stared into the mirror Damian held up, reflecting into the larger one Indigo held at her backside.

"Oh, it's beautiful, so majestic and proud. Thank you!" She beamed at him.

Indigo flashed her a shy smile, nodded at Damian and left the room.

Her lover's jaw dropped as he walked behind her, stared at the tattoo. An exact replica of Damian as wolf, green eyes sharp and intelligent, his gray carriage straight and proud as he gazed into the distance. Like a king surveying his domain.

He came back, squatted down until he was eye level. "Jamie, why me?"

She stroked his cheek with one finger. "I needed something beautiful and noble to cover the ugliness. Now I bear your mark, and everyone will know I'm one of your family, your pack. I'm yours, always."

Emotion flashed in his eyes. Damian pressed a gentle kiss to her lips. "And I am yours, *toujours*."

His cell rang. Damian flipped it open. "We'll

be there in ten." He thumbed the phone off, looking at her with a wide smile.

"Alexandre found the last clue. He's at Rafe's house, waiting for us."

Chapter 16

In the formal living room, Alexandre, Raphael, Gabriel and Etienne waited for them. Seeing their expressions, Jamie clutched Damian's hand. Something was very, very wrong.

The painting of a wolf standing by a cabin in the bayou rested on the cocktail table.

"What took you this long?" Damian demanded.

"I actually found the clue yesterday." Alexandre exchanged glances with his brothers, his expression as foreboding as an executioner's. "We met, and decided…it was best to keep the news from you, and not spoil Jamie's party. We wanted her, and you, to enjoy the time together."

Fear unfurled in her heart. This was going

to be bad. Damian gave her hand a comforting squeeze, but she couldn't stop trembling.

"When I separated the canvas from the frame, I found this."

Alexandre handed Damian a small piece of wood with a tiny carving of a heart. He dropped her hand, took and sniffed the bark.

"Cypress." Damian's fingers trailed over the wood. "I recognize the scent. He hid the book in the old bayou. My father said the tree represented the heart of the Draicon because it stood so long and so proud, and thrived best in the wild."

He set the bark down quietly. His jaw tightened; his eyes were distant.

Excitement bubbled inside Jamie. It couldn't be that bad. True, a bayou was a large place, but they were Draicon and their excellent sense of scent could track it down. The book was within her grasp. She felt death take a few steps backward, hovering, but no longer an in-your-face reality.

Damian braced his hands on the table, hung his head. Alexandre stared at the wide oak floorboards, refusing to meet her gaze. Despair etched Gabriel's face. Raphael and Etienne both dropped a hand on Damian's shoulder.

A blast of frigid air draped the room, as if death decided to come nosing back again.

"What is it? We're close now, it's in the bayou

where your father hunted… So let's go, it's almost nightfall… We can bring lanterns and flashlights.…"

Damian lifted his head. Jamie reeled back at the utter desolation in his eyes. It was like glimpsing hell.

"That bayou no longer exists. They filled it in and developed houses years ago. The book lies beneath pavement and rock."

Hope snapped on a thin thread. Jamie staggered to the nearest chair and sat, burying her face in her hands. Cold sweat gathered in the waistband of her jeans.

Years of ancient knowledge were lost. She was going to die.

Night descended with a sweep of gold shadows. A wolf caged by a Creole mansion, Damian paced, shoving a hand through his sweat-dampened hair. Jamie was upstairs, resting.

He was alone in his misery.

He'd failed, again. He couldn't save the one most precious to him. The book, gone forever. For all his powers, the battles he'd fought, his skill as a warrior, he was totally useless.

He refused to believe in impossibilities. Who was the stranger who had hidden the clue on the *Natchez?* Did he have the book, or was he also dead and buried?

Damian went to Jamie's room. He knocked softly. When there was no answer, he opened the door.

"Jamie?" He walked inside. The bed was neatly made, the closet...

Emptied. A note, neatly folded on the nightstand, caught his eye.

Paper crackled as he unfolded it. *Sorry, I'm bailing. Gotta find another way. I was only on this ride to grab the brass life ring.*

Betrayal, outrage and misery roared through him. He crushed the paper in his trembling fist. Jamie didn't have faith in him, any more than he had in himself right now.

But damn it, she would come back. Even if he sent every last Draicon to find her. Never, ever again would she leave him. Even if he were a worthless, useless fool. He called Rafe.

The search was on.

Damian pocketed the cell, went downstairs to get a vehicle and hunt Jamie down again. But rage and immense grief bellowed through him. He stood in the living room, threw back his head and howled. He shuddered, and shifted. In wolf form he paced back and forth. Then he howled again, shifted.

In human form, he shivered, naked and cold. Tried to clothe himself by magick. Had to go find her, bring her back.

A shoe appeared on one foot. Nothing else.

Oh *merde,* this was just like the night when he'd lost his family, when he couldn't control his powers and they were all crazy, scattering, forcing him to slow progress back to the mansion. Memories assaulted him like knives. He would not lose Jamie. He could control this.

Damian shifted back into a wolf and paced. Changed back to human. He stared at his chest. Well, at least he got the shirt right.

He kept doing it, again and again. Shifting to wolf, back to human.

Desperation clawed at him as he tried to align his powers so he could find Jamie. Eventually the pain of hunger from drained energy gnawed his insides. He closed his eyes, shifted again into wolf form. Physical pain was good. Better than the rawness eating his heart.

He continued the pacing and shape-shifting.

Jamie stepped off the streetcar and shuffled toward City Park. She shifted the backpack's weight, clutched her suitcase and headed for the museum. Just beneath a sheltering oak, she sagged to the ground.

What the hell was she doing?

Nowhere to go, nowhere to hide, to escape. Nothing would stop this. Death was charging toward her like a hurricane, only this one she couldn't escape.

She dropped her face into her hands. In the maelstrom swirling about her, there remained a steady image of calm. Flashing over and over like a neon sign.

Damian. Always he'd cared for her, protected her, cherished her. He'd opened his heart to her and shared his pain. He trusted her, even though she'd given him no reason to do so. He was the anchor in her crazy, whirling world. And she was running from him.

Dummy.

The same old pattern, running away, always fleeing a bad scene, escaping instead of standing up to her problems. Acting on impulse, judging, just as she had that night Damian killed the Morph replicating her brother. Maybe if she'd stopped, thought and asked questions instead of assuming, she wouldn't be in this mess.

Her hair-trigger reactions caused all this. Wasn't it about time to stop? If she had little time left, how did she want to spend it?

"With you, Damian," she whispered. "Every last second."

Standing, she adjusted the backpack over her opened jacket. The streetcar back to the Ursuline Street Station had already left. She'd walk, even if it took her all damn night.

As she picked up her suitcase and started out of the park, a thunderclap of motorcycle engines roared into view. Dismay filled her.

Twenty bikers, all clad in leather, heading right for her. Raphael leading the way. Jamie twisted her backpack's strap as they stopped, swung off the bikes, all but Raphael, who remained seated, the engine humming.

The bikers, including Adam and Ricky, advanced. They enclosed her, a living, breathing Draicon cage, a werewolf army in leather. Their expressions grim, they marched her to Raphael. Adam took her suitcase, lifted her and placed her on the back of Raphael's motorcycle.

Raphael turned, grabbed her chin, forcing her to look at him. His gaze was fierce, dark and cold. "Listen to me carefully, my brother's draicara. As his mate, you're under my protection. But don't you ever try hurting him again."

He gave a soft growl. "You tipped him over the edge when you left. He's very angry."

She swallowed fear as he gunned the engine. She'd been right all along. Damian's family would turn against her. Oh God, she should have kept walking, running away. At least she'd be safe and unhurt.

The werewolves escorted her back to the house like a prisoner to an execution. As they herded her into the pristine living room, Jamie shrugged out of her backpack and jacket, let them drop on the floor. She bit back a startled gasp.

A large gray wolf paced back and forth. The wolf lifted its head, sniffed the air. Looked directly at her, fangs flashing white as it growled.

She tried to shrink back, but Raphael's hand held her steady.

Fast as an eyeblink, the wolf vanished, replaced by a six-foot male. Fully clothed in trousers and a shirt. Looking at him was a bad idea. Jamie dropped her gaze.

His feet were bare.

Damian advanced. Fury boiled from him like a pressure cooker about to explode. His eyes were wild, his wide shoulders rigid as rock.

"Leave us," he ordered.

Raphael and his pack cleared the room as if someone had lit the fuse to a shoe box stuffed with C-4. Jamie hid her shaking hands. Never had she seen him this agitated.

Hands fisted, breath whistled out of his clenched teeth. Muscles locked in tension as he fought for control. It was like facing a muscled, two-hundred-pound time bomb.

"You," he grated out, "will never, ever do that again."

Twisting her hands behind her back, she dragged the words out of a mouth drier than sawdust. "I was on my way back when they found me. It wasn't you, Damian. It was me, and this habit I have, always running off without thinking. And when I stopped running, I realized I had nowhere to go. But back to the only one who's never, ever forsaken me."

He went still, nostrils flaring.

"And I don't think he ever will. Even though I've given him good reason to, time and again. But I'm scared. I don't have much time left, Damian."

"You doubt my ability to save you." He gave her a level look.

"I know you would do everything you can, just as you have, to save me," she whispered. "But even if you could, I don't know if I can take everything that comes with you. How can I ever be sure no one in your family will ever turn on me if I hurt you like I did before?"

Damian released a heavy breath. "Because if they ever dared to lay a single finger on you, they know I'd take them down. One, two, damn it, all of them if necessary. My adopted family and my pack in New Mexico. You come first, Jamie. You always will. Not them. Your happiness, your joy. You matter most to me."

Fierce loyalty to her rang through his words. No one had ever put her at such a high priority. Jamie's heart melted as she stared at him. "Oh, Damian, I'm tired of running. I don't want to be alone anymore. I want you, for whatever little time I have left."

His eyes burned bright as green lasers. He grabbed her by the shoulders, took her mouth, possessive, controlling, claiming. She slid her hands up to clutch him closer.

The low moan of assent rumbling in her throat triggered him.

"I have to get inside you. Now," he muttered into her mouth.

Still kissing her, he swept her into his arms. Taking the stairs, his long, powerful legs eating up the distance. He carried her into his bedroom, and set her down on the floorboards.

Damian stripped off his clothing. Naked, he ripped her blouse apart. Buttons snicked onto the hardwood floor. A low growl rippled in his throat as his claws emerged, and sliced through her bra. He shoved the pants down her hips, sheared off her panties.

She hit the bed and fell backward, as he rolled next to her. Damian rose up, took her nipple into his mouth and suckled her. Little, fast flicks, creating a gush between her legs. Then he reached down, his hands spreading her wide, bent his mouth to her core and licked her. Fast, furious swipes with his tongue, getting her scent on him, all over him. She writhed in ecstasy, making little animalistic sounds.

Pushing her thighs farther apart, he mounted her. His look was intense, determined.

Jamie sagged against the mattress in surrender, recognizing the humming need, the instinctual drive. The grief and anger he felt raged also in her own heart.

The head of his erection pushed at her wetness, then surged inside. He slammed into her, driving up to the hilt. Shocked at the invasion, she writhed. He was bigger, harder than ever. She felt stretched, full, Damian joining them, possessing her in the most primitive way.

"You're mine, mine," he breathed, the powerful muscles of his arms locked as he held himself over her. He thrust forward again, pulled back, thrust again, pressing her deep into the mattress. "Mine. Do you get me, *chère?*"

"Damian…"

"Answer me," he demanded, withdrawing. His slick penis hovered just outside, leaving her empty and aching.

She sobbed, clawing at his shoulders, her need great, so close, so close. "Yes, I'm yours, only yours," she cried out.

Damian gave a satisfied smile. Then he rewarded her by sliding deep into her again, and taking her mouth. His tongue stroked as she pushed her hips up at him, frantic now to come. He pulled away, licking her lips. A bead of sweat popped off his forehead, splashing onto her breast.

She reached up and bit his collarbone. He grunted and pistoned his hips harder, making the bed shake and thump. Jamie strained against him. She stared up at his eyes, dark with passion, his face hardened and intent. He commanded her body now, this big male joining them intimately. The heat of orgasm flickered just out of reach, and she wailed, needing it, wanting it.

"Yes, that's it, come, come for me," he demanded.

The words and the tender command in his husky voice clinched it. Jamie arched, her body rising off the mattress as she shattered, climaxing hard. Her nails dug into his thick muscles, scoring the skin. He threw back his head, the cords and tendons on his neck straining, and roared her name. Coming inside her with powerful spurts of his seed.

She bore his heavy weight as he collapsed onto her with a soft sigh, his head dropping to the pillow beside her. Jamie locked her trembling thighs around his hips, stroked his sweating back.

Damian rolled off her, breaking their contact. He slid an arm around her, as she curled into his shoulder, her heart rate slowing.

"You left me again." His voice was low, anguished.

Jamie stroked the damp hairs on his muscled chest. "I'm sorry. I wouldn't blame you if you wanted to leave me instead."

She dropped her head back onto his shoulder, ashamed. He raised her chin with a finger, forcing her to look at him.

"I could no sooner leave you than bite off my own arm," he gently teased.

"Coyote ugly doesn't apply to wolves?"

Damian laughed, then drew her tighter. He buried his face in her hair. "You won't die, Jamie. You can't. I won't let it happen."

They drowsed a little, then her hand slipped down his muscled thigh. His penis lay against his leg, stiffening. Damian groaned as she gently squeezed, and rolled her over onto her stomach. Jamie tensed as he settled behind her, his hands braced on her hips.

In this position she felt open, vulnerable. But she trusted him.

With reverence, he kissed her tattoo, then she felt him cover her from behind. A big, muscled warrior ready to invade her in his ancient mating tradition. He entered her hard and fast, and began thrusting in a rhythm that sent heat spiraling through her. Damian bent over her, his chest hairs scraping against her back, murmuring to her in French. He reached down between her legs and touched her.

She came apart again, crying out, squeezing him tight as he stroked inside her. He joined her, his big body shuddered as he clenched her hips.

When they lay spent and exhausted, he gave her a warm, lingering kiss. Jamie blinked, her heart beating fast to the pace of his, the breath bellowing out of her lungs slowly easing to normal. Damian wrapped her in his arms. Comforted by his strong embrace, she fell asleep.

Hours later, she woke, the room shrouded in darkness. Her senses screamed danger. Damian snapped back the covers, pulled her off the bed so hard her arm felt like it nearly detached from the socket.

And then she smelled it.

Smoke.

He swore as he jammed his legs into his pants, pulling them on commando style. Jamie grabbed a T-shirt from the drawer, pulled on her sweats and raced to the window. Below on the street were about thirty people. Not people. Morphs.

Fear made her heart race.

"They couldn't get past Rafe's safeguards, so they're flushing us out. Stay with me."

Damian hustled her out into the hallway. The door to the attic burst open, Cindy's face strained as she hustled Michael, Sophie and Sandy down the hallway. Etienne followed, Ana in his arms.

Bare-chested, Gabriel ran toward them, buckling his jeans.

"Fire's on the first floor. Damn it, they tossed a Molotov into a window and the drapes caught. We'll have to go out the back way through the windows." Gabriel herded Etienne's family across the hall toward his room.

"How did they get past our defenses?" Etienne shifted Ana in his arms.

"Someone using magick weakened the shield just enough."

Several pairs of eyes shifted to Jamie. Oh crap. Playing basketball in the house, and practicing her powers secretly in the house, dematerializing when she ran away. With all else, she'd forgotten. And her magick was far more powerful than theirs.

"Where's Rafe?" Gabriel yelled.

"Here," a calm voice answered. In black leather, his face surreally calm. "They're outside. Waiting for us."

"Saw them," Damian said grimly as they crossed the room. "Gabriel, take the children and Cindy, get them onto the Cassidys' property next door. They're away and Rafe and I safeguarded the yard just in case. The Morphs can't touch them there. Then come back, we'll need you to fight. Jamie, go with Cindy and Gabriel."

Smoke clogged her lungs as it thickened the

air. The children came first. Her magick caused this problem. And it would help now.

Gabriel already had the French doors in his bedroom opened to the balcony. Etienne was just about to climb over the railing, a bawling Ana in his arms. With his Draicon strength, he could easily jump. But with the children, he had to climb down.

Damian vaulted over the railing, landing fifteen feet below. He held up his arms, waiting. Waiting to catch her if Etienne dropped her. Damn, this was not good.

Jamie ran over to Etienne, grabbed Ana, snatched up the wailing Sophie and set them down. He shot her a furious look.

"Trust me," she said softly. She bent down to the children. "Hey, guys, remember when we played floater basketball?" When they nodded, eyes huge in their faces, she smiled. "We're going to play another game called flying. It's just like when we played basketball. I'll have you the whole time. Okay?"

Sophie nodded, gripping Ana's hand.

"That's right, hold her hand, she's scared and you're her big sister. Hold on."

Taking a deep breath, Jamie concentrated. Pain speared her temples. The children's feet rose off the balcony, and they floated, safely down, into Damian's arms. At the same time, Etienne herded Cindy to the railing, and she jumped. Damian and Cindy took the children and gently lifted them over the fence. Ran back.

Jamie held a hand to her pounding temple, feeling the pain as if someone shoved an ice pick into her head. Oh God, she couldn't do this twice. The agony was too much.

A scream snapped her attention below.

Cindy was pointing toward the side of their house, where a pack of wolves now slunk toward them. Morphs. The last magick barrier dropped, they breached the yard. Damian didn't hesitate. He grabbed Cindy about the waist, all but hurled her over the neighbor's fence. Then turned, ready to fight.

The wolves ignored him, loped over to the balcony. They waited below, their jaws open, snarling. Their eyes focused on Michael and Sandra on the balcony.

They waited for the children. Their mouths opened, showing rows of razor-sharp teeth. Saliva dripped from their jaws.

Raphael and Gabriel stared below. "We can take them, Etienne, Gabe and I and Damian."

"What if they shift again, and get up here? Stay here. I need you to protect the kids." Etienne's lips were tight, his expression grim. He had a death grip on his offspring. Ready to do anything to keep them safe.

This is what family is about, she realized. It wasn't relatives taking you in for your parents' money and making life hell or a brother who ignored you when you desperately needed attention. It was about bonding together and seeing each other through the worst, and a love so deep that a father would sacrifice all for his children.

Her eyes watered suddenly, and not from smoke.

Ignoring her throbbing temples, Jamie squeezed Etienne's shoulder. "Please, trust me. I won't let anything happen to them."

Etienne brushed a kiss against Michael's and Sandy's foreheads and released his children. "Take them," he said hoarsely.

Jamie focused and the children floated over to the neighbors' yard. The wolves howled in protest as Gabriel, Raphael and Etienne jumped to the ground, joining Damian. The four brothers shape-shifted simultaneously into wolves.

Closing her eyes, Jamie dematerialized. And reappeared in the yard next door. Her limbs felt like cooked noodles. Even now she could feel the poison seeping through her veins, the stone spell working, overpowering Damian's magick in her cells, invading and marching through her system.

Cindy herded her children away from the ugly sights and sounds of violent battle. Her body screaming in pain, Jamie staggered to a tree as the brothers took on the Morphs. It was a grotesque, awesome display of power. Damian and his brothers were vicious, savage killers. They killed to defend their family, take down evil. In minutes it was over.

Summoning her strength, she ran and opened the gate, running toward Damian. He caught her in his arms.

"I'm sorry…it's my fault… I weakened your shield."

Damian stroked her hair. "Shh. It's my fault. I shifted several times. But it's okay. We're all safe."

"It wasn't your fault the first time, either, Damian. If you had been there that night, they would have gotten you, too." Shivering, she touched his cheek. "It's time to let them all go and forgive yourself."

His eyes closed as he leaned against her palm. "I will."

Gabriel, sporting a bruise on one cheek, whipped his head about. "Where's Alex?"

"He went to Bourbon Street for the night," Etienne said, embracing Cindy and the children.

"No, he came back a half hour ago."

Worry tinged Rafe's voice. All of them froze, looked up at the house.

And set against an eerie backdrop of orange

flames at a side window, was a figure standing at the window. Alexandre.

Jamie stuffed a fist in her mouth. Damian yelled.

"Alex, jump!"

His brother made no move to open the window. Damian ran forward, but Raphael caught a fistful of his shirt.

"Too dangerous, *t' frère*. You won't get up the stairs."

"Alex…" Damian's voice was a low moan.

Anguish twisted Damian's expression as he stared at the house. His brother. Dying. The screams of the fire engines sounded down the streets. By the time they got here, it'd be too late.

He glanced at her, touched her mind and his face blanched. "Jamie, no, no…"

"Yes. I have to make up for my past crimes," she said quietly. She reached up, kissed him briefly. And vanished.

Smoke stung her eyes, filled her lungs as she materialized just by the window. Agony splintered her head. Jamie coughed violently, squinted through a gush of tears to see Alexandre whirl, his face blackened by smoke, his eyes hopeless.

"No," he choked out. "Go away, go back to Damian. I want to stay."

"You're coming with me."

"I can't." He wrenched free, his shoulders

slumped, his face haunted. "I'll die...and be free at last," he whispered. "My mate and daughter are waiting for me in the Other Realm. I can't live like this anymore. I have to be with them."

Jamie's eyes watered further. She grasped his hand, feeling pain radiate from him like a throbbing heartbeat. Lost in misery, nothing would snap him out of it. Not pity.

"You selfish bastard," she yelled. "You can only think about what you lost, and not what you'll lose? I'd have given my right arm for a family like yours who loved me like they love you, and Damian? This will shatter him. I'm not going to let you do that to him. No way."

His eyes popped open wide, as if he hadn't considered that. Alex stared.

"Alex, it's not your time," she said softly, and coughed again. Jamie threw open the window, jackhammers of pain pounding rail spikes into her temples and forehead. Her lungs burned. With her mind, she tried to lift him. His feet barely cleared the floor.

Think of Damian. Think of all he's lost, and how it will rip his heart if he loses Alexandre. Jamie concentrated on Damian, his love, courage and loyalty. She closed her eyes, saw Alexandre flying through the opened window into the arms of his family.

Family was all that mattered.

Her eyes flew open to see Alexandre's feet touch the ground next door.

She ran to the window, drew in fresh air, her eyes stinging. Took a deep breath. Jamie materialized behind a sheltering oak. And began falling, distant shouts of alarm raised. Strong arms caught her as a pit of inky darkness yawned before her.

She let herself go into the blackness.

Chapter 17

"You really shouldn't have done that."

The deep male voice sounded accusing. Jamie struggled to open eyes that felt glued shut. Her body was dead weight, arms and legs felt as if lead pumped through her veins. She tried to raise her head, but it took too much effort.

She sagged backward, surprised at the softness beneath her. Bed. She was lying with a pillow under her head. Vaguely she remembered waking up, Damian wiping soot from her face, Damian taking her into the shower and washing her tenderly.

Damian laying her in bed as she fainted again.

"I'm sorry. I'm really— God you have no idea how sorry I am."

With tremendous effort, she opened her eyes. Damian stood by her bed, hands on hips, legs splayed apart. Alexandre faced him. Two vivid blue eyes stared out of a face still blackened with smoke, making him look almost comical, if not for the misery etched there.

Damian hugged his brother. Alexandre looked as if he fought off tears. He pulled back.

"Dai, there has to be an answer, some other way. Your father wouldn't have just left it there to be buried…. We can save her, I have to believe that…."

"It'll be okay. Go on, clean up. You look like something the *caimon* dragged through the bayou." He clapped a hand on his shoulder.

Jamie watched Alexandre leave. Damian turned. "Ah, good, you're awake." The bed sagged beneath his weight. He stroked her forehead. "Better now? No more *faiblesse*? Fainting?"

"I won't faint again. Promise."

"That's my girl," he said softly, leaning down to brush his lips against hers.

"What happened?"

"We're at your house. Everyone's staying here but Etienne, Cindy and the kids. They returned to Paw Paw's."

He kissed her again. Damian stroked his tongue along her bottom lip, nipped playfully.

But his actions contrasted sharply to the weighty sorrow leaking from him like invisible tears.

She reached up, struggling with all her might to cup his face. Damian closed his eyes, turned toward her touch, taking her hands and kissing them.

"No regrets, *mon amour*. None. I needed to do what I did. I don't want to have my life end with regrets," she told him.

Something dark and fierce flashed in his green eyes. "You're not going to die. We'll find another way."

Sadness pulled her, but she managed a smile. "Can you ask Raphael to come here for me? I need to talk with him."

He touched her hand. "Anything." Then he looked down and his eyes widened. Shock.

Jamie glanced down and cried out. "Oh God, my hands!"

Her fingers were stiff, unable to bend, hard as rock.

"It's spreading, fast." Damian drew her into his arms. "We have to find a way, we won't give up."

"I won't," she whispered back.

But she suspected it was already too late.

She dozed lightly, feeling the strong, solid body beside her. Damian lay on her bed in wolf form. He told her before shifting he could guard her better this way. Head between paws, he eyed the door. When it did open, Damian lifted his muzzle, growled.

"Easy," Raphael soothed. He held up his hands. "It's me, *t' frère*. Just wanted to visit your Jamie here. Can you give us a minute?"

Her head felt like her brains were sloshing as she struggled to sit. Grayness covered her arms. How much time did she have?

"Damian, remember? I asked him to come."

He whined a little, licked her stone hand. With a baleful look for Raphael, he jumped off the bed and trotted out the door. In the hallway he paused, growled deep at his brother, then loped off.

Raphael shut the door, leaned against it. Jamie fell on the bed, her hands useless and unfeeling. "He's hurting, badly. I can feel his pain."

"I know."

The Kallan's voice was almost gentle. He sat on her bed. "What do you want, little sister?"

Sister, family. Courage filled her. "You're the Kallan, the Draicon who can kill another without any consequence or retribution. I ask you a favor now." Her gaze met his. "I want you to end it for me now."

No emotion shone in those dark eyes, smooth and ageless as the bayou.

"Soon, before I can't talk. Before I fully turn to stone."

"Why?" Raphael asked quietly.

Jamie struggled to speak. "I saw, when you examined me. I know what awaits."

He remained silent.

"It scares me...but I think I can deal. No choice, right?" She gave a nervous laugh. "What I can't deal with is having him see me, like that. Alive but dead. Not moving, not able to speak. It will tear him apart. Worse than death. I'll suffer, but for him it will be...agony."

She waited, breath heaving in little ragged strips. Staring at his dagger, wondering if he'd do it. End it all now. Spare his brother.

"How much do you love him, little sister?"

The answer came without hesitation. "More than my own life."

Raphael locked gazes with hers. Gone was the watchful suspicion. Respect replaced it. *"Lâche pas la patate, chère,"* he murmured.

As she cocked her head at him, he added, "It's an old Cajun expression. It means don't give up. So don't you. You never know."

"Know what?"

"When little miracles can happen," he said softly. Then he grabbed her face, pulled her forward and kissed her hard.

It felt like kissing a hot blast of air, suctioning off her oxygen. Not arousing in the slightest, just shocking, fusing contact. Speechless, Jamie struggled, whimpering for breath. Raphael released her just as quickly.

A volley of loud French followed, words sounding like curses. Damian stood in the doorway in human form, his glare triggered at Raphael. He bunched his fists.

"I did it just to piss you off so you'd stop moping," Raphael told his brother. "Don't worry, I'm out of your hair. Taking Gabe and Alex to Bourbon. Alex needs a drink."

He angled a dark smile at Jamie as he left the bedroom. "Later, little sister."

Damian growled at him, went to Jamie and pulled her against him, his lips fused to hers. A kiss of ownership and claiming, eradicating thought, reason. The wolf marking his territory. She rested her cheek against his palm.

"How much time do I have left?" Her voice sound like gravel to her ears.

His fingers trailed over her cheek. "Not sure. A few days maybe, if you don't use any more magick." He raised his head, looking bleak, lost. "My magick…won't help anymore."

"Take me downstairs, Damian. I want to feel the sun against my face. Before I can't feel anymore."

Lifting her gently, he carried her to the courtyard, placed her in the comfortable chaise longue. Damian's hand shook as he caressed her cheek.

Then he seemed to gather his strength. "There has to be a way. Father wouldn't leave the book where it might be buried."

"Not without telling someone else." A burst of strength filled her as she sat up. It all fit. "Damian, the clue, the *Natchez*...planted after your father's death. There must be another wolf painting. There has to be. Why would someone plant a new clue if the book was buried under concrete? Maybe that person rescued it."

"And the painting we found was a diversion." He stood up, jamming a hand through his hair, wild excitement dawning in his eyes. "Another wolf painting. I think I know, *Dieu,* I hope it's so. I'm going for a walk by the square."

Jackson Square was bustling with tourists, carriages and artists. Damian raced through the crowds, his heart beating wildly. The artist, surely he was still here...had to be....

"The *loup garou* will never *fais do-do* in the bayou, *mon frère.*"

He whirled. The same artist who'd said the very same thing his first day back. Damian's heart beat faster. He took a hard look at the painting.

The wolf, by a cabin in the bayou. A proud

gray wolf with Alpha markings like his own, jade eyes… His father.

Damian dragged in a deep breath, forcing himself to remember a childhood he'd tried hard to forget. Good times, laughter, friends gathering around, distant kin…French accents. His father's friend, who painted beautiful pictures.

The artist slowly turned, removed his sunglasses. His eyes showed no movement. Damian leaned closer.

"*Mon Dieu.* Jordan?" He grasped the man's upper arms very gently. "*C'est vrai,* you didn't die. *C'est moi.* Damian, Damian Marcel. Andre's oldest."

The man shook with emotion, hugged him. Damian kissed both his cheeks and stared at the man closest to his own father. "What happened to your eyes?"

"Morphs blinded me," Jordan said brokenly. "I was the only one who survived their attack. I had to survive, to keep the secret safe for you. The other pack members had told me you were dead. I refused to believe them. I looked everywhere for you, and couldn't find you. But I never gave up hope."

"The pack drove me away that day to the bayou to die. They banished me. You weren't there." Damian stated a fact, no accusation in his tone.

Jordan put a hand to his face. "I'm sorry. Your father charged me to get the Book of Magick if anything should ever happen to him, and keep it safe for you. I was in town doing that and thought you were safe with the pack."

"First Renee, and now you, alive. *Mon Dieu.*"

"Renee is alive?"

Damian clenched his jaw. "Was. She had disguised her scent all these years and remained in hiding. But the Morphs killed her recently, because she knew about the antique shop, the first clue to finding the book."

"Oh." The Draicon looked visibly shaken. "So much horror and sadness after the Morphs attacked. But I never lost hope you were alive somehow. You, of the whole pack, had to survive. You are strong and your father's son. I waited and waited, not trusting anyone. The Morphs learned to cloak scents and I did not dare trust even your scent alone. I kept asking strangers whose scent seemed familiar. I kept hoping you would return and recognize the painting and remember the words your father always said to you."

"The wolf will never sleep in the bayou, my brother," Damian repeated, then he smiled. "The one who works hard never sleeps. Father always told me that."

Emotion welled up in his throat. He glanced at the painting. "It's in the bayou, *non?*"

"Not exactly." Jordan got to his feet. "We need somewhere safe. Take me there. Now."

Jamie couldn't bring herself to hope as Damian introduced her to his father's friend and set the painting on the nearby table. She watched as Jordan stepped back.

"Touch it, *mon frère*. Touch the painting and say the words," Jordan told him.

Damian closed his eyes, laid a hand on the painting and said the ancient words in the Draicon tongue his father taught him long ago. Iridescent sparks filled the air as the rough surface of the oil painting shifted, turning to...

Red leather. A thick volume, bigger than the New York City phone book. The Book of Magick.

Jamie gasped with wonder. Awe and respect etched Damian's face as he read the contents, flipped through the pages. He frowned.

"I see the heading for the spell, but there's no text below it."

A horrible suspicion came to her. "It's an evil spell and requires either darkness or lack of emotions to decipher the words. Bring it to me. I can read it."

He laid the book very gently in her lap. Jamie blinked, hard.

The dark Morph magick still inside her enabled her to see what Damian could not. Her blood froze. Shock filled her.

"What is it? Tell me so we can heal you."

His expression was desperate. Love poured through her, chasing away a little of the fear. Love. She loved him. And now it was too late.

"We're going to need Raphael and his dagger."

"The sacred Scian?"

For the goodbye ritual. Jamie nodded, and summoned all her strength to seize his wrist. "Kiss me," she whispered.

He replaced the book on the table, and obliged her, his mouth warm and trembling. Jordan hovered in the background, looking thoughtful.

Someone knocked at the gate. Damian went to open it.

"Hey, man, Rafe sent us, said you needed help with something. Is Jamie okay?"

Adam and Ricky walked into the courtyard. Jordan whipped his head around, a snarl curving his upper lip. The Draicon with his well-developed sense of smell scented what Damian could not. What Jamie finally could detect.

The very faint stench of rotting garbage and sewage.

Her heart pounded with fear. "No," she whispered.

The darkness inside her fully opened her eyes

to see his true form just as Adam whirled a dagger out of his back pocket and stabbed Jordan in the chest.

He moved so fast Damian became a blur. He stood before Jamie, hands splayed out behind him, muscled body tensed for fighting. She struggled to get up. Her arms were dead weights, her legs, as well, hard as granite.

She flopped back helplessly, imprisoned by her body and the poison seeping through her veins.

Damian's hand drifted down to his back jeans pocket. He withdrew his phone, his fingers gliding over the buttons as he flipped it open. It lit up as he pressed one. Then he slid it back.

The special number to call in the cavalry.

Adam grinned, flipped the dagger up, catching it by the hilt. He rolled aside Jordan's body.

"Ricky," Damian said in a low voice. "You know what to do. You failed her in the alley, but Jamie needs your help now. Attack him."

"Oh, he won't listen to you. He only obeys me." Adam flicked the flat of the blade at the biker. "Heel, Ricky."

The other Draicon came forward obediently.

"Change," Adam demanded.

Before her horrified gaze, Ricky's face bulged, expanded. Shifted, his body contorting. Ricky vanished. In his place was an exact duplicate of...

Adam.

Oh merciful heaven. Jamie's heart raced with panic.

The original Adam flipped the dagger.

"Did you know that killing a relative gains you power, but killing your own mother makes you practically invincible? You can create clones without draining energy. Human clones, not just animals. Human clones that can look different, kill for you, giving the energy of the kill back to you, their host."

He laughed. "It's the greatest. I could be in eight different places all at once."

His satisfied purr sounded like metal grating against a chalkboard as he walked to the table, ran the dagger's point over the Book of Magick.

"Thanks for finding it for me. Knew you'd find it eventually. I programmed all your moves into the computer. My mother tried to stop me. So I killed her. Poor Renee."

Oh God, Renee's son. "Maurice died in a car crash," Jamie cried out.

"That's what she told everyone. I changed my name and Renee kept me hidden. Needed the cover, see? Poor *maman*. Lost her husband and then her son, when Claude tried murdering you as a baby, Damian. He knew, like I did, just how dangerous you'd be. So when you finally shifted into wolf for the first time, I knew I had to act and kill you and your family."

His smile was a pit of darkness. "I liked their fear—it was very energizing. Especially Annie's. She was so very afraid."

Damian went very still. Waves of fury and sorrow slammed into Jamie, but he looked perfectly in control.

"Renee couldn't bear to part with another son. It was a good arrangement. I'd hunt at night and return to her place by day to hide. Then you came to the shop, you bitch. She told me she couldn't live like that anymore. She'd seen what goodness shining out of darkness was and that was you. She saw nothing in me but blackness. She threatened to expose me."

Adam's smile went dead, like his eyes. "Couldn't have that. I killed her and shapeshifted one of my clones into a black cat like Archimedes. Chased the real Archimedes into the street and waited to see who would show up at the shop. You have a soft spot for animals, Damian, and I needed a spy in Jamie's house. I didn't count on the real Archimedes finding a way into Jamie's house, and you killing my clone when you realized it was a Morph."

He flipped the knife up again. "And now that

I have the book, no one can stop me. I have the greatest power of all."

"You'll never know the greatest power of all, you bastard." Damian's nostrils flared as he clenched his fists. In a flash he shifted into wolf.

Adam snapped an order. Ricky shifted into a black wolf, charged Damian. Damian side-stepped, roared with outrage and the pain of betrayal. When he turned, Adam had morphed into a wolf, all teeth and claws. Damian rushed forward.

Horror shot through her as Adam suddenly divided, again. And again. Now there were five black wolves all charging at Damian.

Two went for his throat, their teeth sinking into Damian's neck. Three others launched onto his hindquarters, trying to bring him down. Blood splashed as Damian growled, trying to shake off the ones at his throat. He wrenched free, teeth snapping and scoring a gash in the other wolf. But the three on his hindquarters were slowly bringing him down.

Damian didn't stand a chance.

Jamie summoned the last of her strength, all her love, and concentrated. She hurled stones from the garden at the wolves. Startled, they drew back, loosening their grip on Damian. Then she lifted the two charging wolves, hurled them backward like rag dolls. They hit the brick

wall with such force they slid down unconscious. Freed from the immediate threat, Damian
whirled, charged the closest of the three.

A loud snarling split the air. Her gaze whipped
to the open doorway. Three large gray wolves
entered the courtyard. Relief filled her. Damian's
brothers joined the fight. It was soon over, and
Adam and his clones were dead.

Damian and his brothers shape-shifted back,
clothed themselves. Raphael went over to Jordan,
checked his pulse. "He's alive. Just missed the
heart. He'll be fine. Help me get him upstairs."

Gabriel and Alexandre helped the older Draicon sit. Jordan looked pale, blood staining his
shirt. Jordan turned his head as if scenting her.

"I'm sorry, but I couldn't help. I can't fight
well enough anymore. I scented Morph as soon
as they entered, and should have warned you."

The Draicon seemed ashamed.

"You did well. Thank you for bringing the
book here," Damian said gently.

Jamie tracked them as they helped Jordan into
the house.

Damian enveloped her in his arms. "It's all
over now," he whispered, holding her. "Everything will be all right now, *chère*."

He drew back, running his thumb along her
lower lip. "You're so cold. It's accelerating too

fast. Tell me now. How can we counteract the spell?"

It felt as if her lungs were filling with concrete. Jamie dragged in a breath, finding it hard to draw in air. The spell was working on her internal organs now, speeding through her body. Soon she'd be fully immobilized.

Raphael, Gabriel and Alexandre returned, gathered around the book.

She went to raise her hand to touch him, but it remained at her side. "Damian, lay me on the ground. Please, it's easier for what you must do."

When he did so, she bit back a sob. Wishing she could touch him, feel his skin against hers one last time. "Kiss me," she whispered hoarsely.

His mouth was soft, warm against her icy lips. She savored him, closing her eyes. One last time.

When he drew away, a frown creased his forehead. "Tell me what I must do to free you. What did the spell say?"

"There is no cure." Jamie gasped for breath. "Only in the b-beginning stages. It's too late. There's nothing you can do except let me go so I can die."

Chapter 18

Damian stared at Jamie lying supine on the ground. Her pallor was gray. Even the whites of her eyes had taken on a shade of dull slate. Her soft lips were turning to granite.

Raphael, Gabriel and Alexandre gathered around him.

Unbearable pain shot through him. "I love you. I can't let you go."

"You must!" Jamie spat out the words with difficulty. "You must. It's...the only way to r-release my spirit...from the spell. The ritual of departure."

Her anguished gaze met his. "Please."

Damian closed his eyes in an agony of indecision for the first time in his life. How could he bear to lose her?

"You're...losing me already," she whispered. "Please. Don't let me...go...like this. I'd rather be dead."

He saw into her thoughts. Didn't want to leave him mourning. Numb and forever grieving. Having her nearby, a stone statue he silently worshipped. Wasting his life, abandoning his pack, searching for miracles to bring her back to life in his arms. His memories of Jamie haunting him until he turned into something as corporeal as her spirit. Trapped forever, locked with her eternally wanting what he couldn't have. Never to stroke her face, feel her lips against his, slide his palm into hers, argue with her about spinach with his steak. Not even existing.

She loved him and wanted him to be free.

Just as his releasing her spirit would set her free.

Damian clutched her hand, his palm sweaty. "Don't do this. Jamie, please, hold on. Please, don't leave. Don't."

Pain flashed in her gray eyes. They glazed over as if life leaked out already. No, she had to hang on, stay with it. Damian glanced at Raphael in desperate hope. His brother's face was expressionless. Then he looked away.

Horror sliced through Damian. He gathered

her in his arms, cradling her tight. Maybe if he held her like this, giving her his enormous strength, his magick, she'd live. Had to live, he couldn't lose her. Not Jamie.

A small, faint sigh sounded against his chest as he stroked her hair. Gently, he lowered her back, afraid he hurt her.

But the resignation in her eyes sliced him apart more.

"I...love you," she choked out. "Please...let me g-go, Damian. Please."

The hollow feeling in his chest amplified. *Don't let her die. I'll do anything. Take my powers, my magick, please. Anything.*

Jamie was making little gasping noises now, like a fish desperately trying to suck in oxygen. Sorrow filled Raphael's gaze.

"Do something, please," Damian begged his brother. He'd never pleaded before. Too proud. Too stubborn.

Now, too desperate.

"*Laissez-faire.* Let her go, *t' frère*," Raphael said quietly. "It's time. Do it. You have to let her go if you ever want her back."

The ritual for releasing a loved one into the afterlife. He must. Had to ensure her spirit would move on, find rest and not be locked inside a body of stone. His love would be a tiny beacon, leading him back to her when his life winked out.

His voice cracking, he recited the sacred, ancient words. *May your journey to the Other Realm be swift, your joy eternal, your spirit free. Forever will you dwell in peace. My love for you is eternal, and I keep you in my heart all my days. Until we meet in another time and place.*

Damian tore open his shirt. His brother withdrew the sacred dagger at his waist and handed it to him. The slash across his palm was clean, pain he barely felt. Blood welled up. The cut across his chest was deeper, a burn he welcomed. He placed his bleeding right hand over the laceration on his chest.

"My heart guards your memory, which will live forever inside me. My hands guard your honor, and will always serve and protect in courage and strength in remembrance of my love for you," he whispered in the Old Language.

His throat closed up, feeling like battery acid splashed over his esophagus. Damian bent over, kissed each of her cheeks. Then finally, her cold, rock-hard mouth.

"I love you," he whispered against her lips. "I'll love you forever. Wait for me on the other side. Someday, somehow we'll be together again. But I have to stay here, and go on. I'm letting you go, Jamie. You're free now, my love."

Jamie began making little sounds of distress as he sat back. "I—I love you, Damian. I'm s-sorry

I couldn't tell you...before. I love y—" Her lips stopped moving, frozen into stone.

"Goodbye, little sister," Rafe said softly, leaning over her.

Rafe kissed her. He shuddered, his chest expanded, his eyes fogging over. Something flashed, like a tremendous burst of energy. Rafe sagged back on his haunches, his gaze distant and unfocused.

Damian saw her chest rise a little. Hope soared like a bird struggling to take wing. Had to work, had to, she couldn't die, just couldn't...

With a tiny exhalation, she went, like a small candle sputtering out. Her eyes, her body.

Stone-cold.

"No," Damian whispered. "You left me."

"Her spirit is safe. She's not locked inside her body any longer," Rafe told him quietly.

From her parted lips, a black cloud suddenly whooshed into the air as the last of the evil Morph magick fled her body. The scent of rotting evil stamped the air. They all winced, turned away.

"Jamie." His whisper grated in his ears like steel wool. Damian stared at his beloved.

This was it. So damn still. So quiet.

He wanted to scream at everything to stop, to grind down, to end. Jamie was dead.

Life ended at this moment. He saw his damned

existence stretching out like train tracks. Breathing but not living. Seeing, but not feeling. The agony in his heart turning to stone, hardening him like granite. Nothing but pain and then finally nothing at all, numb years of living, hunting, breathing, for fifty years, a hundred, a hundred more.

A walking ghost. Waiting, waiting, craving the peace and release of death so he could once more hear her laugh, touch her smile, taste her joy.

Voices murmured, an indistinguishable blur of sound. Wind caressed his hair. Something ran down his cheek. He touched it, brought it to his mouth.

Salty. His tears were salty.

Hers had been sweet.

Damian threw his head back and screamed. He sobbed, tears dripping upon Jamie's granite form. Nothing but an empty shell. His shirt clung to his chest in damp folds.

Had to kiss her again, one last time. Damian pressed his mouth to her icy lips. Raphael made a sound, turned away. Alexandre stomped off. Gabriel squeezed his shoulder silently.

But something wasn't right. Damian stared at Jamie. Blotches of color returned to her body. An effect of death? A tear rolled down his cheek, splashed onto hers.

Leaving on Jamie's cheek a bright spot of fleshy pink. Erasing the stone.

Understanding flashed through him. Damian looked wildly at his brothers. "The spell, *mon Dieu*. Tears. Salt water wears away rock. All those times she cried, I thought it was my magick beating back the spell, but it was tears. Damn it, get buckets of water, salt! Hurry!"

Minutes later, a large container of salt was dumped into buckets of water. They began splashing them over Jamie. Damian's heart beat double time as he gauged her body, the stone melting away from her flesh like layers of watercolor paint erased by rain.

It had to work. It had to restore her, bring her back.

When the last bucket had been poured over her body, Jamie lay on the ground, her body as rosy and seemingly alive as she had been when he'd first met her. First caught her gaze across the crowded bar, and the contact between them sizzled.

He leaned closer, pressed his mouth to hers. And met ice-cold flesh.

No longer stone, but dead. Gone, forever.

Raphael opened her blouse, cut a small pattern over her heart. He slashed his wrist, dripped four drops of his blood into the wound. He licked his wrist, leaned forward. His brother heaved a giant breath and then fused his mouth to Jamie's as if giving her CPR.

"Holy... Look, Damian." Gabriel pointed. "Just look. My God."

Jamie's chest rose half an inch. Fell. The wound in her chest healed as her chest rose again. Raphael tore away from her body. He looked gray, spent. Drained.

Shock slammed into Damian as if someone had bagged him with a pillowcase of bricks. His gaze whipped to Jamie. Her chest rose and fell in a regular rhythm. He didn't dare hope, couldn't think...

A loud gasp filled the air as she opened her mouth and took a breath.

Her eyes, her beautiful ice-gray eyes, flew open. They looked unfocused. Then they blinked and softened as her gaze landed on him. "Damian. Oh, Damian, you're here."

Hoarse and raspy, her voice was sweeter than the purest angel's. Damian took her hand, his heart pounding so hard it felt as if it would leave his chest.

"Please, tell me this isn't a dream," he said thickly.

"Don't push her. Give her a minute," Rafe rasped. "She needs it."

Damian gathered Jamie into his arms, cradling her against him, feeling the solid, steady beat of her heart against his. He buried his face in her hair, rubbed the silky strands against his wet cheeks. He stared at Rafe.

"You gave her your blood. Your magick."

Gabriel's jaw unhinged. "You can't, Rafe. It's forbidden unless it's for your mate. It goes against…"

"Our laws. Yeah, well, I guess my ass is in trouble." Raphael gave a grim smile.

No words would suffice. Damian looked at him steadily, knowing his feelings sang out on his face. Knowing his brother didn't need words.

The silent thank-you hovered in the air.

Gabriel went to the Book of Magick, thumbed through the pages and squinted. "It's hard to read, but it says the spell can be broken only in the beginning stages and life restored to fullness with salt water. Tears shed too late, the body returns to flesh, but the spirit is lost forever unless the ritual of departing is granted by a loved one, releasing the spirit to the Other Realm."

"Tears melt the heart of stone. And love restores a spirit lost," Rafe said quietly.

"The parting ritual… I had to release her and prove my love for her," Damian realized.

"Just as Jamie proved her love by not wanting to see you suffer. That kiss I gave Jamie before, it forged a connection. And just now, before she went, I took her spirit into me." Rafe dragged in another deep breath. "I kept her safe for you. Until the last of the dark Morph magick fled her body."

"You're immortal. You could harbor another spirit inside you."

"Not without consequence." Rafe finally straightened, his color a little better. "And I hate to see what hell there is to pay. Worth it. I couldn't see you going through what Alex did. It just wasn't in your destiny. She's supposed to be with you."

Damian couldn't fathom the sacrifice his brother had made for him.

"As Kallan, I'm permitted it just once, only to save my draicara. But you had to love her enough to let her go. The greatest love of all." Raphael's gaze landed on Alex, who hovered nearby with a look of anguish. "She came back to you because she's yours. I was just the conduit."

Damian kissed Jamie. Her lips were soft, warm. He poured his heart and soul, his life, into the kiss.

When he raised his head, his wondering gaze landed on Alex. His older brother fisted his hands. Something shimmered in his blue eyes.

"Cherish her, *t'frère*. Never let go. Ever." Alex's voice was rough and low, his smile forced.

Pivoting on his heels, he jammed his hands into his pockets and walked away. Raphael's expression sobered as he trailed him. Damian cuddled Jamie close, relishing the sound of her breathing as she reached up to touch his face.

A sickening dread speared him as he glanced at Rafe. "Rafe, your draicara, your one chance to save her…what if…"

The Draicon sighed. "I doubt I'll ever find my mate. It's cool. I couldn't let you suffer while I search for the one meant for me."

But his gaze whipped over to Alex, who hung back, looking anguished.

"Then why me? Why not Alex?" Damian asked quietly.

His brother closed his eyes, flesh tightening over his taut jaw. "I offered. But like I said, it's a one-shot deal. He had to choose between Simone and Amelia. Save the mother, or the child. He couldn't. So he let them both go."

Opening her eyes to life and seeing Damian had been a miracle to Jamie. He'd sacrificed so much for her, but most of all, he'd sacrificed his heart. In doing so, he saved more than her life. He'd restored her spirit and her hope. Never before had anyone risked so much for her, and loved her for who she was.

But it was Raphael who had given back her life, and she'd learned the price he'd paid. Damian's brother, his family. Where her family had only taken away, Damian's family had given. Raphael had accepted her thanks with a very French shrug, hands shoved deep into his jeans pockets. The warmth in his eyes as he regarded them said more than words.

Now, resting in bed, she drowsed in Damian's arms. Alexandre came inside and greeted them.

His smile seemed a little sad. "Seeing Damian lose you felt like losing my beloved all over. I'm glad you were spared."

Though sorrow still shimmered in his eyes, there was also peace. Alexandre was slowly healing.

Alex told them Raphael had already made changes. He'd handed over leadership to Etienne and had given Jordan a new position in his pack. With Jordan's ability to scent Morphs, the blind Draicon would act as a screening device. The hunt for Morphs in the city just became easier.

After Alex left, Damian asked her if there was anything she needed. She whispered her request into his ear.

They waited two days for her to rest and regain full strength. Now they were all waiting downstairs for her. Heart thrumming with nervous excitement, Jamie entered the courtyard, wearing a peacock-green dress and clutching the violets Celine had hand-picked from her greenhouse. An

emerald-green ribbon swept her black hair from
her face.

His family crowded the courtyard. His brothers, including Etienne, Cindy and the children,
his adopted parents–they'd even brought Paw
Paw, who'd insisted on making the arduous trip.
Joy filled her heart. Her family now. But her gaze
riveted to Damian. Breath fled her in an awed
gasp. The dark Armani suit, white shirt with
French cuffs, heavy gold links and polished shoes
reflected the urbane and sophisticated male, but
nothing outshone the love for her reflected in his
jade-green eyes.

Damian spread out his hands, smiling at her.
"Your wish is my command. You wanted to mate
me, I am yours."

It was a simple, poignant ceremony. Damian
couldn't stop touching her, marveling at Jamie
and the rare gift he'd been granted. He could
stare at her for eternity and never grow tired of
seeing Jamie happy.

As the highest-ranking Draicon, Raphael performed the ceremony, uttering words in the Old
Language. Then he withdrew his sacred Scian.
Damian removed his jacket, unfastened his right
cuff link and rolled up his sleeve. Her eyes grew
wide at the sight of the blade.

"It's okay," he reassured her quietly. "Give
Rafe your right hand. Palm up."

His heart turned over at the absolute trust shining on her face. She handed his mother her bouquet. The cut across Jamie's lower palm was swift. She looked a little pale. Damian held out his right hand. Blood welled up from the burning cut Raphael delivered. Gabriel came forward with a white ribbon and a clean white cloth in a small velvet box. Raphael wiped the blade with the cloth, sheathed it. He took their right hands, pressed them together so their blood freely flowed into each other. He tied their hands loosely with a white ribbon.

"Two halves once lost now become one flesh, one heart, one blood made whole again."

Damian's fingers laced through hers. She beamed at him.

Raphael rested his hands on their shoulders. "Go and seal in the flesh the bond which has been created in the blood and the heart."

He stepped back, a wide smile on his face as everyone cheered. A radiant flush raced across Jamie's face as Damian led her into the house. She looked confused as he climbed past her apartment.

"It's a surprise," he murmured. "I had everyone decorate."

The door to the third-floor apartment was open. He led her down the hallway to the master bedroom and opened the door.

Jamie's gasp of shocked wonder made him laugh.

Sky-blue fabric hung from the walls and windows. On the ceiling was a relief of the night sky, with a backdrop of stars. The king-size oak bed was simple and covered with an electric-blue quilt, turned down. A simple oak desk was against the wall.

Dusky light leaked through the white shutters. A light scent of honeysuckle perfumed the air. Jamie, all Jamie, her soft skin, glowing smile and the flush on her cheeks. Alive, free. His, forever. He untied the binding about their wrists, and pulled it free. Damian lifted her palm, tenderly licked her wound closed. Desire burned in her gaze as he pulled the ribbon from her hair, setting the glossy strands free. The thin silk fluttered to the floor.

He wanted to cherish her, wrap her inside himself and never let go.

"There's only one thing missing," he said softly. "Light."

Stretching out his hand, he created a glowing sphere. It danced on the air, shimmering with magick. Jamie cried out, her expression filled with wonder.

The orb floated toward her, and settled on her outstretched palm. She gave a musical laugh and bounced it like a child's red rubber ball. Then she flung it upward. It hovered against the ceiling, illuminating the burst of stars painted there.

"I'm free," she whispered. "Really, truly free. Oh, Damian, thank you. I love you so much."

Her kiss was warm, welcoming. It felt like coming home. He cradled her head in his hands and drew her closer.

Jamie felt the raw emotion in his trembling lips, the untamed need for sex layered with tenderness and awe. He kissed her mouth, his lips then trailing over her chin and neck as she clung to him, giving back everything he gave. Then the intensity took over, the kisses frantic with passion.

They tore off each other's clothing, kissing as they worked their way toward the bed. His skin was warm velvet over layers of powerful muscle, his body hard against her softness. He grazed his mouth over her neck, tasting her, then nipping her lobe. Her hands grasped his taut ass, urging him closer.

She burned for him, her emotions cranking up to an urgent cry to mate, to be one. His mouth blazed down her sensitive skin, then settled on one nipple. Gently he suckled. Jamie gripped the heavy muscles of his shoulders, her head flung back as he stroked with his tongue. Wetness gushed between her thighs.

When they spilled onto the bed, she fell back onto the pillows, her arms stretched open in invitation. Damian mounted her, settling between her opened legs. She felt his thick hardness press against her soft, wet core as he braced himself on his hands on either side of her head. Her pulse quickened with anticipation and yearning. Emotion shone in his green eyes.

"I love you so much. I never want to lose you again, *mon amour*. You are my very life, the air I breathe, the spark in my soul that will never die," he said softly.

She cupped his cheek, watching his eyes close as he savored her touch. "You are my heart. I will never leave and will follow wherever you may go. And when the time comes for us to part again, I will wait for you."

Something warm and wet dripped onto her breast. A single lone tear fell from his eye. She reached up, kissed away another hovering on his jaw.

"Make me yours, Damian. Make us one so nothing will ever part us again," she whispered.

Then he thrust into her, deep.

He was so big he stretched her full. Jamie bent her legs and tilted her hips up to take him, feeling his thick penis penetrate, joining them intimately. She threw her head back and moaned at the sensations, the softness of his chest hair against her flushed skin, the delicious male scent of Damian and musk invading her, his low, sultry murmurs in French. Her nipples felt hard as pearls as he brushed against them.

Jamie wrapped her legs around his waist and pulled him closer. He began hammering his hips, his shoulders moving with fluid strength, his hoarse cries equaling her tiny whimpers of excitement.

She let go, convulsing around him, screaming as she cleaved to him, hearing him cry her name. He threw back his head, tendons and veins bulging, his big body shuddering. The hot wash of his seed spurted inside her as he climaxed.

Barely had she come back down with a blissful sigh when she felt it.

Like a tap switched, all emotion poured out of her like running water, an incredible draining feeling as if she had again died. With it came a blast of heat and strength and an overwhelming feeling of being wrapped in pure love. Sucked into a whirling vortex, emptying everything she was, replacing it with Damian.

Iridescent sparks showered them, bursts of light so brilliant her eyes teared.

"What's happening?" Her anchor, she gripped his biceps, feeling his penis widen and impossibly thicken inside her. Feeling herself replaced by Damian's thoughts, emotions.

Damian raised himself on his elbows, stared down solemnly at her. "The mating lock. Just let it happen, it's okay, *mon amour*."

Then he wrapped her in his arms, rolled over, letting her rest atop his body. She dropped her head on his chest, trusting absolutely. Wondering awe spilled through her as tears dripped down her cheeks. All of Damian, his past, hope and present, and then a surge of heavy masculine power. She felt his magick churning through her body, pushing into her veins, the thrill of becoming wolf, the excitement of the hunt, the heavy, weighty duty of leadership and the quiet pride.

Jamie wept as she absorbed each emotion, each hurt and each joy of his, her tears splashing onto his chest. He stroked her hair gently, murmured assurances. Damian pulled her down and rubbed his own wet cheek against hers, their tears mingling.

Minutes later, the sparks of light faded. The ball of magick hovering against the ceiling winked out, leaving them draped in darkness. Damian ran a hand through her hair.

"I'm fine." She raised herself up to stare at him, realizing she'd answered the question he'd asked telepathically. "And I feel alive. It's weird, I'm still me, but inside me is part of you, like you're there in the background, not interfering, just reassuring like you're stroking me from the inside. It feels wonderful."

"I only feel an absurd urge to play World of Warcraft. While eating pesto."

Jamie punched his arm lightly as he grinned. "Does this mean I'll turn into a wolf?"

"Only if you wish it. You have the ability, but I would never force you."

"I want it, Damian. I want to share everything with you, your family. I feel like this is finally who I'm meant to become."

He rolled over, slowly withdrawing, leaving her body feeling empty. But deep inside she felt his spirit and knew she'd never be alone again.

Damian stroked her face, his fingers lingering over her damp cheeks. "*Ma petite,* I want to take you home to New Mexico. Our home. Our pack. It's time. They need you, what you can bring to them, just as you brought it to me."

"Text messaging?" she teased.

"Hope, and joy again," he said solemnly. "Will you go with me?"

Doubts tugged her. Last time she'd seen his pack, they were shocked she'd tried to kill their leader. Maggie, the pack's empath, and Nicolas, Maggie's mate, who had healed Damian after Nicolas inherited Maggie's abilities, had been kind. But the others might not be as friendly. "I doubt they'll welcome me with open arms. Fangs, yes. Arms, no."

"Maggie and Nicolas will be there. They know how important you are to me, and to all of them. Don't worry. They'll learn to love you, and obey you as they do me."

Obey. The idea sounded tantalizing. "Such as me ordering them to eat greens instead of meat all the time? Okay, I'll go."

A heavy sigh, followed by his deep chuckle, followed. "You'll see. Maybe you can even convince me."

"I don't need to convince you." She leaned down, splaying a hand over his perspiring chest. "Because I don't want to change you one little bit. You're just exactly as I need you."

As she kissed him, she murmured against his mouth. "A very über awesome Alpha I love very much. *Toujours*."

"I do have a surprise for you." Damian rolled out of bed, shrugged into his trousers. He headed for the desk. Shock filled her as he opened a slim laptop and powered up. Jamie dragged the sheet about her, joined him and stared at the screen.

"You like World of Warcraft so much, I decided to learn. While you've been resting these past two days, Gabe signed all of us up, taught me a few computer skills and I've been practicing. It's fun."

"You told me computer games were a frivolous waste of time," Jamie teased.

"Spending time with you isn't. You taught me to feel young again," he said solemnly. Then mischief sparked his green gaze. "Besides, I'm very competitive."

Shock filled her when he confessed what level he'd achieved already. "I'm rusty and I have to level up. Let's play," Jamie suggested.

Mirth filled his boyish grin. He looked years younger, carefree. Her heart turned over as she caressed his cheek. Then she fetched her own laptop, and they played the game.

The sound of Damian's laughter was the most beautiful sound in the world to Jamie.

A few days later they materialized on the rain-soaked field near the pack lodge in New Mexico. Damian staggered, shook his head. Jamie grinned at his stunned expression.

"Takes a little getting used to, having your molecules scrambled like eggs as you travel through space, huh?"

Blinking rapidly, he looked a trifle green. "Now I know why I never watched *Star Trek*." He glanced at her. "No more headaches?"

She shook her head. Since the stone spell had left her body, magick flowed with no ill effects other than needing energy. The pain she'd felt before using her powers had been the darkness inside her fighting against the white magick.

Damian clasped her hand as they walked toward the lodge. She trembled a little, wondering if the pack would be upset at seeing her. Jamie, the one they'd once loathed.

Something in the grass caught her eye. She broke free, ran over. A half-deflated football lodged in the crusty mud. His memories flashed through her. The game he'd played, years ago, when the Morphs attacked. Damian had lost three pack members that day and blamed himself for indulging in recreation instead of scanning his territory for an attack.

It was time to heal that memory, and start again. Jamie pulled it free.

"Hey, wolf, catch!"

Damian caught the muddy, lopsided ball in one hand. He stared at it in bemusement, then looked at her expression.

"Throw it back!" she yelled.

He slowly grinned, ran backward and let it sail. Jamie caught the football, ran forward in a charging tackle.

She spilled him downward into a thick patch of mud, landing atop him with a whuff of air. He growled and wrapped his arms around her. She laughed as they rolled over and over in the mud. Jamie pressed a kiss to his warm lips, needing the contact between them. A sigh wafted out of her as he deepened the kiss.

"I love you," they echoed at the same time, and they both smiled.

Nearby sounds warned they were no longer alone. Damian released her, sat up. Mud clinging to her sweater, she wiped her face, leaving more streaks of dirt.

Astonishment filled her as she gaped at the crowd coming down the hill. She recognized a beaming Maggie and Nicolas flanking two small children holding a large white banner. Painted on the banner was a childish scrawl. "Welcome to our family, Jamie."

Wetness spilled down her cheeks. She didn't check the tears, but let them flow. Oh, hell. Jamie began to cry in earnest. Damian squeezed her hand gently.

The pack stared at her, made sounds of distress. The blond girl holding one edge of the sign let go. She scrambled forward, sank to her knees and touched Jamie's face.

"You're crying," she cried out. "We thought the sign would make you happy."

"It's fine," she said, smiling through her tears. "Really, crying is a very good thing."

She wouldn't have it any other way.

* * * * *

A sneaky peek at next month...

NOCTURNE™

BEYOND DARKNESS...BEYOND DESIRE

My wish list for next month's titles...

In stores from 17th February 2012:

❑ Claim the Night – Rachel Lee
❑ Wolf Whisperer – Karen Whiddon

In stores from 2nd March 2012:

❑ Embraced by Blood – Laurie London

Available at WHSmith, Tesco, Asda, Eason, Amazon and Apple

Just can't wait?

Visit us Online

You can buy our books online a month before they hit the shops! **www.millsandboon.co.uk**

Don't miss Pink Tuesday
One day. 10 hours. 10 deals.

PINK TUESDAY IS COMING!

10 hours...10 unmissable deals!

This Valentine's Day we will be bringing you fantastic offers across a range of our titles—each hour, on the hour!

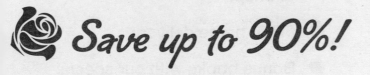

Save up to 90%!

Pink Tuesday starts
9am Tuesday 14th February

MILLS & BOON® Book Club

Free Book!

Get your free book now at
www.millsandboon.co.uk/freebookoffer

Or fill in the form below and post it back to us

THE MILLS & BOON® BOOK CLUB™—HERE'S HOW IT WORKS: Accepting your free book places you under no obligation to buy anything. You may keep the book and return the despatch note marked 'Cancel'. If we do not hear from you, about a month later we'll send you 3 brand-new stories from the Nocturne™ series, two priced at £4.99 and a third, larger, version priced at £6.99 each. There is no extra charge for post and packaging. You may cancel at any time, otherwise we will send you 3 stories a month which you may purchase or return to us—the choice is yours. *Terms and prices subject to change without notice. Offer valid in UK only. Applicants must be 18 or over. Offer expires 31st July 2012. **For full terms and conditions, please go to www.millsandboon.co.uk**

Mrs/Miss/Ms/Mr (please circle)
_____

First Name
_____

Surname
_____

Address
_____

_____

Postcode
_____

E-mail
_____

Send this completed page to: Mills & Boon Book Club, Free Book Offer, FREEPOST NAT 10298, Richmond, Surrey, TW9 1BR

Find out more at
www.millsandboon.co.uk/freebookoffer

Visit us Online

0112/T2XEA